MOONLOCKET

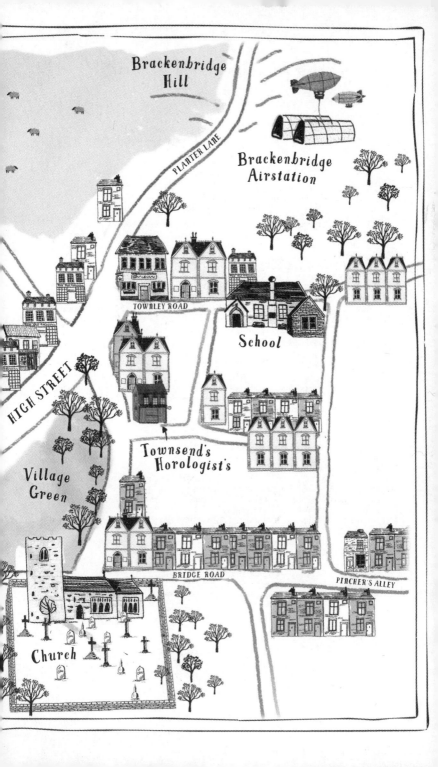

For Hannah, who read this first.

First published in the UK in 2017 by Usborne Publishing Ltd., Usborne House, 83-85 Saffron Hill, London EC1N 8RT, England. www.usborne.com

Text © Peter Bunzl, 2017

Cover and inside illustrations, including map by Becca Stadtlander
© Usborne Publishing, 2017

Extra artwork for map by Antonia Miller
© Usborne Publishing, 2017

Photo credits: Fir trees silhouettes © ok-sana / Thinkstock; Key © VasilyKovalek / Thinkstock; Brick wall © forrest9 / Thinkstock; Wind-up Key © jgroup / Thinkstock; Clock © Vasilius / Shutterstock; Hand drawn border © Lena Pan / Shutterstock; Exposed clockwork © Jelena Aloskina / Shutterstock; Metallic texture © mysondanube / Thinkstock; Plaque © Andrey_Kuzmin / Thinkstock; Burned paper © bdspn / Thinkstock; Crumpled paper © muangsatun / Thinkstock; Newspaper © kraphix / Thinkstock; Old paper © StudioM1 / Thinkstock; Coffee ring stains © Kumer / Thinkstock; Bikes © Ferdiperdozniy / Thinkstock; Picture frame © hayatikayhan / Thinkstock; Playing card © Maystra / Thinkstock; Back of playing card © Maystra / Thinkstock; Wood texture © NatchaS / Thinkstock; Swirl floral retro frames © milkal / Thinkstock; Jack of Diamonds © Teacept / Thinkstock; Wax seal © bmelofo / Thinkstock; Unicorn shield silhouettes © randy-lillegaard / Thinkstock

Published in the United States by Jolly Fish Press, an imprint of North Star Editions, Inc.

First US Edition
First US Printing, 2019

Library of Congress Cataloging-in-Publication Data
Names: Bunzl, Peter, author.
Title: Moonlocket / Peter Bunzl.
Description: First US edition. | Mendota Heights, MN : Published in the
  United States by Jolly Fish Press, an imprint of North Star, [2019] |
  Series: Cogheart adventures ; [2] | Originally published in the United
  Kingdom in 2017 by Usborne Publishing.
Identifiers: LCCN 2019015359 (print) | LCCN 2019019211 (ebook) | ISBN
  9781631633768 (ebook) | ISBN 9781631633751 (print)
Subjects: | CYAC: Adventure and adventurers—Fiction. | Friendship—Fiction.
  | Criminals—Fiction. | Families—Fiction. | Steampunk culture—Fiction |
  Science fiction. | London (England)—History—19th century—Fiction. |
  Great Britain—History—Victoria, 1837-1901—Fiction. | LCGFT: Steampunk
  fiction. | Action and adventure fiction.
Classification: LCC PZ7.1.B867 (ebook) | LCC PZ7.1.B867 Mo 2019 (print) | DDC
  [Fic]—dc23
LC record available at https://lccn.loc.gov/2019015359

Jolly Fish Press
North Star Editions, Inc.
2297 Waters Drive
Mendota Heights, MN 55120
www.jollyfishpress.com

Printed in the United States of America

MOONLOCKET

PETER BUNZL

JOLLY
FiSH
PRESS

PROLOGUE

Jack stepped through the crack into the night. Outside, the yard was quiet and thick dark clouds hid the moon from view.

Squatting beside the door, he scooped handfuls of muck from a puddle and plastered it through his white hair. Muddy lumps dripped down his scarred face, oozing odorously into his eyes, nose, and mouth, making him want to retch.

A spotlight swept past, outlining the barred windows. Jack crouched low to the ground and scanned his surroundings. The prison yard, the cells, the watchtower, the tall perimeter fence, the gatehouse, the iron gates, the high stone wall tipped with iron spikes—all unbreachable. In its long illustrious history, no prisoner had ever escaped the 'Ville…

But he'd conquered worse. After fifteen years in maximum security, under constant surveillance, it had been a mistake for them to transfer him here to Pentonville and a regular cell. This past week the screws had barely looked in on him; they'd even let him out to exercise. They should've known better. Now, because of their stupidity, he'd be The World's Most Infamous Jailbreaker as well as its Greatest Escapologist!

He crawled toward the fence and pulled himself onto its wire surface, scrambled upward vaulted nimbly over the top, and dropped down the far side. Landing with a squelching thump, he raced toward the main gate and exterior walls.

A drainpipe snaked up the side of the gatehouse. Jack brushed his muddy palms against his chest, took a deep breath, and began to climb.

Reaching the top, he hauled himself over the gutter onto the slippery roof and across a patchwork of tar and tiles, the exterior wall looming above him in the dark. Mounds of leaves and globules of green moss gathered in the crevices up here, creating perfect hiding places for small items someone might wish to stash.

Jack rummaged in one such crevice and pulled out a tarry tangle of ropes. They'd been bartered and bargained for outside the oakum shed over the past seven days, and were the makings of a secret escape kit. He began fastening them together, checking each knot carefully and pulling them tight.

Long ago he'd taught Fin to do this. A good knot can be the difference between life and death, he'd told the boy. Especially for an escapologist, or a hanged man. Luckily he'd never yet been threatened with that final rope.

Thoughts of the old times led Jack to remember his wife and the plan they'd made long ago to hide his greatest treasure—the Blood Moon Diamond. Artemisia might be gone, but soon, very soon, that big beautiful stone would be his once more. And, oh, what a diamond day that would be!

Jack checked the last knot and fastened a heavy rock to the rope's end. Then he stood and began whirling it around his head like a lasso, feeding out lengths of line until the stone picked up speed. When it was finally making a wide circle about his head, Jack released his grip.

The stone flew through the air, arcing over the exterior wall. For a second the rope wriggled, trying to snake free, but Jack kept a tight grip on its end, and the stone hit the ground on the wall's far side with a clunk.

He waited a moment, listening…

Awhoo! Awhoo!

An owl hoot—the signal that the line was secure.

The searchlight was fast approaching once more.

Jack dropped flat against the tiled roof and, when it had passed, jumped up and pulled the rope taut, testing his weight against it.

His knots held—as he knew they would.

He scraped the soles of his boots in the roof tar to make them sticky.

Then he began to climb.

The cracks between each stone made strong footholds. The top of the wall was fifteen feet above, but he took mere seconds to reach it and hop nimbly over a row of spikes that guarded the parapet, before lowering himself down the far side into the street.

Finlo stood beneath him wearing a battered bowler hat. He was a little taller than his father, though that wasn't saying much—all the Doors were short. As a teenager, fifteen years ago, he'd been a skinny disappointing runt, but since then he'd added a few inches, filled out into a man. Perhaps, Jack thought, he might be useful on this mission after all.

Jack dropped to the pavement beside his son and embraced him, sniffing the air. "Get a whiff of that peppery smell, Fin. I haven't smelled that in fifteen years!"

Finlo took a deep breath. "What is it?"

"Freedom!"

Jack flashed him a scarred smile. As he strode toward the prison entrance, a few feet away along the wall, a loud alarm bell began to wail.

"Da, please," Finlo called softly. "We have to go."

"Quiet! I've one more trick up my sleeve…" Jack pulled a playing card from thin air, and pinned it to the jail door.

When he lowered his arm, Finlo saw what it was: the Jack of Diamonds.

"And now," said Jack, slipping into the shadows, "we disappear."

CHAPTER 1

In her short life Lily Hartman had come back from the dead not once, but twice. Neither time had been particularly pleasant. The first she didn't like to recall; the second she wished every day she could forget.

Her first near-death occurred when she was six years old. She'd been in a terrible steam-wagon crash, which had killed Mama and left her mortally injured.

Her second near-death took place last winter—barely three months past her thirteenth birthday. On that cold November day Lily was shot by someone she trusted dearly; and it was only thanks to the bravery of her friends, Robert and Malkin, and the enormous strength of the Cogheart—an amazing invention of her papa's—that she'd survived.

Though it had brought her back to life, the Cogheart made Lily different. She was a hybrid, with a clockwork heart that might tick forever. A girl with untold secrets—for who could she tell when, outside her family, everyone regarded hybrids and mechanicals as less than human?

Not that Lily liked to dwell on such things. This morning her troubles felt truly behind her. She lay with her back on the warming earth, enjoying the fizzing feeling of being alive, and let her mind drift to the promise of the long hot summer ahead.

Malkin, her pet mechanical fox, was curled at her side, one black beady eye open, watching. Tall stems of corn towered over him.

"Oughtn't we to be indoors?" he snapped, gnawing disdainfully at a burr-covered leg. "It's practically breakfast time."

"You don't eat breakfast, Malkin," said a second voice.

Robert, Lily's other best friend in the whole world, was picking dandelion clocks a few feet away. He stuck one in his buttonhole. It looked almost as good as the crown of daisies garlanding Lily's flame-red hair. Almost, but not quite.

Malkin spat out a mangy hairball with a sound like

an engine misfiring. "But I can smell breakfast," he persisted. "Chiefly Mrs. Rust's lumpy porridge. It's the most important meal of the day—you wouldn't want to miss that."

They probably would miss it, because they'd risen early and gone out to spot the night-mail zep on its morning flight from London, as they often did. When it passed over Brackenbridge, at half past seven or thereabouts, Lily knew all was right with the world. Then she and Robert would dash for their bicycles and race pell-mell through the village, over hill and dale, and on to the airstation, to collect the mail for Papa.

This morning, however, the night-mail was very late indeed. They'd been sitting a good forty-five minutes in the lower field, waiting for the zep's arrival.

Lily took a sixpence from her pocket and turned it over in her hand. "Heads we stay. Tails we go."

She flipped the coin, letting it land in the curve of her dress.

"Heads. We're staying."

"You didn't let me see," Malkin groused. "It could've gone either way."

"Well, it just so happened to go my way."

"It always does," he huffed.

"Malkin," Robert said, "you're so easily wound up."

Lily laughed. "Yes, anyone would think you were made of clockwork!"

She settled back on her elbows, getting comfortable. The sky had turned bright red over the roof of the house, and she could see the sun and moon simultaneously. If she glanced over her right shoulder there was the sun, slowly rising, and if she gazed to her left, there was the moon. With a large slice of its ghostly white face in shadow, it looked like a bent penny dropped in a wishing fountain. Lily held her sixpence up against it and squinted, making a lunar eclipse.

"The man in the moon looks awfully like Victoria today."

"She should be called the woman in the moon then." Robert snatched the sixpence from Lily and performed the same trick.

"The coin-Queen's got a bigger nose," he declared thoughtfully.

Lily chewed a stem of grass. "But you have to admit, they do look alike."

"How would you know?" Malkin was still quite cross; he gnawed at his other paw. "You've never met the Queen."

Robert handed the coin back and Lily replaced it in her pinafore, beside her pocket watch and a stone with a small ammonite in the center—a gift from her mother that she always carried. "Did you know," she said, "the Queen has two birthdays, like me. What d'you think of *that*?"

"You don't have two birthdays," Malkin snapped.

"Yes, I do." Lily adjusted her crown of daisies, which had slipped to one side. "My real one, and the time Papa brought me back from the dead. Three if you want to count the time I was shot. I'm unique."

"Birthdays don't work like that," Robert said. "Not even if you're…" He whispered the word: "A hybrid."

Lily's hand jumped to her chest, feeling for her scars. "Please don't call me that."

"Why not?"

"I don't like it."

A grasshopper settled on the corner of her dress. She watched it idly. It seemed so real and yet so mechanical at the same time—just like her. She hated the word hybrid; all she ever wanted was to be normal.

Malkin snapped at the insect and it hopped away between the ears of corn.

"What did you do that for?" Lily cried.

"You think too much," he grumbled. "Besides, I missed it, didn't I?"

"Because you're not fast enough." Robert picked another dandelion clock.

"How's this for fast?" Malkin nipped at the fluffy seeds, scattering them.

"Hey!" Robert cried angrily. "Why don't you—"

But before he could finish, a loud *tuk-tuk-tuk* of turning propellers interrupted him. An immense zeppelin, decorated with the insignia of The Royal Dirigible Company, bobbed overhead.

"The night-mail! Finally!" Lily whooped above the din. "I knew it would arrive!" She took out her pocket watch and flipped it open to consult the time. "An hour behind schedule."

"Better late than never!" Robert said, wedging his flat cap onto his head. "Come on, let's go meet it." He snatched up his bicycle, which lay nearby in a flattened ring of corn, and wheeled it to the edge of the field.

"On your feet, Malkin." Lily dusted the earth from the front of her pinny.

"If you insist." The fox leaped up and shook the burrs from his fur as he watched Lily grab her bicycle.

The two of them trotted though the tall grass. By the time they reached the gate, Robert had already pushed it open and was in the lane, sitting on his bike, waiting.

Brackenbridge village was busy with people on their way to work; costermongers, tradesmen, and clusters of shoppers with wicker baskets stood in the lanes, gossiping and exchanging the time of day. A few mechanical servants, owned by the people from the smarter houses, walked in the gutters along the edge of the road, so as not to disturb the crowds.

Robert and Lily sped around the corner to the High Street, where a lamplighter was decorating the lamp posts with ribbons in preparation for the Queen's Jubilee celebration in four days' time. They wove past his ladder, bumping along the cobbles side by side, then whirred up Planter Lane and on over Brackenbridge Hill.

Malkin bounded between them. He may have only been a mechanimal, but he could run twice as fast as a real fox and had no trouble keeping up. His internal clockwork fizzed with joy, keeping time with the rattling spokes of Robert's and Lily's bicycle wheels. His tongue lolled between his teeth as he nipped at their heels, trying to worry them over the brim of the hill.

When they arrived at the airstation the mail-zep was already turning about, casting a long shadow over the landing field. The airmen on its prop platforms loosened a pulley and lowered three red flags.

"That's the signal," Robert said. "In a second they'll drop the mail."

A puffing steam-wagon jerked to a stop in the center of the landing strip and a stocky mechanical porter jumped down from its driver's compartment. The zep lowered him a line and Lily watched as he attached it to the rear of the wagon. Then he gave a brief hand signal and four mailbags came zipping toward him. The porter caught each in turn, and threw them into the wagon's hold. Finally, he unclipped the airship and it floated away, disappearing behind a froth of buttermilk clouds.

The porter got back in his steam-wagon and drove toward the rear of the airstation. Malkin, who'd been stalking up to him this whole time, broke into a sudden gallop, streaking alongside the wagon's wooden wheels.

"What on earth's he up to?" Lily cried, and she and Robert jumped on their bicycles and pedaled as fast as they could to keep up.

They rounded the corner to discover the steam-wagon already parked outside the mail depot. Malkin stood beside it, barking at the mechanical porter, who was trying desperately to unload his sacks of mail. "Shoo!" he cried, waving a fat sheaf of envelopes at the fox.

Letters tumbled free, blowing about the yard.

"Shoo yourself!" Malkin growled, and gave a snort for good measure.

"Stop harassing that mechanical, Malkin!" Robert shouted.

"Is this creature yours, Sir?" The mechanical porter's clothes-brushtache twitched indignantly. "Call him off at once!"

"Malkin, you clonking clot!" Lily cried. "That's enough!"

"He smells funny," Malkin snarled.

Lily waved her arms, hurriedly shooing the fox away from the porter.

"I'm terribly sorry, Sir. I hope we can set things right?"

"I should think so!" The mechanical man began picking up his letters.

As Lily bent to help, she caught a glimpse of the brass number plate bolted to his forearm:

HARTMAN AND SILVERFISH Ltd.

First-class Mechanicals and Mechanimals

The porter was one of Papa's inventions! She handed him the letters, peering closely at his metal face. She was certain she'd seen him somewhere before…

"Weren't you on the airship from Manchester last year?" she asked.

The porter's face lit up. "Bless my bolts! Yes, I was. My faculties might be rusted, but I remember you. Miss Grantham, isn't it?"

"Actually it's Miss Hartman."

"Of course…the professor's daughter!" He took her hand and shook it enthusiastically, until Robert thought her arm might fall off.

"You brightened a dark day for me then," Lily said. "May I ask your name?"

The mechanical man gave a deep sigh. "Alas, I don't have one, just my serial number: Seven-Six-Five-G-B-J-Four-Zero-Seven. It's a bit of a mouthful, so some of the airmen call me Brassnose, on account of, well…my brass nose." He polished it proudly with the sleeve of his jacket until the sun winked off its coppery surface. "Perhaps you'd be kind enough to introduce your friends, Miss Hartman?"

"Of course, Mr. Brassnose, this is Robert and Malkin."

Robert doffed his cap to the mechanical and Malkin gave a non-committal grunt.

"I see you quite regularly 'round the airstation," Mr. Brassnose said.

"I'm no tocking zep-spotter, if that's what you're implying," Malkin snapped back. "Personally, I can't abide airships—such vulgar vehicles! It's these two who are the aficionados. Robert here knows every flight path. He even has a book full of zep registrations. Show him, Robert."

"I do not." Robert bristled. "Besides," he told Mr. Brassnose, "we're not around that often, only once… or twice a week."

"Why's the mail-zep so late today?" Lily asked, trying to change the subject.

"Could be anything…" Mr. Brassnose said. "But I heard on the telegraph they stopped the newspaper presses for some breaking news. And since Fleet Street buys up most of the cabin space for deliveries, that tends to put the whole flight back."

He lugged the last mail sack from the bed of the steam-wagon and Robert saw that it was stamped with the logo of *The Daily Cog*. "Must be a big story to delay the zep an hour," Mr. Brassnose said, opening the bag and handing a paper to Lily. "What's it say?"

Lily read the headline and smiled, for the story was credited to a friend of hers and Robert's.

❀ DAILY COG ❀

STARTLING JAILBREAK FROM PENTONVILLE PRISON

London, morning edition, 16th June 1897.   One penny

Reported by Anna Quinn

Infamous escapologist and thief Jack Door broke out of prison last night, and has been on the loose ever since.

Patriarch of the notorious Door family, renowned for their theatrical divination and escapology routines that wowed crowds across Europe, Mr. Door was serving a life sentence for masterminding the theft of the Blood Moon Diamond. The priceless jewel, owned by Queen Victoria, was stolen from the forehead of her mechanical elephant – the Elephanta – during a royal command performance fifteen years ago.

Last week Mr. Door was moved from the high security of Millbank Prison, where he was kept in solitary confinement under constant supervision, to a standard single cell at Pentonville Jail, pending an appeal hearing. He absconded from there sometime between the hours of twelve and three a.m. The police have found no further trace of him, apart from his calling card – the Jack of Diamonds – discovered pinned to the gate after the great escape.

Lily stopped reading, and pursed her lips. "They know all this and yet they can find not a single clue as to his whereabouts… Who would believe it?"

Malkin shook his head. "Not I."

"Nor I," Robert said. "What else does it say?"

Lily perused the rest of the article. "'The redoubtable

Chief Inspector Fisk of the Metropolitan Police, New Scotland Yard, is of the opinion that the convict was aided in his escape by a third party, and that he, or they, may have procured transport out of the city. Members of the public are advised not to approach Mr. Door as he may well be armed and dangerous. They should instead make a note of his whereabouts and inform their local constabulary forthwith.'"

"Have we any letters today?" Malkin interrupted. "I'd hate to think we came all this way merely to hear you read out choice excerpts of the news. Hardened criminals or no, we deserve our mail."

"Let's see." Mr. Brassnose flipped through the piles of correspondence in one of the other bags, checking the addresses. "You do realize we deliver?" he said.

"I know," Lily said, "but we were in the area…"

"And you wanted to watch the ships come in. I understand!" Mr. Brassnose stopped abruptly and pulled a cream-colored envelope from the bag. "You're in luck. This one's for your father."

Lily took the envelope. It was addressed in scrolled calligraphy to: *Professor John Hartman, Esquire, Brackenbridge Manor*. After that came a long looping flourish—like the swish of a fancy sword—that gave her such a whoosh of excitement in her belly that Lily dearly wished the letter had been addressed to her.

She turned it over. On the other side was a red seal embossed with a lion and unicorn, rearing up on their back legs and facing each other across a large ornate shield topped with a crown. Under their feet were the waxy words: *DIEU ET MON DROIT*.

"Looks important," Robert said, peering over her shoulder.

"Very." Mr. Brassnose's eyes glowed. "You'd best get that to Professor Hartman immediately. That's the Queen's seal—you've got Royal Mail!"

Lily put the letter in the pocket of her pinafore. Malkin grasped the newspaper in his jaws, and the three of them hurried home. As they cycled through the village, Robert hung back, letting the others surge ahead. There was something else he wanted to do.

At the end of the High Street, as they approached Bridge Road, he took a detour across the village green, past the graveyard and the gray stone church where they'd buried Da last winter. The ground had been so frozen beneath their feet it had felt as if it might never thaw.

He felt a pang of apprehension and squeezed the brakes of his bicycle, thinking he might stop, but this was not his destination. Instead, he coasted around the corner and on up the street to Townsend's Horologist's shop.

Once his da's pride and joy, now it hunched, a festering tooth in Brackenbridge—a scorched shell of its former self, its windows boarded up, the glass of its front door broken. The state of it made Robert's chest ache. And yet its dingy presence had become a magnet, pulling him in, until he found himself pining like a lost puppy for Da, and for his former life, lost in the fire.

Sometimes he liked to imagine he was only staying with the Hartmans until Da's return. He'd pretend Thaddeus had popped away on a visit and would be back soon. It was only when he saw the concrete reality of things that he knew this wasn't so.

He'd come to stare at the burned-out shop many times, but he'd yet to muster the courage to go inside. Professor Hartman had warned him not to. The building was unsafe. Anyway, everything he wanted had been taken from him by the flames. This wreckage belonged to his ma, wherever she might be.

Selena. In the ten years since she'd left, she hadn't bothered to send a single card or telegram, not even on his birthday. She probably hadn't heard about Da's death—that was how little she cared. And yet she'd been named owner of the shop in his will… When Robert first heard that surprising news six months ago, he'd waited for her to return and clear things up. She hadn't appeared, and Townsend's sat empty, while he remained with the Hartmans. Well, he was done. There would be no more waiting. He would turn away from his past.

He was about to do just that when his eye was caught by his old bedroom window, and his heart leaped to his throat.

Something had moved behind the smoky pane of glass. A figure in the gloom…

He peered closer.

There was no doubt about it. There it was. Staring right back at him.

Its face was pale and moon-shaped, with a square nose, graying hair, and piercing dark eyes. Da? Could it be?

He stepped toward it, but the figure disappeared, vanishing as quickly as it had come, as if it was a ghost. For a moment Robert expected it to materialize in the downstairs doorway and beckon him over to open the shop. He waited, but it never did.

Suddenly Malkin skittered to a stop at his feet and, seconds later, Lily screeched to a halt beside him on her bicycle.

"Where have you been?" she asked breathlessly.

"We were heading home but, when we looked behind, you weren't following."

"I was right here," Robert replied. *I was heading home,* he wanted to add. *This is it.*

It was on the tip of his tongue to tell her about the ghost, but he didn't. Because it could've been wish fulfillment, a fantasy. Hadn't he just been thinking of Da? Maybe he'd conjured a picture of him looking down…

"What's the matter?" Lily asked. "You seem lost."

"Not lost," he replied. "But I…I had a vision."

"A memory?" she persisted.

"Perhaps."

Was that what it was?

Lily nodded at the house. "If you're planning to go in there—"

Malkin dropped the newspaper in the road. "No, no, no," he barked loudly. "John said the building could collapse at any moment. Come on." He nudged their legs with his dry nose. "Let's get back to Brackenbridge Manor. There's breakfast waiting. Delicious porridge! Besides, we still have the Queen's letter to deliver."

"I'd almost forgotten." Robert gave a ponderous smile and watched Malkin pick up the paper.

But as they cycled off, he couldn't help glancing briefly

over his shoulder one last time. There, in the shrinking gloom of the shop window, he swore he saw the shadowy face of his da again, watching them from behind the soot-stained glass.

CHAPTER 2

Lily and Robert swerved up the drive of Brackenbridge Manor, with Malkin scampering along behind them. They aimed their bicycles through the open doors of the stable block and came clattering to a stop.

Malkin sniffed at a pair of metal feet sticking from beneath the front of a steam-wagon.

"Leave it out!" Captain Springer rolled himself out from beneath the vehicle's chassis. His metal face was covered in engine oil, but that wasn't unusual given that he was a mechanical. He dropped his spanner into his big tin toolbox and rooted around for something else. "Your father's looking for you," he told Lily. "You're late for breakfast again." He gave a tut like a ticking clock.

"An engine can't run without fuel, you know, tiddlers."

"We know," Lily told him. She and Robert left their bikes against the wall in an empty stall and hurried through the yard into the house.

They arrived in the dining room to find Papa already seated and tucking into a plate of kippers.

"Ah, the wanderers return!" he cried. "Zep-spotting, I take it?"

Malkin jumped up onto a chair and deposited *The Daily Cog* on the table. "Merely collecting the paper. Here you go—it's hardly mauled." He nudged the paper toward John with his nose, then jumped down and slunk under the table.

Papa smoothed out the crinkled pages. Lily half-expected him to start in straight away on the sensational story about the jailbreak, but instead he opened the technology section and, taking up his half-moon glasses, peered through them at the tiny printed articles.

"Aren't you going to read the headlines?" she asked, as she reached over and snatched the puzzle pages for herself.

"This item's far more interesting," Papa muttered.

Lily gave a big sigh; she was too hungry to argue. Besides, she knew he wasn't listening. He'd be lost in reports of the new inventions being built around Britain.

Mr. Wingnut, the mechanical butler, bustled in. His metal brow furrowed in concentration as he set down a silver tray and gave a bowl of porridge and a plate of bacon, eggs, and toast to each of them.

There was too much food again. Mrs. Rust, the cook, had never quite gotten the hang of quantities and consequently would overdo things a little in the kitchen. But two breakfasts suited Lily down to the ground; she sat at her place and ate up immediately. After so much cycling she felt as if a hungry army was marching around the pit of her stomach demanding to be fed.

She scoffed down alternate mouthfuls of porridge, toast, bacon, and eggs, and glanced at Robert across the table. He gave her the wannest of smiles. His complexion had turned terribly pale and he was barely eating. Lily hadn't noticed before, but tired gray circles had grown under his eyes.

She was sure it was visiting the shop that did it. For a while a suspicion had been growing in her that Robert had been making secret excursions there regularly. He tended to disappear at odd times, when he imagined no one would notice. But Lily did. She always noticed where he was—it was as if she was extra sensitive to it. Catching him at Townsend's today had only confirmed her suspicions: he was aching for his old life. She knew what that was like, but dwelling on the past could only make you upset. Her heart went out to him.

Lily missed Mama every day. It could be a pain in her chest, as if a cord that once tied them had been broken, or the tiniest itch of a memory. Half-forgotten hugs and faded conversations—they rattled around inside her and came out sometimes, like catching the slightest whiff of a faded scent that you can't quite place.

The pain of loss must've been keener for Robert, since the cut was fresh and deep. He probably thought of his da every hour of the day. And perhaps he felt he couldn't say, or worried she, or Papa, would see that as ungrateful. But Robert was silly to imagine he couldn't be truthful with them.

"Listen to this." Papa shook out the newspaper. "Parliament today voted to build a new power station on Lots Road, in the London borough of Kensington and Chelsea, with plans to move ahead with electric power for the whole Underground and West London."

"That's not interesting," Lily said.

Papa straightened his glasses, which had gone wonky on his nose. "Of course it's interesting, Lily. Electricity is the future. Why, ever since Edison first lit up the street lamps on the Holborn Viaduct fifteen years ago, engineers in London have been striving for bigger and better power stations that will transport electricity efficiently around the city and, one day, around the country."

He began moving condiments around on the table. "I mean, imagine this pepper pot is the power station, and this fork a railway train, or better yet, this knife."

"That's my knife!" Lily cried. "Give it back! I'm eating!"

Papa waved it at her. "But listen, Lily...this is important. Within your lifetime, there may be no more clockwork engines, or steam-wagons. The fact is, soon, everything will run on electricity."

Lily snatched her knife from him and cut another slice of bacon.

"After that," Papa continued, "mechanists like me will be out of a job. Mechanicals too. A multitude of electrical appliances will take their place."

There was a crash in the background as Mr. Wingnut dropped his silver tray, spilling a plate of kippers on the floor.

"Sorry!" he mumbled, and Lily heard him muttering, "What clacking nonsense," under his breath as he bustled around picking up the tiny fish bones that were stuck to the carpet.

"In the meantime," Lily said, tapping the front of the newspaper frustratedly with her eggy fork, "you're ignoring the most exciting story of the year, right under your nose. The daring jailbreak of a vicious convict named Jack Door, written by our friend Anna."

Papa stared at the headline splashed beneath the masthead. "Well, well, I see she's their lead reporter now. A female lead, whatever next!"

Lily tutted. "Plenty of ladies are lead reporters, Papa. Haven't you heard of Nellie Bly, or Elizabeth Bisland?"

"Why bless my soul, of course I have!" Papa peered at the article. "Who's this blackguard Jack? He robbed the Queen, it says…"

"Yes," Lily replied. "He was given a life sentence. And then he wrote a book in prison called *The Notorious Jack Door: Escapologist and Thief Extraordinaire*! It was serialized in the penny dreadfuls, but I read it as a book last year. It's marvelous!"

"Sounds more scandalous than marvelous," Malkin said.

"And a mite scary, if Anna's article is anything to go by," Robert added. "How'd he sneak a novel out of jail, anyhow, if he was being held in maximum security?"

Lily took a big bite of toast. "Nobody knows. But he managed it somehow—if you're an escapologist you have those kind of skills, Robert."

Robert pushed his food aside; he hadn't eaten much,

he was too busy thinking about the ghost at the window. At least Lily's story was a distraction. "That's what Jack's book's about then?" he asked. "His famous tricks and robberies?"

"Not really," Lily said, spraying toast crumbs across her plate. "It mostly tells you how to pick locks. That and how to break unbreakable chains...oh, and how to tie untie-able knots."

"Why on earth would you need to know any of that?" Papa asked.

Lily licked the end of her finger and picked up the crumbs one by one. "It came in handy when we rescued you, didn't it?"

"If I recall correctly," came a voice from beneath the table, "I was the one who did the better part of the rescuing on that occasion."

Lily ignored Malkin and examined page two of the paper. "There's a little more about Jack's history here... It says he once had a show in the West End with his family. His wife was a spiritualist, and he was some sort of a magician and expert in escapology. When he got bored with that, he started using his skills to steal from country estates—that was before he pinched the Queen's diamond."

"How'd they know he did those other robberies?"

Robert asked. "It could've been anyone."

"Ah." Lily smiled. "He had a calling card. At every house he burgled, he left a Jack of Diamonds pinned to the wall. That's how they got him in the end. Well, that and someone gave up his location to the police."

"What a tockingly stupid way to incriminate oneself!" Malkin exclaimed.

"Quite," she agreed. "He even tied a playing card to the Elephanta's tail, when he stole the Blood Moon Diamond live onstage. So there was no need for the police to use their new fingerprinting techniques to prove his guilt. They locked him up for life on the strength of those cards." She peered down at the article. "Anna's called his jailbreak the most audacious ever."

"Zeppelins and zoetropes!" said Mrs. Rust, who'd come in with a plate of muffins during Lily's chatter. "Let's hope he never comes 'round here. That rogue's probably gone right back into the burgling business." She stooped on her way back to the kitchen to help Mr. Wingnut clear up the dropped kippers.

"He's not interested in inventions, Rusty. He only stole jewelry, and we don't have any of that."

"Houndstooth and herring bones! I should think not," Mrs. Rust spluttered.

"And thank tock for that!" Mr. Wingnut added.

"There's more," Papa said. He was fascinated now, and perusing the article himself. "It says the diamond was never recovered, despite a ten-thousand-pound reward, and during his fifteen long years in prison the Jack of Diamonds never revealed its whereabouts."

"That's his nickname," Lily whispered to Robert. "Because of the playing cards."

Papa gave a loud cough, for he hadn't finished reading. "On top of the original reward for the recovery of the Blood Moon Diamond, a further reward of five thousand pounds has been offered for any information that would lead to the rearrest of Jack." He pushed the paper away and took a contemplative bite of his toast. "We could do with a little of that money ourselves!"

Lily realized he was probably right. Despite Papa trying to hide it, things had been a little sparse of late. Perhaps it was because Madame Verdigris and Mr. Sunder had run off with a lot of Papa's valuable patent papers last year, and they still hadn't gotten them back.

That last thought seemed to jolt Papa from his chair, and he stood, folding the paper under his arm.

"Enough of this," he said. "I've work to do. I have to finish repairing Miss Tock."

Normally after breakfast Lily and Robert had lessons in the nursery, supervised by Mrs. Rust, but halfway through a particularly boring reading comprehension they'd been doing, the mechanical had wound down, and they'd taken the opportunity to sneak off and see what Papa was up to.

The lightning bolt on the workshop door was supposed to symbolize danger, but Lily liked to imagine it represented the inspiring things that filled Papa's workshop. She turned the door handle and she and Robert stepped inside.

It was an amazing space, bigger than Robert's da's old workshop and filled with more clockwork than the insides of Big Ben, but a certain cozy quality was absent. Robert found the rest of Brackenbridge Manor like that as well—a little too grand, a little too imposing. It never quite felt like home, because everyone was spread so far apart.

"Done with your schooling already, are you?" Papa glanced up, and Malkin, who lay underneath his chair, nipped at his shoelaces. He brushed the fox away and stood, beckoning them over. "Come and look at this, a proper clockwork brain!" he said, indicating Miss Tock, the mechanical maid, who sat wound down on the workbench, her stilled legs dangling beneath her, a panel in the front of her skull open. She had banged her head while dusting and doing the housework, knocking a cog loose, and it had been rattling around and making her act strangely ever since.

Papa fished out the troublesome cog and waved it at them. "These cogs connect up, much like the synaptic links in your heads. Their turning allows ideas to pass through her consciousness. One piece out of place and she'd never remember what day it was!"

Papa's talk of clockwork made Lily's mind drift to her own clockwork innards and worries. Her sense of not fitting in, of being a square peg in a round hole. It wasn't just the Cogheart, pumping blood around her body with each mechanical heartbeat, that made her feel that way. Even before she knew she had a perpetual motion machine for a heart, she'd always felt different from other children. The truth was, discovering she might live forever had only made her feel more out of sync with the world. She glanced at Robert, but he didn't seem to be concentrating either.

Robert's trouble was that he couldn't shake the image of his da's face at the window. Could it really have been a ghost? For a second Robert wondered if he should ask Professor Hartman, but then he decided against it. He didn't want to worry him unduly. The professor would probably say he'd been imagining things, or was going mad. He tried, instead, to focus on what John was saying, but all this talk of clockwork made him think of his old life as Da's apprentice and that made him miss Thaddeus even more.

"There." John replaced the final gears. "That's the last of these complications. She'll be ticking royally once again in no time."

"Oh my goodness! I forgot!" Lily pulled her purse from her pinafore with such force that the letter, her ammonite, watch, and money flew from her pocket and scattered across the table. She scooped up her things and handed Papa the letter. "We received this in the post— Mr. Brassnose at the airstation said it was from the Queen."

"You forgot a letter from the Queen?" John looked incredulous.

"I…" Lily looked embarrassed. "I was so intrigued by the jailbreak story that it clean escaped my memory."

"Never mind." John put the letter on the workbench beside Miss Tock and carefully finished screwing the panel on her head up tight.

"Well," cried Lily, "aren't you going to open it?"

"I can, if you like…" Robert reached for the letter.

"In a moment." John propped his elbows on the workbench and steepled his hands, as he always did when he was trying to give a lesson. "Patience, you know, is a virtue. First, we have to finish with Miss Tock here."

"This is hardly the time for lectures, Papa." Lily stepped toward him, so that she might lunge forward and see the letter.

"Yes," said Robert. "Please, let's hear what it says."

John sighed and picked up the envelope, breaking the seal and slitting it open with his screwdriver.

Lily and Robert leaned in close. Even Malkin—who was the sort to pretend he received letters from the Queen every day—jumped up onto the workbench, so he might see what was going on.

John put down the screwdriver and, with a grand flourish for his audience, reached into the envelope and pulled out a thick chunk of cream paper.

He unfolded it carefully but, as he began to read, his smile faded. "Good heavens!" he muttered.

"What is it?" Robert asked. "What's the matter?

"Yes," Lily said. "Tell us."

John cleared his throat. "The Queen wants me to travel to London, to the Mechanists' Guild, and repair the Elephanta."

"You mean the mechanimal Jack stole the diamond from?" Robert asked.

"That's right." John nodded. "She was the first mechanical creature ever created. Prince Albert had her made for the Coronation. The missing Blood Moon Diamond is what powered her. The Queen seems to think I, as a renowned mechanist and maker of mechanimals, might find a way to bring the Elephanta back to life so she can take part in the Jubilee."

Robert was aghast. "But that's only four days away! An impossible task!"

"Not for Papa," Lily said. "If anyone can fix the Elephanta, he can."

"I don't know, Lily…" Papa replied.

"Of course you can. You're the greatest inventor in the land. And if the Queen's requested you, she must think so too." Lily wondered if she was brave enough to make her next suggestion. "But with so little time you'll need us to come to London and help with the work."

Papa shook his head. "No, Lily, you and Robert will stay at home. I don't want you getting into any new trouble. I'll be in London under my own name and I don't want to draw attention to us. Besides, you've everything you could wish for here, haven't you?"

"But, Papa…"

"No buts; my mind is made up. And, as for being the greatest inventor in the land…I want people to forget me. Forget us. It's the only way we can ever hope to remain hidden. There are greedy opportunists about, Lily, and if they discovered how unique you are, then you'd have a price on your head—or, to be more exact, on your heart. I can't risk losing you like that. I've already seen you at death's door twice, and lost your poor mama. You're the only thing I have left, all I'm holding on to."

He turned away and gave a sniff. Then folded the letter, and replaced it in the envelope. "So I think it best you stay at home."

"Can we at least go to the village school while you're away?" Robert asked. "We'd come to no harm there, surely?"

"Mrs. Rust and the mechanicals can continue to teach you," Papa countered. "Meantime, I shall go undertake the Queen's work. Were it not for the money, I would not risk drawing attention to myself, but I shall complete the task and return as quickly and quietly as possible. Then we can catch up with extra lessons."

Lily listened to his speech with a heavy feeling of doubt. Papa was living in the past, trying to keep them hidden. Those dangers were gone now, she was sure of it. And in any case, couldn't he see she was almost grown, and perfectly capable of taking care of herself? Why, she even helped him with his work. But Papa didn't think in those terms. In his world she would stay squirrelled away forever, like some sort of secret.

"I think we're done." Papa wound Miss Tock up with

her winding key, and they waited…as slowly, very slowly, she jittered to life.

"By all that ticks!" she exclaimed. "It feels as if I slept for a thousand years. What did I miss?"

"Nothing much." Malkin yawned. "Just a letter from the Queen."

"Is that all!" Miss Tock clucked. "Well, thank clank for that!"

Lily wondered if she had understood Malkin entirely, but Papa seemed sure she was fine.

"You should run as good as new now," he told Miss Tock. "Lily will show you out, won't you, Lily?"

"Of course."

After Lily had assisted Miss Tock to the door, she and Robert helped Papa pack away his tools. Suddenly, Papa stopped and stared at them.

"Robert, I wonder if you might accompany me to my study after this? There's something I wish to discuss with you…about your, er, situation."

Robert's stomach gave a sudden lurch. He knew exactly what the professor meant—a mercurial mixture of ghosts, burned shops, and visions of his missing ma sloshed about inside him, threatening to overflow. Ever since Da's death six months ago, the professor had been trying to help Robert trace his ma so she could be alerted to his predicament and they could sort out this mess with Townsend's Horologist's. Could he have made a discovery? If he would only reveal it in private, Robert was pretty sure it must be bad news.

CHAPTER 3

"Come in, come in, my boy." Professor Hartman ushered Robert to a comfortable chair, moving a sheaf of papers to make room for him to sit down. "I'm sorry I couldn't be more specific before, but there's something rather delicate I wanted to discuss with you."

He held the papers aloft for a moment as if he wasn't quite sure where to put them. Finally, he settled on a side table beside an old battered gong suspended between a pair of tusks. Then he returned to his desk, banging his knee on its underside as he sat down.

While the professor was fidgeting, Robert glanced around the study. It was his favorite room in the house. The oak-paneled window and the glass-fronted cupboards somehow reminded him of his old shop home, and its myriad display cabinets. At the far end of the room, on the mantel of a big stone fireplace, stood a small brass urn. Above it a large gilt-framed portrait of a woman smiled down at them both from on high. She was Lily's mama, Grace Rose Hartman, who had died when Lily was only six years old, and she had a kindly and understanding face that Robert rather liked.

Robert's da had never told him the reason for his own ma's departure. She'd left when Robert was only three years old, and when he was big enough, Robert had felt such resentment toward her that he never asked. At least he'd had Thaddeus—he'd cared for Robert; he'd stayed. But now his da was gone, Robert felt entirely alone.

The professor had finished his fussing. He leaned forward and looked at Robert with his piercing bright eyes. "I'm afraid," he said, "we've received no answer to the classified ad I placed in *The Daily Cog* searching for your mother. And the police have apparently had scant luck tracing her. I've asked about the village too—they're all terrible gossips, of course, but none of them have any information. Except the rector. He remembered your parents' wedding in the church, and I thought it might be useful to get your mother's maiden name from their records. But when we searched the marriage register, it was the oddest thing… The page where they should've been recorded was nowhere to be found. It had been ripped out."

Robert leaned forward in his chair. "What does that mean?"

"It means someone removed it illegally," John said, "perhaps because they didn't want your mother's maiden name to be found."

Robert took a deep breath and slumped in his seat. He felt rather deflated by this new revelation. "How curious," he said finally.

"Isn't it?" John said. "Is there anything else you remember about her? Anything that might help us?"

Robert thought again. Hard. There was one other thing. "I think Da said when they met, Ma spoke to spirits, and that she was an actress in the theater." Was that right? Surely not—it sounded far too strange… And yet he remembered it distinctly.

"The truth is," he told John, "Da barely talked of her after she was gone. And why should he? It was she who left us. What I don't understand is why he gave her the shop."

"I couldn't tell you." John sighed. "But at least we have something more to go on. Though I don't hold out much hope of sorting this mess, if I'm honest. It seems Selena, or someone associated with her, has been attempting to keep her whereabouts secret for a long time." He gave a cough. "Ironic, really, since I've been trying to keep this family hidden too. Maybe she also had troubles in her past that she's still trying to escape."

Selena's story just got stranger and stranger. Was John right? Had she disappeared deliberately to escape some unknown trouble? Robert couldn't even begin to guess at the truth.

John capped a fountain pen that lay across the blotter on his desk. "Anyway, Robert, without any new information about your ma, there seems little more we can do to find her, despite my best efforts."

Robert shifted uncomfortably in his seat. "What does that mean for me?"

John sighed. "That you're left an orphan, I suppose. But I have another suggestion to solve that problem…"

"And what might that be, Sir?"

John smiled, his brown eyes twinkling behind the half-moon lenses of his glasses. "No 'Sirs' anymore please, Robert, my boy. You can call me John, or…" He cleared his throat. "You can even call me Papa, if you like—we're practically family. And that's what I wanted to speak to you about…the practical part, I mean… That is to say…I've been thinking a lot about your place with us at Brackenbridge since your da…since poor old Thaddeus died… And I've decided the best thing for

you—for us, Lily and myself too, you understand?—
would be if we…if I…adopted you. How would you feel
about that?"

Adopted! The word was an electric jolt he'd not been
expecting, not in the least. The truth was he'd barely
come to terms with the changes that had taken place
since he'd moved here. Then to think they'd be
permanent…

John had been so very kind, and Lily too, everybody
in fact. And it was a beautiful house… But, if the past
was anything to go by, life might fall apart at any
moment… Surely it was safer to keep things as they were?

He opened his mouth to speak, but John raised a
hand. "Uh, now, you haven't to decide immediately.
While I'm away I shall speak to a lawyer, then if you
resolve to join our family we can make the formal
arrangements."

John blew out a deep breath. It seemed he'd planned
all of this, this speech, far in advance and had finally
gotten through what he wanted to say.

Robert tried to formulate a reply. The words were
on the tip of his tongue, but they wouldn't quite come.
A gulf of silence was opening up between them and he
didn't know how to fill it. He liked the professor very
much—felt nearly as fond of him as he did Lily. It was

almost as if they were family. But there was still that *almost* there. A bump in the road. Or a brick wall, stopping him in his tracks.

"The thing is, Sir," he said, and as he did so, he realized he was supposed to call John "John"—not Sir, or Professor Hartman. "It's not…I would like to, a lot, but, to me, it doesn't quite feel like my da is gone. I don't mean to be ungrateful. But it's just…"

He didn't know what else to say; he hated to seem rude. A part of him would love for John to be his father and Lily his sister. But another fragment felt it would be a betrayal of his da. And a small insidious voice whispered in his ear: *And what if my ma comes looking for me, what then?*

To be part of another family would feel wrong, he realized. He wanted his old life back, to be where he belonged. Though he was angry at Selena for abandoning him those many years ago, for leaving without saying goodbye, and for the fact he'd not heard a peep from her since, to be her son was somehow to still be Da's son as well. And he didn't want to let Da go, not yet.

He knew it was likely, from the way things stood, that his mother had made her choice long ago and never wanted to see him again. They were strangers, and she'd probably reject him if he ever did find him. But he had to keep trying. He had to know why she'd left. Had to tell her everything that had happened since. Give her one final opportunity to change her mind. Or, if not, then at least hear her side of the story. Learn how she came to meet his da so he could fill in the gaps Thaddeus's death had left unanswered. Because, at the moment, his life was a cogless machine—an empty home—and how could he be expected to function with so many pieces missing?

No, before he accepted John's offer, he would have to find his ma—get to the bottom of where she'd disappeared to. And he should start by investigating the shop. His da had said Ma talked to spirits, perhaps he could too? If the figure really was a spirit—maybe it was more of a vision, a sign there was something he needed at Townsend's? Either way, he'd visit tonight and find out. John would've set off on his trip by then, the mechanicals would be wound down, and Lily asleep—no one would realize he was gone.

"I don't think I'm ready to give up the search for Selena just yet," he said. "I need to close one door before I open another." He stood abruptly, and as he turned to walk away, he glanced back at John. The professor smiled at him, but, behind the lenses of his half-moon glasses, his eyes looked sad.

That afternoon, Lily found Papa in his room, packing.

"You're leaving already?" she asked, as she watched him take down his shirts from the wardrobe and fold them away in his suitcase.

"I have to," he replied. "The Jubilee's in four days, that's barely time to complete the work."

It was disappointing to see him going off alone. Lily held out a hand for Malkin, who butted his wiry head against her palm. "Take us with you," she said. "The work will be easier with our help."

Papa paused halfway through folding a shirt. "I've decided Captain Springer will accompany me for that purpose. He's the most practically minded."

"Robert and I are practically minded too."

"Lily, I don't want to argue. There isn't time. I have to get this done, or I'll miss my airship." He gave up folding and stuffed the shirt into his case. "Besides, you and Robert would never be packed and ready to leave in time."

"I thought you might say that," Lily told him. "So I prepared a bag while you two were having your talk. It's got everything we need, both of us, and it's waiting in the hall. See how practical I am? I made sure we'd be ready, and with as little fuss as possible. You've got to stop treating me with kid gloves, Papa."

Papa shook his head. "Why don't you listen, Lily?

You're not coming, and neither is Robert. He's still hurt about his da, and as for you, the worst threats to you may be gone, but we can't be sure that Silverfish, or those murderous blackguards, Roach and Mould, didn't tell others about your Cogheart. After all, they were prepared to stop at nothing to try and steal it. We must assume there are still people who wish you harm."

Lily helped Papa close his case and buckle up the straps. Why did he always treat her like a little girl? She'd done more this past year than she'd ever thought possible, and yet he was too shortsighted to see it. Was he going to hide her away forever? What kind of a life was that anyway?

She slammed herself down on the bed. "I don't care, Papa. It's time we stopped concealing things. There's no point living in fear of what *might* be when it prevents you enjoying the freedom of what *is*."

Papa took his case from the bed. "It's not just that someone might try to steal your heart—as if that wasn't bad enough! Mechanicals are property; hybrids are disapproved of—I've even heard of cases where they were harassed in the streets."

"I don't think that's true," Lily said. "And I think you underestimate my ability to cope."

"Perhaps," Papa said. "But it's easier this way. I've made up my mind and nothing you can say will change it." He paused and gazed at her. "There's something else I haven't told you, Lily… I asked Robert if he wanted to be a part of our family permanently. While I'm in London, I intend to speak with a lawyer about the possibility of adopting him."

Lily jumped up from her seat, excitedly. "That's a splendid idea," she said. Then she remembered how sad Robert had seemed lately, how she guessed he was aching for his old life. "But shouldn't we give his ma one last chance to find him?"

"Robert's mother made her choice when she abandoned him. I'm not sure she's ever coming back."

"Everyone deserves the benefit of the doubt, surely?"

"Look, I must go," Papa said, "or I'll be late for my flight."

Then, when he saw the cloudy, confused thoughts flitting across Lily's face, he stopped, dropped his bag and came over to her. He placed a hand on her shoulder and looked her in the eye.

"Robert needs time without me around to think about what he wants, to get used to the idea that this is his home. And you need to get used to how things are changing too. I don't want to pressure him, Lily. I want *him* to decide. Meanwhile, you must make him feel welcome, let him know he belongs."

He squeezed her into a hug. "This is your mission while I'm away. Do things together, treat him like a brother."

"Is that all?"

"That's all." He kissed her forehead.

Lily felt her anger still bubbling as they walked together to the top of the stairs. Being nice to Robert wasn't a mission. She would do that anyway because she liked him. But them both going to London with Papa, that would've been a real adventure.

She hated being sidelined like this. She hung back and lingered at the bannisters pretending she'd something else to do and observed Papa descending the staircase, alone, to greet Mrs. Rust, Miss Tock, Malkin, and Robert in the hall.

Papa kissed Robert goodbye, nodded to the mechanicals, and ruffled Malkin's ears. Then he looked around for Lily, and when he realized she was still standing on the landing, gave an amused smile, before he waved and blew her a kiss.

Lily's heart softened a little, but she let her face stay set, and folded her arms across her chest so she wouldn't be tempted to wave back to him.

She watched as he stepped onto the porch, and out the front door, held open by Mr. Wingnut.

When she ran to the picture window, Papa was already climbing into the passenger compartment of the steam-wagon, along with Captain Springer. Meanwhile, Mr. Wingnut had settled himself in the driver's cabin. He had some trouble starting the engine as this wasn't his usual job.

Malkin slunk in beside Lily and jumped up onto the window sill. He cocked his head and regarded the steam-wagon as it puttered away down the tree-lined drive.

Lily stroked his ears and stared at the plumes of smoke emanating from the wagon's chimney. She suddenly wished she'd gone down to see Papa off properly. She'd tried hard to be the daughter he wanted, but it made no difference because he never seemed to notice.

If he'd only stop treating her like a broken machine, then maybe she'd stand a chance. He needed to let go, quit being so stubborn, and, most importantly, stop believing he was the only one in the world who could fix things.

Next time they spoke, she would prove him wrong. Make him realize she could be her own person, beyond the doors of Brackenbridge Manor. She was strong enough to take care of herself. And fearless too—braver than him, anyway.

What was it Robert's da had said…? *No one conquers*

fear easily; it takes a brave heart to win great battles. Yes...
that was it! And though Papa might fear the fact that
people would dismiss her as only a hybrid, deep down Lily
knew she could achieve anything she set her heart to.

CHAPTER 4

Robert was woken by a stream of moonlight. He'd left the curtains open for that precise reason. He sat up and rubbed his eyes. The moon's waxy pockmarked face peered through the window, pale and pithy as a piece of fruit, stars sprinkled behind her like spilled sugar. Her gaze silvered the room, the heavy wood furniture and the books and pieces of a train set that lay scattered about.

Although it had everything he'd ever wanted, Robert could never get used to the splendor of this space, or to the quiet. His first night sleeping here, he'd stopped the clocks; their quiet ticking had been unbearable. It was too much a reminder of the shop filled with Da's timepieces, their shapes and sounds engrained in him like old friends, before they were lost in the fire. Besides, he didn't need clocks to tell the hour; he'd lived side by side with time his whole life. He could read it in the sun's shadows, or the arc of the moon and stars.

He jumped out of bed and pressed his nose to the glass, ticking off the names of the constellations in his head: Hercules, Virgo, Libra, Scorpio, Delphinus, Aquila, Ophiuchus, and Serpens. He knew them by heart, thanks to Da's summer star charts, and from their position in the sky tonight he estimated the hour to be around midnight. Time to be off.

Robert dressed swiftly, pulling on his trousers, shirt, and socks, before lacing up his boots. He paused to swipe the lucifer matches and the candle stub from its tin holder by his bedside. He'd refrain from lighting them until he left the house. He didn't want to wake Lily next door, or alert any of the mechanicals who might not have wound down for the night.

His da's coat hung on the back of the door, as it had since he'd first arrived. He took it down and put it on. He'd need its warm comfort tonight—with a sky as bare and cloudless as a shorn sheep, it was sure to be cold out.

As he buttoned the coat a ghostly trace of pipe tobacco wafted from its lining. Da's smell. It made Robert feel

Thaddeus was nearby, watching. And that thought fortified him for the journey he was about to make.

He opened the door and crept out, past the entrance to the library, so full of books that the new ones awaiting shelf space were piled outside. The high-ceilinged landing was lined with rows of gilt-framed paintings. Between them heavy oak doors led to various rooms whose functions Robert had trouble remembering at the best of times, let alone half-asleep, in the dead of night, with a head full of worries. Luckily, he wasn't aiming for any of those spaces. He was heading home.

He took the servants' staircase to the basement and sneaked along the tiled back corridor to the kitchen. There he paused in the darkness to light his candle.

His heart jumped as a face appeared in the blaze.

It was Mrs. Rust, sitting ramrod straight in a wooden chair beside the scrubbed oak table. Her metal eyes were closed and her paint-chipped brow furrowed. Being a mechanical, she only functioned for about sixteen hours a day and, right now, with the springs and cogs inside her run down, there was no chance she'd wake—not until she was wound again in the morning.

Even so, Robert couldn't help but creep past. Something about her face in the flicker of the candle looked so human, as if she was frozen in deep sleep, which, if you thought of her as alive, he supposed she probably was. But it made him fear she might wake at any moment and demand to know where he was sneaking off to.

If that happened there'd be pitiful excuses and explanations, then disappointed looks, and telegraphs to John. Because, if you take someone in and give them a nice place to live, you don't expect them to sneak off at midnight, when no one's watching, to visit their old home.

But maybe Robert *did* want someone to stop him from slipping away into the dark. Perhaps he wanted a friend to notice how bereft he felt, perhaps he needed their advice…because, the more he thought about it, the surer he was that the face at the window was an echo of the past. A signal there was something at the shop to do with his parents he needed to find. And with John's talk of adoption this might be his final chance.

He unlocked the back door and was about to open it, when a loud cough behind him made him almost jump out of his skin.

He turned, expecting to find Mrs. Rust awake and eyeing him with an inquisitive and disapproving stare. But instead he saw someone else…

Lily.

She was leaning on the door jamb of the open pantry,

dressed in her long green coat and walking boots, almost as if she intended to go out. Behind her, half-hidden in the shadows cast by flour sacks and baskets of vegetables, was Malkin. He yawned and gave a little sneeze that sounded like the fizzing springs of a pocket watch.

"Where are you off to in the middle of the night, pray tell?" Lily asked.

"Nowhere," Robert replied.

"Liar." She stepped forward until her freckled face filled with candlelight.

Malkin came too, his claws scratching on the tiled kitchen floor. "Don't think we tocking well don't know what you're up to, Robert Townsend. You're sneaking off to visit your old home."

"So what if I am?" Robert said.

Malkin sniffed. "We want to know why."

"I can't tell you."

"Yes, you can." Lily squeezed his arm and Malkin snapped at his shoelaces.

"All right!" Robert gave up. "It's the vision I spoke of earlier."

"What about it?" Lily asked.

"Mmm, whtt?" said Malkin, with a mouthful of laces.

"It was a face at the window. Eyes looking directly at me. I think it might be a ghost."

"A ghost!" Lily's eyes went wide. "Of who?"

"Da." Robert shooed Malkin away. "It doesn't sound very plausible, does it? I thought you might think I was mad, that's why I was sneaking home. To prove I wasn't daydreaming, and to find out if the spirit was real…or just some kind of sign."

"I can't believe you would leave us out of a ghost hunt!" Lily said. "No, alone would definitely *not* be best. What would be best is if *we* came with you."

Robert gave her a defiant stare. But Lily was having none of it.

"We need an oil lamp," she said, taking one down from the shelf of the kitchen dresser. Prizing the candle from his hand, she removed the lamp's glass chimney and lit the wick. "Now," she said, "let's go and investigate."

The night was pitch-black, but the stars and gibbous moon shone bright. Lily rode her bicycle ahead along the drive, toward the gates of the manor, the lamp in the basket on the front. Malkin trotted beside her, Robert following behind. He was rather cross that Lily was taking charge, but that was just her way—always trying to turn everything into her adventure. He pedaled faster to catch up.

Cycling in the dark, it took them almost twenty minutes to cover the distance to Brackenbridge village. The road brought them down Bridge Lane, past a scattering of houses. In the distance Robert could make out the vague curving shape of the river. They crossed the Bracken Bridge and passed along Bridge Road. The golden glow of bunting-strewn street lamps illuminated the length of the High Street. As they crossed the green, and neared his home, Robert's body gave a small, involuntary shiver.

He tugged at his shirt collar, darting nervous glances across the lane, up at the window of Townsend's Horologist's. It was too dark to be sure, but he sensed no one inside.

As they propped their bicycles against the street lamp opposite the shop, a distant owl gave a screeching hoot.

"The place is empty," Robert mumbled. "Whatever I saw, I must've imagined it."

"There's only one way to be sure." Malkin pricked up his ears and scampered into the door well, sniffing at the planks nailed across the door. "I can't smell anything strange, except singed metal."

The fox stood on his hind legs, placing his paws on the ledge beneath the boarded-up window, and peered through a narrow slit. "It could've been someone breaking into the house, but it doesn't look like anything inside's been tampered with."

"Perhaps we should check 'round the back?" Lily proposed.

The three of them squeezed down the narrow passageway between the buildings and stepped into the yard at the rear of the shop. Behind the gloomy silhouette of the outside privy and a small pile of old packing cases, the back door had been boarded over with sheets of plywood, to hide the panes of glass Roach and Mould had broken on that fateful night when they'd followed Lily, set the fire, and killed his da.

Lily felt around in the inky shadows and grasped the door handle. The door swung easily inward. "Clinking chronometers!" she whispered, brushing her fingers against the side of the lock. "It's been picked! It wasn't a ghost, or a figment of your imagination. There really has been a visitor, Robert."

Robert leaned against the cold brick wall and gave a sickening cough. Suddenly he felt rather sick at the thought of going inside. He remembered what John had said about his ma, how she could've been in hiding for years for some mysterious reason. If she came back at all she'd probably have to do it secretly. Could it be her in the house, or was it someone else? "What should we do?"

he asked. "We can't venture in without reconnaissance."

"Malkin can sniff around," Lily said. "If he scares up anything he can flee quick enough. Whoever it is might even imagine he's a wild fox that's got in by mistake."

"I *am* a wild fox," Malkin said. "You've never seen my wild side—and thank goodness, because it's positively tocking ferocious!" With that, he stepped through the door and disappeared into the sooty darkness.

"Don't fall down any holes," Lily called after him softly, remembering the danger they'd been warned about.

Robert waited for his sarcastic reply, but it didn't come.

Silence. The night was so still that Robert could hear his own heartbeat…or was that Lily's, stood beside him? He listened for her tick amongst the booms. And then it came, but it was only Malkin, his fizzing clockwork echoing from inside the house, until his nose appeared in the narrow gap between the door and the jamb.

"The coast's clear," he yapped. "I heard a few creaks, but it must be this old house, because no one's here. There is evidence someone was sleeping rough for a day or two. But they must've seen you through the window, Robert, got scared, and moved on."

Robert felt a wave of surprise. He'd been right then…
The only difference was the face had been real, not the
ghost or vision he'd imagined. Perhaps it had been his
ma, secretly returned?

"What kind of evidence?" Lily was asking Malkin.

Malkin nipped at a charcoal smear on his orange fur.
"Oh, you know…footprints in the dust, scratches on the
walls, fingermarks on the paneling—that kind of thing.
The front bedroom seems to contain a bed on the floor,
made from pieces of cardboard and an old blanket."

"Is there anything that could've been left intentionally?"
Robert asked. He was still in shock, and wondering if the
visitor had been looking for him.

"I don't think so." Malkin sniffed. "Why don't you
come and see for yourself? If there's a significant clue,
you're more likely to find it."

"You're sure we won't get caught?" Lily asked.

"I told you, didn't I?" Malkin snapped. "The smell of
humans is unmistakable. There's no one here. I checked."

"Fine." Lily pushed the door wide, her lamp flickered
and dimmed and she turned to Robert. "It's nearly out
of oil."

"Then we'll need more light." Robert took his candle
and matches from his jacket. His hand shook as he struck
a match, and the flame danced and jigged so he had

trouble finding the candle. When he finally got it lit, he nodded to Lily.

The pair of them stepped into the ravaged house with trepidation. Robert took a deep breath...and suddenly his past was upon him, seeping sootily into every bone and sinew of his body.

CHAPTER 5

Robert and Lily followed Malkin through the burned-out husk of Townsend's Horologist's. The fox skipped daintily ahead along the hallway, leaving tiny paw prints in the dust.

Robert held his breath as he and Lily dodged beneath a fallen joist that must have once been a roof beam. Everywhere he looked he saw traces of the fire that had raged through the house six months ago: walls begrimed with mold, paint pimpled and boiled like greasy skin, and plaster that had flaked away to expose broken wooden lathes, like ribs. It was as if his home had been mauled by a flaming beast.

Peering into the workshop, his stomach heaved at the

sight of the crumbled cupboard he and Lily had pushed across the doorway to try and stop Roach and Mould's attack. He tried not to think about what had happened in that room on the night of the fire, but that was impossible. The air was thick with damp, sooty sadness; bitter memories.

Through the skeletal remains of the cupboard, Robert glimpsed the humped, charcoaled frame of Da's workbench. The tools on the wall were warped beyond recognition—white ash and twisted metal was all that remained of them.

"Look." Lily pointed at the outline of a space where a screwdriver had been removed from its hook. The soot on the floor beneath it was newly scuffed. "What do you think it means?"

"I don't know," Robert replied hoarsely. "But I don't like it. Someone's been rifling through this room."

They ducked back through the doorway, and walked down the corridor to what had once been the clock shop. Smashed cabinets lay overturned everywhere. The heavy iron till was tipped over on the counter, but otherwise fine. Funny how some things came through a fire practically unscathed, while others were reduced to ash.

"This room's been searched too, by the looks of things." Lily bent down, examining a scattering of fresh footprints, and then froze as they heard a low creak from the floor above.

"What was that?" Robert asked.

"I told you—old houses." Malkin pointed with his nose at the ceiling. "There's more evidence of your visitor on the first floor. If you come with me, I'll show you."

The three of them returned to the hall, and stared up the stairs. They were in a terrible state—the bannisters dwindled to twiggy stumps and the risers ringed in black.

"Is it too dangerous to climb them?" Lily asked.

"Keep to the sides," Malkin advised, "the wood'll be stronger."

He trotted ahead, skirting the damage in each step.

Robert and Lily followed cautiously.

Lily's pulse echoed in her ears, sputtering like an overwound watch. She clutched the ammonite stone in her pocket and its cold shape against her palm calmed her down.

Robert coughed. There was a dry scratchiness at the back of his throat. This place—he could taste the closeness of it in every breath.

The floor of the upstairs passage was riddled with scorched holes. Edging carefully around them, they took care to keep only to the main joists, which were almost all whole. They passed the dilapidated kitchen, where

Robert had spent his days eating with his da, then his blackened old bedroom and, finally, they stepped into what had once been Thaddeus's sleeping quarters.

A few stray shards of moonlight filtered through an opening in the roof, revealing a broken iron bedstead, teetering on the edge of a thicket of loose boards that stuck out over a jagged abyss. In the far corner, beside the chimney breast, a pile of charred rags lay on one of the few surviving islands of floor.

The room had been almost completely destroyed. The only thing that had survived unscathed was the cast-iron fireplace. Even in winter, Robert remembered, Da never lit himself a fire. He preferred to save their coal for the kitchen range, or let his son have it for his room—he'd been generous that way, always attending to others' needs over his own.

Robert's eyes watered—maybe it was the dust? He brushed a hand across his face. "Let's go," he said. "There's nothing anyone wants here."

"Wait," Lily replied.

"What?"

"That mound of rags just moved."

Malkin tensed, pricking up his ears. "Probably a mouse."

"I think it's bigger than that," Lily said.

74

The fox gave a loud sniff. "A rat then."

Robert held out his candle and crept along the crooked surviving center beam of the floor, peering at the pile of wretched blankets.

"I don't see anything... Oh..."

He was looking up now at the fireplace; there was something odd about it. The small grate and the stone hearth looked incongruously clean compared to everything else, as if it had been dusted. Robert stepped gingerly onto the island of intact floor and waved his candle beneath the fireplace's arch.

"That's odd," he said. "The back's been pushed aside to access the chimney. And here's the missing screwdriver from the workshop, resting in the grate..."

"What's it doing there?" Lily hugged her arms and tiptoed along the singed beam towards him.

Robert crouched, placing a palm on the iron surround, and leaned in closer. The screwdriver was covered in dust. "Why," he said, "it's almost as if someone's been poking around in the chimney."

He pushed at the fireback. A storm of dust fell from it, guttering the candle flame, almost putting it out. Robert bent forward as far as he could, until he could see directly up the flue. "Something's stuck here, but I'll need more light to get it out."

Lily moved closer, across the wobbly floor. Her lamp was fading but she set it by his shoulder so he could see.

Malkin joined them on the ridge of boards. Then he gave a start, and trotted over to the mound of rags, snarling and poking at it with his nose. Lily swore she saw it twitch again.

"Rob...ert!" she whispered in a strangled voice.

"Hmm? What?" Robert was busily poking at the chimney. His body, stretched sideways, threw the room into awkward shadow.

"I-I..." Lily stuttered, stepping back.

Malkin raised his hackles and bared his teeth, snapping at the rags.

Finally, Robert turned.

The mound of rags was undulating upward. Growing taller, and more human-shaped by the second. Shirts, trousers, and sheets slipped from its shoulders, until, suddenly, all that was left was a man, wrapped in a dirty wool blanket. Beneath his cowl, his unshaven face was caked in mud and a long white scar ran down his right cheek.

Malkin lunged at him. But the ragged man stepped quickly out of his way, and made for Robert.

Robert scrambled backward dropping his candle. The

flame went out, and then the ragged man grabbed his throat.

Soot-blackened nails scratched his skin and bony fingers tugged him toward the ceiling. "*GARGGHH!*" Robert cried. "Let go!"

"Never!" the ragged man growled.

Malkin was on him again, but the ragged man kicked him aside and pulled Robert into the corner, throwing him against the wall.

"Call off your fox," he whispered, his breath hot and angry in Robert's ear.

"First let me go." Robert coughed. He tried to shake himself free, but the man's fingers tightened against his windpipe, until his breath felt sharp and jagged.

"Call off your fox and we'll see." The ragged man's eyes were wild with anger.

"Malkin, get back!" Robert wheezed.

Malkin froze, then retreated to Lily's side.

"Good." The man's gravelly voice grew calmer, but he didn't stop staring at the fox.

Robert motioned to the door. *Go get help*, he mouthed at Lily.

Lily tried to keep her face neutral. Giving him the slightest nod, she stepped sideways, edging herself back along the central beam.

"No, you don't!" The ragged man grasped Robert tighter and jumped across the gap, blocking Lily's path. He lunged at her.

Malkin snapped at the man's boot, darting between his feet.

Lily hopped sideways, grappling for a steady piece of floor. The man tried to follow, stumbling forward, dragging Robert with him, but he was too heavy. *KKKCRrrAaaaccCKKK!* went the boards beneath him.

He stopped and looked down. "What the...?" he spluttered, clutching Robert against his chest.

With a sudden *WHOOOOOOOSSSSSHHHHHHH*, the entire floor gave way, the boards splintering and splitting and spitting, until they finally collapsed. Lily and Malkin leaped for the safety of the doorway, but Robert and the man tumbled through the gap, along with the bedstead and a cloud of soot and plaster that exploded in their wake.

The rushing pitter-patter of falling rubble soon gave way to a loud ringing in Robert's ears. He felt as if someone had smacked his head with a hammer. As the dust cleared, he looked around.

He was in the small storeroom. Once there'd been

shelves along its wall, filled with devices and clocks, but they'd since turned to wreckage and relics. The bed and the upstairs boards lay broken on the floor around him. He looked up.

The hole through which he'd tumbled was almost as wide as the entire ceiling. Sharp ragged knives of wood stuck out around its circumference, and two little faces peered over its edge, an oil lamp perched between them. One face had red hair hanging down around it; the other, with coal-black eyes and scruffy ears, had a hairy orange snout.

Lily held the lamp high. It rattled in her hand.

"Are you all right?" she called out.

Robert tried to reply but every ounce of air had been pushed from him. He patted at his limbs and found them to be present and correct. It didn't feel as if anything had been broken; in fact, he seemed to have fallen on something soft.

Then he realized what it was: the man.

Robert was lying across his chest. They must've twisted around in the air so the man hit the floor first, beneath him. Robert rolled away from him and crawled to his hands and knees. The man didn't react.

He stood and tried the door. It was locked. Maybe he could climb the shelves, or the bedstead, like a ladder and get back to his friends. It would be difficult, plus the edge of the hole looked jagged and uninviting.

He cleared his throat and shouted hoarsely up to Lily. "I don't think I can get out!"

"What about him?" Lily hollered down.

Robert nudged the man with a foot, kicking up a sweaty stench that made him recoil. The man didn't move. "He's out cold," Robert called. "Bring the police, or someone, before he comes 'round."

Lily nodded. "Let me try something first." She disappeared over the edge of the hole, taking Malkin and the light with her. Robert heard their feet on the stairs, and moments later the door rattled as Lily grappled with it from the other side.

"The cover's melted shut across the keyhole. I won't be able to pick the lock from out here."

"Funny, it seems fine on this side," Robert said. "But go and get help!" he begged. "And quickly!"

"All right," she yelled, and she and Malkin crunched away through the house.

Then Robert found himself left alone in the storeroom, in darkness, with this dangerous, unconscious stranger.

Time passed—it could've been minutes or hours. The only illumination was moonlight glancing through the hole in the roof far above. Robert huddled in the corner of the room, as far from the man as possible, sucking in deep breaths. A cloud of fear bubbled. He shut his eyes and tried to exhale it away.

"Where are we, boy?" the man whispered, suddenly close by his side. He had woken and Robert hadn't even heard, or noticed him move!

"We fell through the floor." Robert tried to keep his voice from shaking and muster some bravery from the slush inside. "We're in a locked room. Lily's gone for help."

"Lily, is it?" the man purred.

"It. Is." Robert spat the words like bullets, but inwardly he cursed himself for giving her name away. "And when she gets back with the police you'll be charged with trespassing. Then we'll see what's what."

The man gave a hearty laugh that set Robert's teeth on edge. "But I won't be here, boy." He leaned in close until Robert could feel the man's breath against his face.

"You still don't know who I am, do you?"

"N-no." Robert shook his head, then watched in horror as the man ran a finger down his scarred cheek.

"Need a clue? Ah, you'll know soon enough." The man stepped away to the ill-lit far corner of the small room and Robert heard him rattle the door handle.

"You won't open that before they return," he said,

with more confidence than he felt. "Thaddeus Townsend built that lock and it's fail—"

"—safe," the man finished for him. "You're talking to someone who's cracked them all, lad! Let's have some light, shall we?" He struck a match and the flame illuminated his grin as he held it up to the lock for a second. Then it went out.

"What're you doing here?" Robert asked.

"Looking for something that belongs to me." The man grunted. "Something stolen," he hissed under his breath. "But I'll catch up with that traitor Selena. She'll regret the day she ever crossed me."

Robert felt a wave of shock. The man was talking about his ma! Suddenly he was glad the room was lit solely by moonlight. It would hide his surprise.

The man struck a second match and stared intently at the lock. The flame burned slowly, down to his fingertips, but he didn't flinch, merely poked the match into the keyhole until it fizzled away. Then Robert heard the distinctive click of tumblers.

The man smiled and shook the matchbox in his fist. When he opened his fingers his palm was empty. The box had disappeared into thin air.

Those matches—they were his, Robert realized. The man must've taken them from him without him even noticing. Surely he couldn't do that, could he?

Robert thrust his hands into his pockets. The matchbox *was* gone. Instead, he felt something else—a card with curved corners.

He pulled it out and turned it over, peering at it in the gloom. A Jack of Diamonds.

His stomach gave a flip. "You're Jack Door," he gasped. "The greatest escape artist in all the land!"

Jack laughed. "Ah, the penny drops! Mere locks can't hold me!" He stepped through the now-open doorway with his arms outstretched and gave a little bow, as a magician might to end a show. He hovered for a moment, as if he was waiting for some sign of recognition, some applause from an invisible audience. And then Robert realized who the audience was. It was him.

"Well, lad," said Jack Door. "It's been a pleasure meeting you, but I'll have to be off. I shall return, so be sure to tell no one of my visit—if you value your life."

Before Robert could respond, he stepped through the doorway and was gone, leaving only moon shadows behind.

Robert stumbled toward the dark square of the open doorway. The ground-floor corridor of the shop was empty—Jack had completely disappeared. He looked down at the card, which was shaking in his hand. The Jack of Diamonds. What on earth had he been looking for? And could he really have known Selena? Professor Hartman had suggested that Robert's ma might have run away to escape trouble—and surely there was no greater trouble than getting on the wrong side of a notorious criminal like Jack Door? But if Jack was after Selena, could that mean she was actually alive, and somewhere in England…?

Robert felt a wave of something like relief. He had no idea if his guesses were right but they made a strange sort of sense. Although even if they were right, there were still so many questions… Jack Door obviously didn't know where Selena was, but what had she stolen from him, and what would Jack do if he ever found her? Robert's knees quivered beneath him—from the fellow's fearsome reputation, he felt sure that, whatever it was, it would be bad.

Then he remembered that the newspaper article had mentioned Jack was fifteen years into a life sentence for masterminding the theft of the Blood Moon Diamond—could that be the thing Jack was looking for, that had been stolen from him? And by Selena? Surely not…?

How would his ma have gotten hold of such a valuable jewel? And why would Jack think she'd left it at Townsend's all those years ago?

Anyway, everything had been consumed by the fire... And yet, Jack had been searching the house when they'd interrupted him. He must've hidden in Thaddeus's room and hoped they'd go away, but instead Malkin had stumbled on him. Which meant what he was looking for could still be up there...

Then Robert remembered the thing stuck in the chimney.

Carefully, he made his way back upstairs. The jagged hole in his da's room cut right across the floor. The cross-beam was still intact, but barely visible in the moonlight; he managed to inch his way across it and soon he was standing at the fireplace once more.

He crouched down and pushed his hand past the cast-iron fireback and into the chimney. The flue was far too narrow for a grown man to reach up—even a contortionist like Jack wouldn't be able to manage. But for Robert, with his smaller hands, it was easy.

He stretched his fingers as far as he could...and felt something.

It was fluffy and disintegrating, covered in dust. A dead bird? Robert brushed his fingertips across the thing again. He could feel it rocking back and forth in the place where it was wedged. He pulled his hand back and then pushed at it hard, and it loosened somewhat…

Then it fell, toppling out of the chimney in a cloud of coal dust that flew straight up Robert's nose and made him sneeze. The object came to a rest at his feet. He picked it up.

It was a small bundle of gray rags, and though it looked as if it had been wedged for some years up the chimney, it was still a lot cleaner than anything else in the crumbling room.

Quickly he unrolled the bundle to reveal a tattered envelope. Two raggedy words were scrawled in black ink on its yellowing surface:

Queen's Crescent

A heavy and misshapen object was scrunched inside. He tipped it out and rubbed his sleeve across its surface. It glinted in his hand. It wasn't the Blood Moon Diamond, as he'd hoped, but a silver C-shaped locket.

The front, inlaid with ivory, showed the sickle-shaped profile of a man in the moon. He'd a round bulbous nose and a crater-y smile like Jack's. On the tip of his head a long chain looped through an eyelet, so you could wear the crescent around your neck. Robert turned it over. A single red jewel flashed from its back, embedded in a spindly tree-like drawing. Underneath that was a pair of engraved words. He peered at them closely in the moonlight. They looked to be in a foreign language, and were followed by a small triangle:

fmqzw uofhvlxvcwn △

"Is this what you were looking for, Jack?" Robert whispered, fingering the locket. "Because I have it now."

A rush of footsteps on the landing interrupted his thoughts. He jumped to his feet and dipped his head, clipping the chain round his neck. The locket swung cold against his chest. He'd barely time to button up his shirt collar and hide its silvery glint, before a creaking figure stepped through the doorway toward him.

"Robert?" a soft voice called.

With relief, he saw it was not Jack, but Lily, closely followed by Malkin and Mrs. Rust.

"Frying pans and fish kettles!" Mrs. Rust exclaimed. "Thank goodness we've found you!"

"We thought you were locked in the storeroom," Lily yelled. "But when we got back it was empty. How did you get out?"

"That man picked the lock," Robert shouted.

"Then it's a good thing we brought help," Malkin growled. "Where is he?"

"Gone."

"Good." Lily grinned and waved over at him exuberantly. "I rode home as fast as I could! Mr. Wingnut's waiting outside in the steam-wagon." She looked around. "Where did the man go?"

"Disappeared." Robert edged his way toward them along the cross-beam. "Apparently it's his specialty!" He arrived at Lily's side and pulled out the Jack of Diamonds, presenting it to her with a flourish.

Lily's eyes went wide. "I can't believe it!" she whispered. "Jack Door? And he gave you this?"

"Not exactly," Robert replied. "More like hid it about my person when he stole my matches."

"Spinning wheels and spice racks!" Mrs. Rust whispered. "He could've robbed any one of you without you even realizing."

"Oh tosh!" Malkin said. "I think not!"

Lily handed the card back. "He was looking for something though, wasn't he, Robert? Something stuck up that chimney?"

"I wonder if he found it?" Malkin mused.

Robert touched a hand to his collar. The Moonlocket rested under it, nestling against his breastbone. A cold, sharp curve hanging between his shirt and skin.

"Somehow," he said, "I don't think he did."

CHAPTER 6

Robert stumbled through dream doorways, half-asleep. A fiery Jack of Diamonds floated before him, edged with silvery moonlight. He chased it, arms outstretched, but it flitted from reach and the ground tumbled away beneath him, pulling him from slumber into the bright blue morning, and landing him with a lurch in his bed.

He lay for a moment, catching his breath. Light streamed through the open curtains. The sun was at its midday zenith. A strange cold shape was crushed against his breast. He sat up and it swung from side to side. The Moonlocket! It had made a red C-shaped pattern on his bare skin.

Of course, it was all returning to him… How Lily and the mechanicals had brought him to Brackenbridge. When they'd gotten back, Mrs. Rust had made a posset of milk, and Lily and Malkin had hung around to check he was feeling better, before they were shooed off to bed—that had been around five o'clock in the morning.

There was a knock at the door.

"Come in," he called, pulling the sheets up over his chest to hide the locket.

Miss Tock entered with a steaming jug.

"Finally awake, are you, you clanking criminal?" she chided, as she poured water out into the basin on the washstand. "I ought to box your ears for the bother you caused! We were a-jitter with worry last night… Going out with Lily like that…getting tangled up in trouble… having such a tumble and covering your clothes in a dozen different kinds of dirt!"

"Sorry," Robert mumbled.

"Sorry won't cut the mustard with me, I'm afraid." Miss Tock sighed and began picking up his dirty clothes from the floor. Her face was set in anger but Robert could detect a twitch of worry in the corner of her mouth.

"Bless my brackets!" she said at last. "I can't be cross any longer. Not for the world. We were so worried about you, Robert. You could've died!"

"I'm fine, honest."

"Well, thank tock for that!" She gathered up the last of his things. "I'll take these and have them washed. And when you're done dressing, leave your shoes outside the door—I'll get those cleaned as well."

"Thank you."

After she'd gone Robert got out of bed and tested the water in the washbowl gingerly with the tips of his fingers—it was almost as hot as her scolding! He added a little cold from the jug at his bedside and, lathering up his hands with the scented soap, proceeded to wash his face.

He took a towel from the rail and dried himself; making black sooty stains on the fluffy white wool. When he'd finished, he regarded his reflection in the round mirror of the washstand. The silver Moonlocket glinted against his chest in a shaft of afternoon sunlight.

Robert turned it back and forth, twisting the chain worriedly around his fingers. Where had it come from, before he'd found it in the chimney at Townsend's? The most pressing worry was if Jack was still looking for it, and found out where Robert lived, what would happen then? Robert knew it wouldn't be pleasant.

He let the locket drop and it thumped cold and hard against his breastbone, sending a shiver through his ribcage, like a stone dropped in water.

Suddenly it felt too heavy. He took it off and laid it on

the bed. The silver sides and the ivory inlay actually did make it look like a crescent moon, suspended in a blue bedspread sky.

The profile face seemed to be laughing at him. What he'd thought were cheeks above the mouth were actually sort of craters. It was almost as if the man in the locket-moon had the features of the real moon itself.

Suddenly Robert felt a tiny hidden catch beneath the moon man's nose. He held his breath and gave it a flick, half-expecting it to be locked. But, with a click, the front face of the locket swung open smoothly, revealing a tiny compartment filled with a miniature portrait, brightly colored and barely bigger than his thumb.

Robert peered closely at it and let out a low gasp.

It showed a baby with dark curly hair and hazel eyes—just like Robert's—clasped in a woman's arms. Beside her stood a young man, his arm placed protectively around her shoulders, looking content. He was cut away slightly by the sickle C-shaped frame, but there was no doubt in Robert's mind that it was Thaddeus, or that this picture was done by his hand. The baby must be him, and the woman must be his mother, Selena Townsend.

He felt a rush of elation. This Moonlocket was hers.

A clue to learning more about his ma. But who'd hidden the locket in the fireplace? His da? Did that mean he was planning to give it to Robert someday, or never at all? This was more complicated than he'd first thought.

He closed the locket and turned it over to examine the back once again, to distract himself. The leafless tree looked clearer in the daylight. Its main trunk had many branches leading off it, and stood on a sort of wavy line that perhaps represented a hillside. Then there was the red stone inlaid on the uppermost branch, and the two strange foreign-looking words underneath:

fmqzw uofhvlxvcwn △

What did they mean? Robert ran his fingers over the letters. They felt raised, like tiny pimples, cold to the touch. When he took his finger away he found he had left a greasy print on the locket's surface. He turned the engraving round and wiped the mark away with his cuff. There, in the other corner, was a cross capped with a small arrowhead and a capital N for north. He hadn't noticed it the night before.

All at once it occurred to him that this drawing was a map. A map Jack needed desperately. And maybe Selena knew something about the place it represented?

Robert felt sick. He couldn't decide what was a worse prospect; him running into Jack again, or Jack threatening Selena. But he knew he had to find his ma urgently, to ask her about the locket, and warn her about Jack. Although she probably didn't know it, Selena was all the family Robert had left, and he felt a sudden need to protect her from harm.

He took out the envelope the locket had come in and read it carefully a second time.

Queen's Crescent

Were those two words part of the mystery as well? Connected to the pair of foreign words on the locket? And, if so, how?

As he was thinking these things, Lily and Malkin came tumbling through the door.

"Good morning!" Lily cried. "Or is it afternoon? I must say, you look much better." She sat down on the foot of the bed. Malkin hopped up beside her, leaving muddy footprints over the covers, and padded over to wash Robert's face with a sandpapery tongue. Robert reached under his wagging brush, pulled out the Moonlocket, and handed it to Lily.

Lily's mouth fell open. She held it up to the light, staring incredulously. "It's beautiful. What is it?"

"Something valuable," Robert said. "I found it last night at the shop, after you went for help. It was hidden in the chimney in my da's room. I think it's what Jack was after. It was in this." He showed her the envelope.

"Queen's Crescent," Lily read. "Do you think it belonged to the Queen then?"

"No, I think it belonged to my ma."

Lily flicked the locket open and examined the picture inside. "It's only a partial portrait."

"True," Robert said. "But I remember that face. It's definitely her. That other figure with his arm around her is Da, and the baby she's holding is me."

"How can you be sure?" Malkin asked.

Robert pursed his lips. "Two things: the painting's done by my da's hand. And the second thing is, my ma's name was Selena."

"So?" Lily asked.

"Selena comes from Selene," Robert explained, "which is the Latin name for moon. If she owned a locket it would be a Moonlocket, don't you think?"

Lily closed the locket and pressed the points between her fingers, turning it around. "These markings on the back, and the two words, what can they mean?"

"At first I thought it was an engraving of a tree or a river," Robert said. "But then I saw this little compass here in the corner, and realized it must be a map."

Malkin leaned in close, poking at the locket with his nose. "These two words must be the key, but they aren't in any language I know of."

"Maybe they're a code?" Lily traced them with a finger. "The trouble is they butt up to the edge here. The map lines too. And this red jewel that's sort of diamond-shaped—it could be like an X marks the spot…" She sat up straight with a jolt. "Of course! This must be a map to where the Blood Moon Diamond is—that's got to be why Jack came for the locket! He's trying to recover his greatest treasure."

"You think so?" Robert's pulse quickened. He felt awash with giddy excitement.

"Of course," Lily said. "Why else would he have come? Although I don't understand why Selena had such a clue in the first place. Or what it was doing hidden up a chimney in your da's shop…"

But that thought was interrupted by a knock at the door. Hurriedly, Lily handed him back the locket. Robert looped it around his neck, and tucked it quickly beneath his shirt collar, while Malkin jumped down off the bed.

"Come in," he cried out finally, and the door opened to reveal Miss Tock.

"By all that ticks!" she grumbled, trundling into the room. "Was there ever such a day? There are two gentlemen to see you, Master Robert and Miss Lily. Policemen—by every account—and they're waiting in the drawing room."

She handed Lily a calling card.

"Inspector Fisk," Lily read out, her brow crinkling. "Serious Crimes Squad. Scotland Yard." Why did that name feel familiar? She pursed her lips. Of course, he was the policeman mentioned in Anna's newspaper article.

Robert shuddered and thought immediately of Roach and Mould—those two villains had disguised themselves as the police many times when they'd tried to steal Lily's Cogheart. Jack Door seemed just as tricksy. But surely he wouldn't call in broad daylight? Announcing himself as the very man chasing him? That sort of show-off theatrical flourish was too much, wasn't it…?

"You're sure they're police?" he asked Miss Tock.

"One of them is in uniform," she replied. "Are you well enough disposed to receive them, Master Robert? Or shall I send Miss Lily alone? You still look rather pale."

"I'm fine." Robert grabbed his jacket. Only one way to find out.

"So shall I relay that the pair of you will be down shortly?"

"The three of us," Malkin said.

"Very good." Miss Tock stepped out into the hall.

Robert steeled himself. He did not yet know how much he wanted to reveal about the Moonlocket, and he didn't have much time to decide.

He put a hand up to it, hanging against his chest. "For

the moment," he told Lily and Malkin, "I think we should keep this a secret."

"As you wish," Lily said.

"We shall follow your lead," Malkin added.

The two policemen were sitting in the drawing room on the chaise longue, enjoying a spot of tea and a plate of Mrs. Rust's homemade almond thins, which was perched on the coffee table along with a manila folder. When Lily, Robert and Malkin entered they put down their cups and stood up.

The first man was tall and stately, with a long white beard and wearing a plain gray tweed suit rather than a uniform. Lily was certain he was Inspector Fisk. Beside him was a second fellow, who was clean-shaven except for a neatly coiffed moustache. He was decked out in a constable's blue uniform and wore the domed hard hat of a beat bobbie, with its silver star-and-crown badge. She noticed he carried a truncheon, a rattle, and a set of handcuffs in his belt.

"Ah, here's the young gentleman and lady now," the bearded tweedy man said.

"And a...er...fox," added the other, noticing Malkin.

"Mechanimal," Malkin corrected.

"Are you here to arrest us for breaking into my home?" Robert asked.

"We're here about Jack Door." The tweedy man stepped forward, shaking first Robert's and then Lily's hand. "I'm Chief Inspector Fisk of Scotland Yard, at your service. I'd be much obliged if you could tell us everything about your encounter with the escaped prisoner. My colleague here will take notes. Won't you, Jenkins?"

"Yes, Sir." Constable Jenkins took a pad and pencil from about his person.

"Please do include any incidental observations, no matter how small or insignificant," the inspector said. "It may be vital to our investigation. We need to apprehend the suspect as soon as possible. He's highly dangerous. You're lucky to have got away with your lives."

Inspector Fisk returned to his seat and took up his cup of tea. Constable Jenkins sat back down beside him, pencil poised at the ready.

"How do you know we met Jack?" Lily asked, as she and Robert settled themselves on the seat opposite the two policemen. Malkin jumped up onto her lap and she stroked his ears.

"Your father wired me." Inspector Fisk crossed his legs and sat forward, reaching for his manila folder.

"He's not my father," Robert interrupted. "My da was Thaddeus Townsend."

The inspector nodded. "Yes, of course. I'm sorry, I meant Professor Hartman."

"He was telegraphed by one of the mechanicals in the household very early this morning," Constable Jenkins explained. "He was worried for your safety, and asked if we could look in on you. We traveled up from London immediately."

The inspector gave an agitated cough and pretended to consult some notes in his folder. Lily could see he didn't like to be interrupted. "You say you saw Mr. Door at the burned-out premises, Townsend's Horologist's? What exactly happened?"

"We wrestled with him," Lily explained. "He and Robert fell through the floor…"

"Then he picked a lock and escaped," Robert finished for her.

"I see." The inspector shuffled his papers skeptically.

Robert bristled. "I'm telling the truth, that's what happened!"

"He *is* an escapologist," Lily added. "If you don't believe us, go to the shop and you'll see for yourself."

"Oh, we believe you." The inspector waved a hand at Constable Jenkins who wrote something down on his pad. "But we want to confirm every detail. A lot of people have been crying wolf about Mr. Door since his jailbreak. What with the rewards and suchlike, you know how it is? At first I thought this might be similar," he continued, "but then, when I looked at the…surrounding information, I had reason to believe your story might stack up."

Robert shifted uncomfortably in his seat. "What surrounding information?"

"Things to do with the Doors," the inspector said cryptically. He leaned forward in his chair again. "Have either of you asked yourselves why Jack would come all the way to Brackenbridge to visit a destroyed shop? Who…or what was he looking for?"

"That's obvious," Lily said. "The Blood Moon Diamond."

"No," the inspector corrected. "We think he was looking for Selena Townsend—your mother, Robert. But we've only a few clues to go on."

"She left when I was quite small," Robert said. "I haven't seen her since."

"So I've heard." The inspector's face was grave. "Professor Hartman told me he tried to contact her following your father's death. He placed advertisements in newspaper classifieds, but nothing showed up."

"That's right," Lily said.

"Do you know your mother's maiden name, by any chance? The one she had before she was married?"

Robert shook his head. "Is it important?"

"It might be. If what we surmise is correct." The inspector picked some lint from his trousers. Robert could see he knew more than he was letting on. All of a sudden he decided, quite abruptly, that he didn't like the inspector at all. Selena was *his* ma, he'd a right to hear everything the police knew about her. He resolved he would only tell the inspector about the locket if it was absolutely necessary.

"If you've discovered anything about my mother," he said rather brusquely, "then you must inform me of it."

"Of course." The inspector produced a folded piece of paper from the manila folder. "When I was a boy, I was a big fan of the vaudeville—are either of you familiar with it?"

Robert shook his head.

"It means sideshows," Lily said. "Revues, magic performances—that sort of thing."

"Very good!" said the inspector. "I used to collect the lobby cards for every act I saw back then. There was one in particular that I adored." He unfolded the paper and showed it to them.

Robert's eyes widened. It was an old theater poster,

depicting a family—man, woman, son, and daughter—each one decked out in a unique stage outfit. Above them on a scrolled banner were written the words:

THE DOOR FAMILY PLAYERS
ENTERTAINMENTS FEATURING EMINENT
PSYCHICS AND ESCAPE ARTISTS

"You recognize him, of course," the inspector said, tapping the picture of the father. "This was the man you saw?"

"Yes," they said in unison. It was Jack.

"Except he was stubblier and older—more disheveled," Malkin added.

"Fifteen years at Her Majesty's pleasure will do that to a man," Constable Jenkins said.

The inspector pointed out another figure in the picture. "And how about this lady? Have you ever met her, Robert—it would be years ago, if at all?"

"Why, that's Jack's wife!" Lily exclaimed. "Her name was Artemisia Door. She was a renowned medium, who Jack met in a theater revue."

"She looks more of a small to me," said Malkin poking at the poster with his nose.

"Medium just means she talked to spirits and ghosts," Lily explained.

"Oh."

Robert was feeling more and more funny. "Where is this going?" he asked the inspector.

"Just answer the question, please," the inspector told him.

So he examined the woman's face. "Never seen her."

"It was a long shot. She died ten years ago. I only thought…on the off chance…" The inspector moved his finger down the flyer to the two children standing in front of Jack and Artemisia. "It's their children I'm more interested in. Have you met this fellow, their son, Finlo?"

Robert shook his head.

"Or their daughter, Selena?"

Robert held his breath.

"Take a closer look." The inspector handed him the flyer. "Do you recognize her?"

Robert peered at the inky printed face of the girl. She looked exactly like a younger version of the woman in the locket, the woman he remembered.

"Why," he whispered, softly, "it's my ma."

CHAPTER 7

Robert's face had turned very pale and he looked aghast. Lily knew how he felt—it was horrible to find out a secret about yourself like that, a secret that has been buried for years like a seed and that one day blooms into the open.

The inspector nodded. "I thought so. But I wanted to make sure. We think your ma, Selena, is still a stage performer today. She's no longer in touch with Jack or Finlo, but we've reason to believe she's in London."

"Why?" Lily asked.

"That I can't tell you, I'm afraid, but let's call it a concrete hunch."

The constable was writing something in his notebook.

"Can I keep this?" Robert asked, gripping the flyer of the Door family tightly in his hand.

"Of course," the inspector said.

"Thank you." Robert put it in his pocket. Then he realized something. "If my ma's Jack's daughter…" he said, "that makes me…"

"His grandson." The inspector uncrossed his legs and straightened the creases of his trousers. "There's something more, Robert… When she was but a few years older than you are, Selena gave her father up to the police for his theft of the Blood Moon Diamond. The stone was never recovered," the inspector confided. "We're certain that, before she died, Artemisia Door— Jack's wife—hid the diamond, and we've come to believe Mr. Door suspects Selena of having a clue to its whereabouts."

"What kind of a clue?" Robert asked.

The inspector shook his head. "I'm afraid we don't know. And unfortunately we found nothing in the shop to indicate Jack's next move. Very disappointing." He stroked his beard thoughtfully. "If you know anything more, or have something of his, then you must tell us. Anything he left behind?"

Lily shook her head.

"And you, Robert?" the inspector asked.

Immediately, Robert thought of the Moonlocket

around his neck. It had to be the clue the inspector was talking about—the map to the location of the Blood Moon Diamond.

He reached up and fiddled with his shirt buttons, feeling the locket's bumpy surface against his hand. Should he mention it…? He didn't want to give it up, not yet. It'd been his ma's, after all—perhaps she too once wore it close to her heart? His gut instinct was to keep it, at least until he'd learned more.

He didn't trust the police, not after what had happened with Roach and Mould last year, and the investigation into his da's death by the local force that had come to nothing. No, he'd keep quiet about the locket for the present, investigate himself and reveal his discoveries when the time was right. If only there was some small thing he could provide them with to show he was cooperating…

Then he remembered the card. He took it out and handed it to the inspector.

"Jack gave me this. He hid it on me without me even noticing."

The inspector examined the Jack of Diamonds. Then turned it over and looked at the back. "It's the brand of cards he favors."

"Does it mean anything?" Lily asked. "Anything specific? He's not coming to get us, is he?"

The inspector laughed reassuringly. "Don't worry about that! You didn't give him your names or address, did you?"

"No," Robert said—but, with a start, he remembered he *had* given Jack Lily's name.

"Then," said the inspector, "he probably hasn't even realized who you are. D'you mind if I have this?" He was already putting the playing card in his folder. "We might be able to take a fingerprint from it."

Robert shrugged. "I suppose so."

"Good! Good!" the inspector replied. "And you may keep the flyer. Now that we've pooled our resources—as we like to say—I'm sure we'll catch the blighter in no time!" He stood. "Oh, and one more thing—if Jack or even Selena or Finlo come calling, it's imperative you telegraph me straight away, do you understand? Those Doors are far more dangerous than you could possibly imagine. Especially if they're cornered and desperate."

Robert nodded and so did Lily.

"Good. My address is on my calling card. In the meantime, stay safe, and don't let anyone into the house. I promise we'll send someone local 'round to check on you tomorrow morning." The inspector tucked his manila folder under one arm and tipped his hat, and then, ushering the constable out first, he took his leave of them.

"He was a shrewd customer," Malkin growled, once the door had closed behind him.

"But you told him all we knew," Lily added. "Except about the Moonlocket. Why did you still decide to keep that quiet, Robert?"

"I don't know," Robert said. "It just didn't feel right to give it to them."

He stepped toward the window and stared at the constable and inspector getting into the police steam-wagon sat in the drive.

Robert pressed his hand to the Moonlocket again, flattening it against his chest. He'd been right to keep it to himself. The inspector would only have taken it, like everything else was always taken from him.

He didn't need their help. The locket was his and *he* was going to find out what it meant. It was a map to the location of the Blood Moon Diamond, that much was clear now. That's why Jack needed it. But why had his ma left the locket behind? And why had she left *him*, as if he didn't even matter? As soon as he found her that's what he'd ask.

In the meantime he intended to use the locket to recover the diamond. But not only that—he was going to recapture Jack too. Because that would prove to her that he mattered. That would prove he mattered more than anything in the whole wide world.

When the police steam-wagon had finally disappeared up the drive, Robert flipped the Moonlocket over and opened the catch, staring at the portrait inside once more. The woman the inspector had pointed out on the flyer was definitely Selena. She was slightly older in the miniature locket painting, of course, but there could be no mistaking they were one and the same person.

So she had left her family to come and live with Thaddeus, after she'd given her father Jack up to the police. Then she had left Thaddeus and him behind too—but why? Was she not happy with Da? And if that was so, why did she leave the Moonlocket behind, when it was so important? Robert closed it. He felt a little sick.

"We should show the locket and envelope to John when he gets back," Malkin advised. "Maybe he can work out the map, or what *Queen's Crescent* means and the cryptogram—he was always good at cracking codes."

"I'm good at cracking codes too!" Lily said. "But we need the cypher key really to work it out." She stopped. "Or, we could take it to London to show Papa. It's a good excuse for us to go and visit him. Maybe we could look for your ma at the same time, Robert? Anna might help us; I imagine she knows plenty about the Doors from her article."

"Your papa would only hand the locket over to the inspector," Robert said. "And it's the only clue we've got."

"We'd make them return it," Lily promised.

"I don't think so."

"Then we'll have to do some investigating ourselves. Did your da ever mention Jack, or anything about codes or maps?"

"Never." Robert stroked the engraved surface of the Moonlocket. "If only we could understand what all this meant. It's almost as if there's a piece missing."

Lily took an almond thin from the plate on the coffee table and bit into it as she thought. "I've got it," she said, spraying biscuit crumbs at him. "The locket's a crescent moon…"

"So?" Robert said.

"So there's no such thing as a crescent moon," Lily mumbled with her mouth full. "It's a trick of the light. An illusion. In actuality there's only a whole moon."

"Because," Robert said, "the rest of it is hidden in shadow." He picked up a biscuit and broke it into two halves. "So what you're saying is there's another piece of the Moonlocket hidden somewhere? Another part of the map and code?"

"It makes sense." Lily examined the edge of the locket. "These lines could match up to a missing piece, which would be…"

"…shaped like a gibbous moon." Robert finished her sentence and, at the same time, the last of the biscuits. "And if we had both parts, we might have a solid clue to finding the Blood Moon Diamond, and my ma." He brushed the crumbs from his fingers. "It's definitely not at the shop. If it was, Da would've kept the pieces together."

"Maybe we can deduce what these code words mean anyway," Lily said. "They must have something to do with the Door family, wouldn't you say?"

"I know!" Robert said. "We can look in Jack's autobiography!"

Lily clapped her hands. "Why didn't I think of that?"

"Yes, why didn't you?" Malkin said. "And where, pray, is this legendary book?"

"In my room, of course!"

Lily searched through the pile of books on her bedside table, while Robert and Malkin collapsed on the bed, leaning their backs against the yellow wallpaper, which was pinned with plentiful illustrations from the pages of Lily's penny dreadfuls. Each one had been judiciously hand-tinted with red watercolor paint by Lily to make the crimes they depicted look even more bloody.

"Here it is! *The Notorious Jack Door: Escapologist and*

Thief Extraordinaire!" Lily pulled a book from the bottom of the pile.

Malkin yelped as the rest of the books balanced on top of it came tumbling down around him in a rain of flapping pages.

"What does it say?" Robert asked.

Lily flipped through the pages, scanning the text. "Just as I remembered—I'm afraid it's mostly about lock-picking. Nothing on codes, and barely anything about his family. It mentions his wife Artemisia and their son Finlo. But there's nothing about Selena. That's why I never thought…"

Malkin had climbed out from under the pile of books. He snuffled in beside Lily and licked a few pages of this volume for good measure. "He could have expunged her from his life?" he suggested. "After she gave him up to the police?"

"You could be right," Robert said. "In which case Jack's manual is worse than useless."

"Mama used to have some books on magic and the theater," Lily said. "And Papa has some on codes. They'll be in the library. And we can see if there are any maps in the atlas that match the one on the locket while we're at it…" She looked down at Malkin, who had settled on her bed as if he intended to laze about all evening.

"Malkin," she said, but he didn't respond. "You'd better get up and help, or I'll turn you into a fox-fur scarf."

"You wouldn't dare," Malkin blustered.

"Then you'll come with us, and aid our investigations."

"Do I have a choice?"

"Unquestionably not," Robert said. "But it'll be fun—you can go through the books on the lower shelves."

"Oh, goody!" Malkin leaped to his feet with a roll of his eyes. "In that case, what are we waiting for?"

Lily's mama and papa had collected a lot of books in their lives. The oak shelves of the library were crammed two deep with tomes from floor to ceiling, and even more volumes lay sideways on top of the others. Most of these were scientific papers that explained how mechanicals worked, but if you knew where to look and understood the erratic filing system, there was a lot of information on other subjects as well.

"Right," said Lily. "Let's get down to business. One person can research codes, another maps, and the last one the theater. Who wants to take what?"

"I'll take whichever one of those subjects is on the lowest shelf," Malkin said. "Since I can't reach the high ones."

"Maps then," Lily told him. "All the atlases are down

there. Robert, you had best take theater, since the Doors are your family. I shall take codes and cyphers, my area of expertise."

And they were off.

Malkin pulled the atlases out of the lower shelves and flipped through the lower pages with his teeth, looking for maps that matched the one on the locket. But he soon became distracted by a big book called *Henry McGuffin's Amazing Atlas of the World* and by trying to find out which country was the chewiest.

Lily pushed the stepladder up against the far shelves, where the books on cryptography were kept. She got down as many as she could carry, even balancing one on her head as she'd been taught long ago at her old boarding school, and brought them to the long polished table in the center of the room. But after searching through every one, she could find no key that could help her decipher the two words on the back of the locket.

Robert wasn't having much luck with his research either. He'd examined various theatrical books for pieces on spiritualism or escapology, and finally checked *The Secrets of Stage Conjuring* by Jean Eugène Robert-Houdin for any mention of the Doors, but there was none in any of them. It was almost twilight—outside the window the moon was rising in the gloaming—but he was not yet ready to give up his search.

Malkin had long ago abandoned the atlases and map catalogs in distaste. He would, he decided, rather be chewing on a real cat than a catalog—at least they were chaseable, which was a lot more fun. "Let me know when you've finished your perusing and blunderings," he muttered. "Then we might indulge in something a little more productive."

While he waited, he gave a few other books on the lower shelf a jolly good gnawing, though they were not to his taste. John would surely be upset if he ever discovered his handiwork, but Malkin carried on mauling at them despite this. He was five large mouthfuls into shredding a particularly distasteful volume called *Why Modern Mechanicals Don't Think As We Do* by a man named Victor K. Plunk, when Robert jumped to his feet and shouted: "Look at this!"

Lily glanced up from an encyclopedia page about Morse codes. "Have you solved the cypher?" she asked hopefully.

"Better than that," Robert said. "I've found a photograph of where the Doors used to live…"

It was a pamphlet called *A Popular History of Modern Magicians* by Sir Edward Le-Mesmer, with a short biography on the whole Door family, and it included a large black-and-white photograph that showed Jack and his wife, Artemisia, outside a terraced house with their son Finlo and daughter Selena.

The house was covered in tiny fronds of ivy, from which clean windows peeped out, shining in the sun. Three steps led up to a smart front door, and in the front garden, behind a row of black railings, a flourishing apple tree grew. The Doors stood in front of the house in a row, arms around each other, all smiling.

This was his family. Robert couldn't quite wrap his head around it.

Then, fixed to the wall on the corner of the house in the picture, he spotted a street sign. He peered closely at it, but couldn't quite read what it said.

Lily took a magnifying glass from a drawer beneath the library table and handed it to him, and in the eye of the lens the words became clear.

"Queen's Crescent—like the envelope!" he shouted. "And there's something underneath, I can't make it out…"

He let Lily look. She held back her hair and examined the picture, squinting and holding the magnifying glass up close to her eye.

"London Borough of Camden." She slammed the glass down. "That's it! That's where the Doors used to live. Queen's Crescent, Camden—there must be all kinds of clues in that house, Robert. We might solve the cypher, find the other half of the locket, or even discover where your mother is. We need to visit it right away and investigate!"

"But your papa told us not to leave Brackenbridge," Robert said.

"Oh, fiddlesticks to him!"

"Perhaps we could telegraph," Malkin proposed. "It would be a long way to go on a whim."

Lily shook her head. "Telegraphing's no good. Whatever clues there are, we'll need to be there to find them."

"Jack might've been already," Robert said.

"Or he might not," Lily replied. "We can but try."

She pushed a loose lock of hair back behind her ear. This business felt like the start of a new adventure. Something told her it would be as dangerous as their last—after all, they were going up against Scotland Yard's most wanted criminal. But Lily wasn't scared; she knew what she had to do.

It was as her mama had always said: *Trust your heart. It will make the right choices.*

Sometimes Lily found these words hard to keep in mind, but today she was glad she remembered them. Papa may have decided it wasn't safe for her to be out in the world with the Cogheart. He may have thought she wasn't able to look after herself. But she was going to prove him wrong.

She didn't need to hide away and she didn't want to. She had decided. She would help her friend Robert solve his mystery, and find his ma and the diamond, no matter what. But they would need to act quick if they were to stay a step ahead of Jack.

"We'll go to London in the morning," Lily said. "And find the next clue."

After all, there was really no excuse not to. They'd half a locket, with a map and a secret code, a theater flyer, and an address in Queen's Crescent. It was enough to get started. And if they needed help, they could always look in on Papa, or Anna, when they arrived.

CHAPTER 8

Lily lit a fresh candle, then stood and replaced *A Popular History of Modern Magicians* on the shelf. "If we're going to leave first thing tomorrow," she said, "we should probably ask Mrs. Rust to make us a packed luncheon to take, or a picnic basket."

"Good idea," Robert said. "And, while we're at it, I'm rather peckish now."

"Me too." Lily's stomach rumbled hungrily at the thought of eating. She consulted the clock on the mantel. It was almost ten thirty. They'd been so busy working that they'd missed out on their evening meal. "That's strange," she muttered. "I wonder why no one called us to dinner?"

"Let's go and find out, shall we?" Robert opened the door.

Out on the landing, all the lamps were unlit.

"Something's up," Lily whispered. "It's too quiet."

They slunk silently downstairs to the main hall and Malkin sniffed about a bit. Finally he wandered off down the corridor and jumped up, scratching the surface of the kitchen door.

"This way," he barked.

Robert and Lily pushed open the door and found Miss Tock and Mr. Wingnut sitting frozen still at the kitchen table.

"We were so busy all day," Robert said, "that we forgot to wind them. They must've wound down extra-quick from all the worry."

"I'll get their keys," Lily said. "I think I left them in Papa's study."

She was interrupted by Mrs. Rust, who walked across the room, juddering slowly toward her. The mechanical cook had not quite wound down yet. Each step was more creaky than the last, and she had started to repeat movements and words.

"Water…tanks and watch…dogs!" she said. "Someone knocked…but when I opened…when I opened the door… I saw nobody… And…all…I could…find…found… was…this…stuck…th…ere."

She held out her arm to Lily but jittered to a stop a few feet away. Lily stared at the object in Mrs. Rust's stilled hand and her breath quickened, her pulse thudding in her ears. It was a Jack of Diamonds.

"He's here!" Lily snatched the card from Mrs. Rust's fingers and looked around queasily for any sign of Jack.

Malkin scampered about, snuffling at the four corners of the kitchen. "He may have been," he said. "But he never set foot inside."

"That's a relief," said Robert.

Then they heard a smashing sound coming from the study upstairs and slow, quiet footsteps creeping along the hall.

Lily doused their candle and they stood in the dark. Listening.

The footsteps were coming closer.

A hinge creaked directly above them.

"That's your room, Robert," Lily whispered.

A floorboard groaned. Jack was getting closer, coming down the servants' staircase behind them. Lily's eyes darted toward it. It was too late to get out of the house, but in the far corner, the cellar door stood ajar.

"Quick!" she hissed. "Down there!"

Robert shook his head. "It's the first place he'll look." He scanned the room. "Jack can't possibly know how many mechanicals we have," he whispered, snatching an old coat from the back of a chair, and a colander from the drying rack. "Put these on and sit at the table," he told Lily. "Between Mr. Wingnut and Miss Tock. Try to keep as still as possible, like you've run down."

Lily did as she was told.

Robert swiped a saucepan from a hook above the range and stuck it on his head, then he stood behind Mrs. Rust, and froze.

A moment later Jack stepped into the kitchen. His eyes flitted about the room. Lily's stomach clenched fearfully, but she stayed frozen. Luckily they were lit only by moonlight, hidden enough in the shadows.

Jack noticed the open cellar door and stalked toward it. "You can't fool me, boy," he called, peering around its edge. "I know you're hiding down there with my Moonlocket. I was watching, and I saw you take it from the shop."

Lily counted the steps as he descended—ten in total. As soon as they heard him reach the bottom, she and Robert ran across the kitchen and slammed the door. Jack came pounding back up the stairs, but Lily turned the key in the lock just in time, as he rattled the handle on the other side.

Robert leaned against the door and wiped a bead of

sweat from his brow. Horrible to think that this person who seemed to wish them harm was technically his grandfather. The only thing worse would be if Jack discovered Robert was his grandson. He fervently hoped that never happened.

"That won't hold him for long," Lily said. "How quickly did he pick the lock last time?"

"In a few minutes."

"We need to slow him down."

They took in the room. On the counter was a bowl covered in a tea towel. Robert whipped the tea towel aside and discovered a lump of dough that Mrs. Rust had left to rise for tomorrow's bread in the bottom of the bowl.

"That!" He pinched off a large piece, and stuffed it in the keyhole, while Lily grabbed a chair and wedged it under the door handle. "We need to leave at once," she whispered, stepping away from the door so there was no chance Jack might hear. "We shall go to Papa in London as we planned. We'll be safe there."

"What about the mechanicals?" Robert asked. The cellar door handle was shaking. He put a hand up to still it.

"We'll hide them in the pantry," Lily said quietly. "No harm will come to them there. They can sleep until

125

we get back. Malkin, you guard the cellar, bark if the door starts to open."

Malkin nodded and took up an alert position beside the rattling chair.

Meanwhile, quick as they could, Lily and Robert dragged the three mechanicals into the pantry. All the time the handle on the cellar door rattled as Jack fiddled with the lock. They hadn't long. Finally, when all the mechanicals stood upright among the baskets of vegetables and canned food, Lily drew a curtain across the doorway to hide them and beckoned to the fox.

"That'll have to do," she said.

Malkin glanced at the Moonlocket around Robert's neck. "Anyway," he said, "they won't be Jack's first thought when he gets out."

Robert put a hand on the locket. It felt comforting, but Malkin was right, it was also a magnet drawing Jack to him—of that he was certain.

They ran to the hall, and into the vestibule. Robert took down a light jacket and Lily her summer coat. Malkin only needed his winding key, which was kept on a chain around his neck. There was some money for emergencies in the hall dresser, and this was definitely an emergency! Lily counted out the bills and stuffed them into her purse, before wedging it into her pocket beside her watch, coins, and her precious ammonite stone. She picked up the carpet bag, with the items she'd packed for Robert and herself the day before. "Is that everything?" she asked.

Robert nodded. "Yes, let's go."

If they hurried to the airfield on their bicycles, they'd be in time to catch the last overnight zep to London, and then they could make their way to Queen's Crescent. What they'd find there, nobody knew. But perhaps, for Robert, it would bring him a step closer to his family.

The church clock in the village read quarter to midnight. Lily, Robert, and Malkin cycled past it and rushed toward the airstation. Lily had the bag in the basket on the front of her bicycle, Robert pedaled along at her side and Malkin ran ahead.

As they approached the airfield, they could see the bulging shape of the airship tethered beside the docking platform. The last of the passengers were already making their way up the gangplank.

They sped to a stop outside the gates of the main building and concealed their bicycles in some raggedy bushes nearby.

"We'll just have to hope they're still here when we get back," Lily said.

Malkin trotted toward the door of the ticket office,

but Lily grabbed him by the scruff of the neck. "Wait, Malkin," she cried. "You're not allowed on the passenger deck of an airship, you're going to have to be smuggled aboard in my carpet bag."

There was much struggling and argument, with Malkin complaining about being squashed away with their scruffy clothes. But in the end he agreed, curling up in the carpet bag, and they managed to close it over him.

Lily bought the two cheapest tickets from the clerk at the bookings window, then they ran breathlessly through the doors and onto the platform where the airship was waiting to depart. They arrived as the gangplank was about to be taken away, and ran up it just in time.

The mechanical porter took Robert's and Lily's tickets, examined them, and stamped them with a metallic stamp on the end of his finger, then returned them.

"You're in third class, Master, Miss. Cabin Five. Unreserved seating. Second on your left, off the main passageway. Please mind your heads on the beams as you pass through to your cabin!" he said as he closed the door behind them.

"Thank you," Robert called back. He and Lily followed the narrow corridor in the direction the mechanical steward had indicated, toward the bow of the ship. Robert glanced out of the portholes at the waiting room and platform below, and the depot behind it, half-expecting Mr. Wingnut, Miss Tock, and Mrs. Rust to arrive and try to stop them. He couldn't wait to travel by airship again—it'd been six months since his last flight, and he'd never been on a public zep like this before. He hoped there would be time to look around while they were airborne. He was still a little scared of heights of course, but as long as he didn't look down while they were taking off, he'd be all right.

"Here it is!" Lily had found Cabin Five and slid open the door. Third class was a lot more rudimentary than Robert was expecting—an oblong space with a large porthole window, which framed a view of the airdock, and banks of wooden bench seating down either wall with luggage racks above. The compartment was full to the brim with overnight travelers in gray suits, who sat packed together on the wooden benches, facing one another with stony expressions. Some had felt blankets to cover their knees; one hunched fellow, slouched at the end of the row, had a bowler hat pulled down over his face and was trying to sleep.

Robert and Lily fought their way through a tangle of feet toward the last two seats near the porthole at the far end. The luggage rack opposite them was nearly full and they needed all their strength to lift their heavy carpet bag into it. The man with the bowler hat over his face tutted at the inconvenience they were causing, but didn't get up to offer help, and neither did anyone else.

Finally, with both of them standing on tiptoes, Robert managed to gain that extra bit of leverage to shove the carpet bag in between two suitcases. A little mechanical groan came from inside it but Lily covered it with a yawn.

When they turned to sit they discovered a woman with a gray swirling bun of hair had arrived, and taken one of their spaces. "That's our spot," Lily complained.

"You should've sat in it then," the woman admonished. She settled herself in, shutting her eyes. "Could you be a little quieter! I need my sleep."

"We were stowing our baggage, you old baggage," Lily grumbled, but she made sure it wasn't loud enough for the woman to hear.

She and Robert struggled into the single free space, sharing it between them. Despite the time it had taken them to get settled, and the fact that the engines were puttering, the airship hadn't moved yet. Robert peered out the window. A steam-wagon was parked up on the airfield. It looked almost like John's, but surely it couldn't be? Before Robert could get a closer look, someone dashed across and began moving it from the flight path. And finally the airship began to lift off.

Robert gripped his armrest, butterflies fluttering inside him. In spite of everything they'd been through, he was still a nervous flier, and the events of this evening were making him more so. He wanted to be up in the sky and as far away from danger as possible.

Their take-off turned out to be smooth, with barely any crosswind. Soon the zep's engines were at full power and she rose steadily, in a slow and stately motion, like a soap bubble.

Lily fell asleep almost immediately, her head lolling on Robert's shoulder, her tresses of hair bright red against the gray wool of his coat. Robert wanted to join her in a doze, but what with the shudder of the wooden benches and the pistons and pipes pounding and gurgling in the wall, he found he just couldn't drop off.

Instead, his mind drifted back to the incredible revelations about his family. How could Jack Door, the criminal they'd had to lock in the cellar, be his grandfather? And what about his ma? Jack had disowned Selena, but by cutting Robert out of her life, she'd essentially done the same thing to him. Why?

He fiddled with the chain around his neck, making the Moonlocket dance against his chest. Jack knew Robert had it. The thought ran through him like a chill. Glancing up, he checked Malkin and the bag were still safe before shutting his eyes and tipping his head to one side, leaning it against Lily's. He smelled the fresh buttery fragrance of her hair, and felt her chest rising and falling with each breath, beside his. He knew he needed to come up with some sort of plan for the dangers that lay ahead, but he was too tired to concentrate now...and, pretty soon, he too fell into a deep sleep.

CHAPTER 9

Robert woke to find a bright light blinking down on them through the luggage rack. Beside him, Lily's head lolled against the headrest of the seat. He checked her pocket watch. Nearly four o'clock in the morning— they would be arriving in London soon, if all was well.

At the far end of the cabin, a figure in a black coat and battered bowler hat was stepping out into the passage, pulling the door shut behind him. Instinctively, Robert felt for the Moonlocket around his neck. It was still there, thank goodness! But something wasn't quite right…

He stood and took his cap from the coat hook above him, glancing up at the luggage rack. It was empty!

He shook Lily awake. "Someone's taken Malkin!" he cried.

Blearily, Lily pushed the hair from her face. "What? When?" The words came tightly from her throat.

"Just now. Look!"

She squeezed from their shared seat and surveyed the cabin. "The man who was sitting at the far end…"

"He's left," Robert said.

Lily's chest ticked with panic as she tried to recall what the man looked like. It was no use—all she could remember was a few tufts of black hair curled around the edge of his bowler, which he'd pushed down to hide his face.

She gripped the arm of the woman next to them. "Where did that man go?" she asked, pointing at the place where he'd sat.

The woman yawned and considered the question.

"How would I know?" she said finally. "He ain't returning, though. He took his bag. There's been such comings and goings, some of these fellows get up every few minutes to use the water closet. It's quite unbelievable."

"Which way is the water closet?" Robert asked.

"Right…no, left!"

"Oh, for goodness' sake!" Lily squeezed up the narrow footway to the door, kicking people's feet and bags out of the way. Robert followed, almost tripping over the shoes of the last man in the row, who jolted awake, and watched with uninvolved interest as Lily pulled aside the sliding door of the compartment and let in the cold air.

"Quick!" she cried, and she and Robert raced down the corridor.

Turning sharply at the starboard end, the corridor rose up a short flight of stairs into the first-class lounge. It was dark, except for the moonlight coming in through the large viewing windows.

"There he is," cried Robert, pointing out the man in the bowler, who was walking across the far side of the room, pulling their bag along behind him. Robert felt confused. Who was this new villain? He looked taller than Jack…

Over the soft rumble of the engine, Lily could make out Malkin's muffled cries from within the bag. "Where's that man taking Malkin?" she exclaimed, pushing past empty tables and chairs.

"And what'll we do if we catch him?" Robert raced behind her, accidentally tipping over a trolley filled with cutlery, which clattered to the floor.

"Fight!"

"D'you think we can fight such a big fellow?"

"We have to! We need to get Malkin back."

They sprinted after the figure in the dark and stumbled into another corridor that ran along the port side of the ship. The man was already far ahead of them, nearing the stern. He threw their bag down a stairwell and, holding onto his hat, hopped after it with one balletic jump that reminded Lily of a mechanical monkey.

When they arrived at the bottom of the ill-lit stairwell, they found that a narrow hatch had been forced open and could hear the man's footsteps echoing along the passage beyond it. Robert read the sign above the doorway.

GOODS COMPARTMENT AND ENGINE ROOM—
AUTHORIZED PERSONNEL ONLY!

As they struggled through the hatch a hot wave of stale air hit them and the hairs on the back of Robert's neck rose involuntarily.

Lily gripped the ammonite stone in her pocket. A sense of apprehension was growing inside her. For once, she wished Papa was here to tell them the right thing to do, or Anna to encourage them.

The short passage ended in a long open chamber filled with towering stacks of trunks, roped to cleats that crisscrossed the floor. Pipes ran along the metal-riveted walls, making the room feel uncomfortably hot. A strong musty smell of steam and oil wafted over everything and, far off, they heard the clanging and chuffing of the airship's engines.

The bag thief had disappeared; he had to be hiding somewhere in the shadowy gaps between the rows of luggage. Lily motioned to Robert and the pair of them stepped deeper into the darkness of the room.

"Where is he?" she whispered.

Robert shrugged and shook his head. "I don't know."

A loud shriek broke out, then a bark. A streak of orangey-white flew out from behind a traveling trunk.

Malkin! He came skittering toward Robert and Lily, scraps of torn coat clasped between his teeth.

"I bhff hmm whnn hh pppnnd thhh bgg!" he garbled.

"What?" Lily asked him.

Malkin spat the scraps out. "I said, I bit him when he opened the bag!"

The thief stepped out from behind a travel trunk, waving his hand in front of him as if he'd just burned it on the stove. His hair was dark and curly and his face was worried and pinched, but his eyes were wide and gray, the same as Jack's. One of his sleeves was now raggedy, and blood dripped from his fingers. Who on earth was he?

"Finlo, you worm, I told you not to alert them to your presence."

Finlo bristled and clenched a bleeding fist, as a second man stepped from the shadows behind him, blocking their exit—Jack!

A stony expression clouded his scarred face. How had he made it onto the airship? It had been delayed taking off, but only by minutes, surely? Unless…Robert remembered John's steam-wagon on the airfield…

Jack stepped toward Robert and Lily. "You took a locket from Thaddeus's house."

"What's it to you?" Lily asked.

"Merely a keepsake, a remembrance, a small memento to help me recall that which I've lost. We all like to recall our lost ones, don't we, Miss Hartman? Your mother, for instance…"

Lily shook with silent rage.

"We don't have anything of yours." Robert raised a hand and clasped involuntarily at the Moonlocket. It felt warm and safe, tucked against his chest, beneath his shirt.

"Oh, but I think you do." Jack's gray eyes bored into him. "Do you know what a tell is, boy?"

Robert shook his head. He hadn't a clue what Jack was talking about.

"It's when you tip your hand," Jack Door explained.

"Let the other player know he holds the winning trick." He gave a lopsided grin. "You see, I may not have taken the Moonlocket from you at Townsend's, or at Brackenbridge, and it may not be in your bag." He kicked it viciously and Lily was glad Malkin was no longer hidden inside. "But I know exactly where it is now. You just told me, Robert. It's around your neck. And this time you're going to give it up of your own free will."

"I don't know what you're on about." Robert brazened it out. "This locket belongs to my family."

Jack laughed. "But we *are* your family, Robert. I'm your poor old long-lost grandpapa. And this idiot is your wayward uncle… Surely Inspector Fisk, who visited you the other day, told you that much?" He searched Robert's face for an answer and smirked drily when he saw he was right. "He did? Jolly good!"

"No, I—"

"Don't bother to lie to me again, Robert. I can read your face like a pack of cards. It's always easier when everyone's laid their hand on the table."

"I won't give you the locket," Robert told him. "Whatever you say… It's for my ma when we meet again." He spoke loudly, but sweat was pouring down the back of his neck, and the words seemed more confident in his head. He and Lily may have escaped Jack when he was alone, but this time he had Finlo to help him. Two hard-nosed criminals and no one to come to their aid. But whatever they threatened, whatever terrible things they might be capable of, he, Lily, and Malkin had to stand their ground.

"You think, if you give her the locket, she'll be pleased to see you?" Jack motioned to Finlo, who began advancing on Robert, Lily, and Malkin. "She won't be, son. She doesn't care. Never did. Why do you think she left in the first place, with no explanation? There's only one reason: betrayal. She betrayed us all over the years—you most terribly, poor, dear child. And she'll do exactly the same the next time…"

"That's not true." Robert felt tears gathering unbidden behind his eyes.

"Yes," Jack said, "it is. So why put yourself at risk of that hurt? And from your own mother too? When the only thing you need to do is give me the Moonlocket." He held out a palm.

Robert couldn't stop. Almost as if he was hypnotized, he found himself reaching for the locket, pulling it from beneath his shirt and fumbling with the catch on the chain around his neck to take it off. Jack's eyes gleamed at the sight of it.

"Robert?" Lily whispered. "What are you doing?"

The locket sat glistening on Robert's palm.

"That's it," Jack said. "Hand it over, then you can all go home."

Robert shook the glare from his head. "I have no home." He closed his fingers around the locket. He would keep it. For his ma. And he would fight for that right if need be. He squared up to the men.

Jack shrugged and stepped aside; reaching Robert in an instant, he pulled at his fingers. Robert held tight to the locket, but Jack was crushing his hand. The sharp points of the moon dug into his palm like two nails.

He couldn't grasp it much longer. He needed help, but Finlo was holding Lily and Malkin at bay. Jack pried harder, loosening Robert's digits. For a second his fingers twitched, and Jack snatched the locket away from him.

"I have it!" Jack crowed. "The prize!" Then he saw the crescent. "Where's the rest?" he cried. "This is only half a moon. Half the map!"

Malkin raised his hackles and growled, pulling back his lips to reveal sharp teeth. He dodged past Finlo and was on Jack, snapping at his hand, pulling the locket away in his jaws. Finlo tried to grapple it from the fox, but Lily kicked the villain in the shins and he let out a yelp and let go.

"Come on," she cried, taking Robert's hand. "Down this way."

They hopped a metal joist in the floor, and squeezed through the narrow gap between towering piles of luggage. Malkin galloped in their wake, clasping the locket in his mouth.

As they emerged behind the trunks, Robert nearly tripped over a tangle of loose straps tethering them to cleats along the floor.

"Quick," he cried to Lily. "Push!"

Robert kneeled down and undid each strap, one by one.

Lily threw her shoulder against the tower and shoved hard.

"Malkin, get behind me!" she shouted.

The cases began to shift, but they weren't quite toppling. Not yet…

Lily butted her shoulder hard against them once more, as Robert freed the last of the ropes that held them tight, and stood to help.

Finlo and Jack were stalking around either side of the trunks toward them, when, with a loud *CrRRreaaaAAakkkk!* the trunks collapsed.

Jack and Finlo threw up their arms to protect themselves, but they were caught on one side by a huge canvas trunk, which had fallen on their feet with a crash, and on the other by a heavy wooden box plastered in customs labels. The box smashed open, scattering hundreds of Edison's talking dolls all around them.

"Hello, pleased to meet you!" the dolls squealed in high-pitched cheerful voices, their glass eyes spinning and their arms flailing wildly as they fell.

"Will you be my friend?" they cooed, their mechanical insides rattling as they bounced across the curved floor of the airship's hull.

"Are you my mummy?" one in a pink dress and straw hat spouted.

"Dolly wants to play!" said another, hanging by her hair from a nail on the corner of the box.

"Please sing me a song," said a third with ribbons in her hair.

"Clanging chronometers!" Malkin cried. "It's like teatime at the orphanage! Quiet, you blathering metal babies!"

The dolls didn't hear, or take any notice, just carried on spouting their set phrases…

Finlo and Jack tried to struggle through the mound of dolls, which crawled around their feet, waggling their little arms and grabbing at the men's trouser legs.

"Sing with us," pleaded one red-cheeked doll, as Jack

booted her across the aisle. "Twinkle-twinkle. Twinkle, twinkle…"

Lily and Robert didn't wait for Jack to try the same with them, but turned and ran off down the length of the luggage compartment.

Drenched in sweat, Lily searched for an exit…

"There's no escape pod, clank it!" Malkin barked.

"They never have one on commercial zeps," Robert wheezed, his chest aching with worry.

"Where to now?" Lily cried.

"There!" Robert shouted. "The mail hatch!"

They barreled over to it. Robert fought with the stiff bolts and then, pulling them aside, threw the hatch open, revealing a black hole of darkness.

The airship tipped toward the port side, its nose dropping suddenly. A large box slid from behind them and toppled through the opening. After a moment there was a loud splash.

Lily ducked down, dipping her head through the hatch; screwing up her eyes against the battering wind, she glanced about.

They were somewhere over the northern outskirts of London. The zeppelin had started its slow descent, aiming for St. Pancras airstation in the distance. It hung barely fifty feet above the treetops, passing over what looked like a large lake of shimmering silver water, nestled in the dip of a hilly heath.

Malkin shook Lily by the shoulder. "Hurry," he cried. "We need a plan!"

Jack and Finlo had pushed aside the broken trunks and were wading angrily toward them through the rest of the strewn luggage and squawking dolls.

Robert picked up a stray doll and threw it at them…

It missed.

"I love you," it said mournfully. "Will you be my mama?"

"Drop the mail line!" Lily cried as she ducked back into the gondola. "We're going to slide down into the lake…"

"You know I can't swim," Robert told her.

"Neither can I," Malkin cried. "But never mind that, you demented doohickeys, the fall will probably kill us! If you think I'm getting in another bag to be thrown out of another airship and plunged into a lake," he snapped, "then you've got more cogs loose in your cranium than I'd have credited."

"Quiet!" Robert cried. "I have to think!" He quickly tied three heavy sandbags onto the end of the mail line and threw them out of the hatch. The sandbags plopped into the lake, sinking fast.

Finlo and Jack were almost on top of them now. They were nearly out of time.

Robert let out as much line as he could. The sandbags sank deeper, reeling out the rope, which creaked and cracked. The chugging zeppelin dipped lower over the pond until it was only thirty feet above the water's surface.

Robert snatched two large empty mailbags from the pile beside the hatch and fastened them to the line by their metal C-clips; they were good and strong, made of sturdy sacking.

"Get in," he told Lily and Malkin.

"Here we go again," Malkin muttered. Lily covered his snout and stuffed him into the mail sack, then she clambered in after him. The instant both her feet were in the bag, Robert pushed her off. Lily held her breath as she and Malkin went whooshing down the anchor line.

The airship rocked as the anchor rope reached the end of its tether, pulling taut. Finlo and Jack threw out their arms to steady themselves.

Robert gulped, feeling momentarily dizzy at the thought of jumping out into the dark sky. Panic washed over him—he had to go now, the others had done it, and he needed to get away from Jack and Finlo. They weren't safe, even though they were family! He took a deep breath and climbed into the other mailbag just as Jack reached out to grab him.

Jack's hand snatched out a hair's breadth above Robert's head as he shoved off against the corner of the hatch. And then, in a flurry of cold air, Robert was sliding like a shooting star across the night sky...

CHAPTER 10

Lily clasped Malkin close to her chest. A whoosh of wind pounded around them, feathering Malkin's fur and blustering against her face.

There was a ripping sound and she looked up anxiously. Where it was rubbing against the anchor line, the mail sack had begun to tear open at the seams, unraveling under their weight.

She swallowed back a lurch of panic and fumbled with her numb fingers for the metal clip, clasping it just in time. The bag whisked away beneath them, blowing across the sky like a kite in a gale.

Her grip tightening on the clip and her other hand around Malkin, Lily sped down the line.

Branches swished past and the moonlit lake streaked toward her, the dropped box floating in its center. She was only a few feet from the water now... Malkin gave a loud growl, but didn't let go of the locket, and then—

SPLAAAASH!

They were in.

The water gurgled ice-cold around them, deep as the sky above. Lily tried to pull herself to the surface, but she couldn't tell which way was up. She choked for breath, and struck out for a shimmering reflection of light, thrusting with her legs and arms. Pushing her head high, she broke the surface near the bobbing box and threw Malkin up onto its lid.

He'd barely been in the water more than a few seconds, and seemed all right, thank tock. He shook the water from his fur and gave her a most disgusted look.

She was about to apologize when, with a gigantic splash, another mailbag containing Robert fell into the water beside her.

"Clattering clockwork!" she cried, as she pulled him free from the tangled sacking. "There you are! Grab onto the box!"

She thrust the box toward him and its corner knocked against his head. He grasped it with one flailing arm, laid his cheek upon the lid like it was a float, and took a deep breath.

"For a second it felt like I was swimming in the air and flying in water," Robert spluttered.

Malkin spat the locket out into his hand. "How poetic," he groused, pacing the lid of the box. "But the unvarnished truth is we all could have drowned. Me especially! So far on this trip I have been stuffed in a suitcase and thrown from a moving airship. From now on in, I shall listen to neither of you jangling idiots. However cunning you might protest your plans to be!"

Robert tried to ignore his moaning and instead concentrated on getting the locket over his head and back around his neck.

"Stop shifting about, you meat-muppet!" the fox growled. "You're rocking the box! You'll tip me in. Don't you know foxes hate water?"

Robert pushed the locket beneath his wet shirt and spat out a mouthful of silty slosh. "You're nothing like a real fox."

"Then mechanimals HATE water," Malkin said. "It messes with their insides."

"It messes with my insides too," Robert cried.

Lily ignored them, looking instead for the Doors. With relief she realized they'd not followed. Understandable really. You'd have to be crazy to jump out of a nice warm moving airship into a freezing pond, especially if you didn't like to swim.

Someone had cut the line and the zep was floating freely again, over the hills toward London. Time to make for land.

"Thrash your legs—like this," Lily told Robert, grasping the corner of the box and pushing the three of them toward the edge of the lake.

Robert did as he was told, kicking along with her. When he finally looked up, they were closing in on the bank. He was getting the hang of this swimming lark, even managing to keep his eyes and nose above the waterline—though not his mouth, unfortunately.

They reached the shallows and Malkin leaped daintily from the lid onto the bank; barely a drop of water had touched him.

Robert flopped down on the muddy incline and guzzled the air. It was good to feel the earth beneath him once more. Sky was one thing, but water quite another.

Lastly, Lily clambered out onto the lakeside and stood shivering, her skin goose-pimpled and cold. The box grazed against the bank, making horrible sludgy sucking sounds.

"Well," said Malkin, "at least we're all still in one piece."

Lily nodded. Then she realized something. "The Doors have our bag! It's still in the airship! It has the Queen's Crescent envelope, the inspector's card and Papa's address at the Mechanists' Guild. They'll know everywhere we're going."

"At least we still have the Moonlocket," Robert said. So why did it feel as if they had lost the battle *and* the war?

He scrambled to his feet and brushed a hand across his wet face. His cap was gone! Then he spotted it floating on the surface of the water by the shoreline, a few feet away. He picked it up and stuffed it back on his head. It dripped drops down the back of his neck.

They seemed to be on a heath at the outskirts of a village. Far off, he could see the odd twinkle of a street lamp, and the London skyline edged in the orange glow of the rising sun. The zep was floating above it, dipping toward the tall spired clocktower of St. Pancras airstation. The Doors would reach the city far before them, with all their possessions. "We have to do what they'd least expect," he said at last.

"How?" Lily asked.

"Well, they probably think we'll head straight to the police, or your papa, so we should go to Queen's Crescent first."

"And confound their expectations, you mean?" Lily

wrung the water from her dress. "I suppose it's the only advantage we have."

"And the locket. Don't forget we have the locket!"

"Much good it's done us," Malkin muttered.

They stumbled downhill and along a path that took them to the edge of the heath, the early morning light warming their backs. Lily's belly made empty, gnawing complaints and her head was void of ideas. Her cold wet clothes clung to her skin, tugging on her limbs and weighing her down. She took out her pocket watch, but the hands were stuck at four thirty.

It must've stopped when they fell in the lake. That being so, it was a miracle that Malkin was still working. Thank goodness she'd fished him out of the water when she did!

She tried winding the watch, but it only made a sad clicking sound. She would have to remember to ask Papa to fix it once they were all home again. Or Robert. She glanced over at him. His brow was furrowed with worry.

How would they ever find his ma in time to warn her that Jack was looking for her? Lily wondered. All they had to go on was a single street name for a place where Selena had lived years ago.

The trees thinned and they reached the edge of the

heath, where a railway bridge crossed over an empty branch line. On the other side of the railway tracks was a street of tall houses.

They crossed the bridge and, as they ran down the steep set of steps on its far side, a boy turned the corner sharply at the bottom and began coming up the other way. Lily crashed straight into him.

"Careful!" the boy admonished, but it was too late. He'd dropped his pile of newspapers. They scattered on the ground around them.

"Oh my goodness!" Lily muttered, and she stooped and began to help him pick them up.

Robert joined in, and Malkin tried too, but some compulsion made him tear at every paper he took in his mouth.

"Your dog's ruining my early editions!" the boy cried. "They're only just hot off the press!"

"Sorry," Robert said, and he tried to pull the pages from Malkin's mouth.

Lily joined in with the tug of war, but the newspapers were fast becoming a shredded mess. They floated like confetti to the ground, until all that was left in her hand was the masthead banner—*The Daily Cog*.

She handed that paper scrap back to the boy, apologizing again. He stuffed it under his arm, along with the few issues he had managed to protect.

"Sorry's no good to me!" he whispered mournfully, staring at the shredded sheets with a tinge of disgust, and scratching his thatch of curly brown hair. His tanned face, covered in roadside dust, looked utterly disheartened. "Sorry don't bring nothing back."

"Oh," Lily replied. Then she noticed that his clothes looked rather threadbare. His bony elbows were practically poking through the sleeves of his raggedy shirt.

"What happened to you, anyway?" the boy asked, giving them the once-over. "It ain't raining but you look like you've been in the cats and dogs. You're all wet."

"Let's just say we fell in a pond on that heath and leave it at that," Malkin muttered.

The boy brightened. "Well I never!" he said. "Your dog can talk. Is he a mechanimal then…? Looks almost real."

"I'm a mechanical fox, I'll have you know!" Malkin gave a snort of derision, but that didn't stop the boy's questions.

"Right-o!" he said. "And what were you all doing in Highgate Ponds? Taking a dip, I suppose? Most people bring a bathing suit for that, or they're in the altogether! You lot look like you jumped in with all your mufti on. Besides I thought mechs and swimming didn't mix?"

"They don't," Malkin said. "Neither do mechanimals and airships."

"We fell out of an airship," Lily explained. Although the boy now looked even more confused, and she realized it probably wasn't much of an explanation.

"Look, can we move on?" Malkin said. "It's been clattering good fun—all this biting and running, jumping and drowning, and bumping and chit-chat, but where are we actually headed?"

Robert stepped away from the boy, who was still fussing with his papers, and touched the locket around his neck. "Queen's Crescent, Camden, remember?" he whispered to the other two. "I don't suppose either of you have any idea how to find it?"

Malkin tutted. "Perhaps we should've thought of that before we left?"

Lily felt downhearted. If it hadn't been for Jack forcing them to rush from the house last night, they probably would have thought to bring a map. "It's no use," she muttered darkly. "We haven't a clue where we're going." She turned around, and was about to ask the paper boy if he knew any such place, when she saw that he'd stopped picking up his papers and was eavesdropping.

"Queen's Crescent is only twenty minutes away," he said, his hazel eyes glinting. "For a penny, I can show you the fastest route. That's if you'd like?" He gave her a smile, and his cherubic cheeks dimpled at the sides as he watched Lily fish the coins from her purse.

"Name's Bartholomew Mudlark, by the way," the boy said. "What's yours?"

"Nice to meet you, Bartholomew," Robert said. "I'm Robert."

"Bartholomew's a bit of a mouthful, so most people call me Tolly." Tolly wiped the newsprint from his hands on the tails of his coat and shook Robert's hand, and then Lily's.

"Pleased to make your acquaintance, Tolly," Lily said. "I'm Lily, and this is my pet mechanimal; he's called Malkin."

Malkin offered Tolly a muddy paw and a friendly yap.

Tolly stuffed his papers in his canvas bag, and slung the strap over his shoulder. "All right," he said. "That's the introductions over, so let's be off…"

He crooked out his right elbow for Lily, as if they were about to step out together for a promenade. After a moment's hesitation, she looped her arm through his and they set off down the street, with Robert and Malkin following behind.

The sun was almost fully up and the sky bright. The early morning air had a pleasant brisk quality to it and a light refreshing wind blew about them, throwing up the odd gust of dust. They dripped water as they walked the pavements of Camden, the wind and sunlight slowly drying them off.

"What are you looking for in Queen's Crescent?" Tolly asked as they strolled along.

"Clues to a mystery," Lily explained.

"That's exciting," Tolly said. "I enjoy a good mystery, me."

"Why?" Robert asked. He wasn't sure yet just how much they should tell Tolly, or whether they even needed another companion.

"I dunno. Just find them gripping. 'Specially the penny dreadfuls—sell a few of them on occasion. Full of intrigue, they are. I always dreamed of getting involved in some skullduggerous adventures like that!"

"Then you're in luck," Lily told him. "We're slap bang in the middle of one and it's a wealth of trouble!"

"How so?" Tolly asked.

"Well," she explained. "We forgot our map of London, lost our luggage, were chased by the Jack of Diamonds and, to top it off, we don't know where we're going. But we'd be glad to have someone as clever as you along, Tolly, to aid us."

Tolly looked pleased as punch about this. "That's a proper frightful story, and no mistake," he said. "If the Jack of Diamonds really was after you, then you're lucky to be in one piece. Naturally, I'll do my bit to help you, as best I can. Which, I might add, will be considerable—since I know this area like the back of my hand."

"Thank you," Lily said, cheerily. She felt pleased to have stumbled on such an ally, and relieved that he had evidently taken a shine to her. London felt a huge and scary place to navigate on one's own, despite them having visited once before.

Malkin didn't say anything, and neither did Robert. He was still a little unsure about Tolly, but they did need help, he decided.

Tolly seemed much more concerned with putting them at their ease than making further inquiries about their predicament. He took inordinate care to point out all the little things they passed on their journey and offered up explanations of every one.

"There's the fountain where the pigeons congregate…" he said, of a disused horses' water trough. "And there's old Pete the sniffling lamp-snuffer," he added, nodding at a man carrying a long stick with a tin hat on the end, who was dousing the street lamps. The man gave Tolly a snort of recognition.

"And here comes Artie, the knocker-upper, getting folks out for the daily grind…"

The rows of detached red-brick houses had become low terraced cottages. They saw a man with a peashooter, shooting peas at the top-floor windows to wake people for work.

"How do you know everyone?" Lily asked. "Are your family from 'round here?"

"Nope. I'm an orphan."

"So where do you live?"

"At the Camden Working Lads' Mission," Tolly explained. "They took me in when I was young. I'd run away from the poorhouse, see? And got into a bit of crime…but the geezers at the mission took me in. Taught me to read and write, from old newspapers mostly, and then they found me gainful employment. In return I got a roof over my head—I share a room with four other lads. It's a bit of a squeeze but I prefer it to the poorhouse. And I like selling papers—it's much better than washing smalls in the mission laundry, because I get to read while I work. I like the investigative stories best…"

Lily could barely imagine what that sort of life was like. She was relieved she had a home, and didn't live in a whirlwind all the time as Tolly seemed to. He even walked as fast as he talked—not slowing for anything, kicking his feet up high as he strode along, and chatting all the time. He stopped only once at an old drain cover, leaning down toward it.

"Listen," he said. "D'you hear that?"

"Water!" she cried in delight.

Tolly nodded. "This road we're walking on used to be part of the Fleet River. It ran from Highgate Ponds—what you fell into on the heath—right under these cobblestones and Queen's Crescent, and then flows onwards through North London, all the way down past Fleet Street—that street was named for it—along Farringdon Street, and finally tumbles into the Thames near Blackfriars Bridge. My grandfather used to sail down it, transporting stuff on the longboats."

"But where is it now?" Lily asked. "A whole river can't just disappear."

Tolly shrugged. "Bazalgette and that lot paved over it."

"Bazalgette?"

"The fella who built the London sewer," he explained. "The Fleet's part of it. Flowing underground. Instead of boats, it floats sewage downstream. Pretty profitable for him, I heard. But you know what they say—'Where there's muck there's brass'." He laughed at his own joke, and Lily decided she'd better join in, out of politeness.

Robert couldn't hear much of what Tolly was saying, because the other boy was walking too fast. He and Malkin had to hustle to keep up. But he was thinking about other things in any case—whatever clue might

161

be at Queen's Crescent, Robert was worried that Jack would have got to it first. And even if they made it to Lily's papa at the Mechanists' Guild, there was a good chance Jack would show up there too. So far, it seemed as if he'd been one move ahead of them every step of the way.

Finally they turned into another street lined with elm trees and, behind them, flat-fronted houses coated in white rendering, like cracked royal icing. Every house was framed by wrought-iron railings and a worn set of stone steps led up to each front door.

"This is Queen's Crescent," Tolly announced. "What number are you after?"

"We're not exactly sure," Lily admitted.

"I see." Tolly's face creased in confusion.

"I think their plan is to knock at each house," Malkin sneered. "If there's any other way to announce our presence more blatantly, I'd like to know what it is?"

Robert shook his head. "We don't need to knock on the door of each house. I can remember what it looks like from the picture."

He began to walk up the road. A lot of curtains were still drawn, but people had decorated their windows with bright red and white flowers and blue bunting in preparation for the Queen's Diamond Jubilee in two days' time. All the homes were very smart, but then the one in the photograph had been too, Robert remembered, with its jolly little apple tree in the front yard.

He stared at each place in turn, waiting for a sign of recognition, and yet none came—until he arrived at the scruffiest property on the street. Trailing vines of dead ivy hung from its guttering, fringing dusty, rotten-framed windows.

"This house needs a haircut," Malkin muttered.

"And a fresh bit of slap," Tolly added.

Robert frowned. He was inclined to agree, but there was something about the place—even in its run-down state—that looked remarkably similar to the photograph in *A Popular History of Modern Magicians*.

He peered between the broken railings; the front garden was a spiderweb of cracked concrete and weeds, and growing among them was an ill-tended, scraggy apple tree. It had only a handful of hard little apples, and a few wilted leaves, but he remembered it blooming in the photograph. He looked up above the green flaking front door and found the plaque with the street name, hidden beneath the dead ivy and screwed to the side of the house.

"This is definitely it," he said. "The Door family home."

At least, it had been once, a long time ago; now it was no longer. His ma had lived here in her youth, he knew that much. And he could only hope that she'd somehow left another clue to help him find her—like the rest of the locket perhaps... Instinctively he reached for the chain around his neck, then pulled his hand away. It was his "tell" Jack had said, and though the house looked dark and empty, someone in there might still be watching. "I do hope this isn't a trap," he said quietly to himself.

"You mean a trap Door?" Malkin butted in.

"It's rather early to be paying calls," Lily reassured them both. "That's probably the only reason it's so quiet..."

"Blimmin' heck," said Tolly. "You really do reckon the Doors are after you, don't you? Do you want me to do the talking? Whoever's in there won't know me from Adam. I can say it's a newspaper delivery..."

"No. No, thank you," Robert interrupted. "I'll be fine on my own. Don't worry. I don't think they'll be here yet anyway. And besides, I'll think of something." He threw his shoulders back and, with more confidence than he felt, jostled past them and strode up the garden path.

As he climbed the steps to the entrance, his guts gave a twist. The stone steps had worn away and the number forty-five was daubed in dripping white paint on the glass of the transom window above the front door. He took a deep breath and reached for the knocker.

There was none. Nor a letter box. So he knocked instead, three times, on the peeling paneled door with his fist, and waited for someone, anyone, to come and answer...

CHAPTER 11

Robert shifted impatiently on the doorstep. The locket hung heavy around his neck as he listened to a set of shuffling footsteps approaching through the house. Eventually the feet stopped, and he heard the click and clack of multiple locks being turned…and then, with a creak, the door opened.

It had barely swung in a few inches when five chains clattered across the opening, and it juddered to a stop. A pair of beady eyes peered around its edge, blinking at him from an inky-black hallway.

"Who's calling?" trilled a woman's voice.

"Robert Townsend," he said.

"Who?" The woman leaned farther out through the narrow gap, revealing a puff of white cotton-like hair trussed up in curling papers, and a wrinkled face. She pursed her lips and examined him closely. "You woke me up. Ordinarily, I sleep like the dead, but you knocked loud enough to waken them… Look, what d'you want? If it's about a room, you'd best come back later." She glanced back into the house, to what must have been a clock. "A lot later. I don't normally see renters till well past nine."

"It's not that." Robert pinched his fingers together. "It's…I'm…I mean, we're looking for someone… Selena. Perhaps you remember her? She lived here with her family, the Doors."

The woman perked up at that name. Her eyes swiveled and she tugged her dressing gown tight, peering up and down the street. "The Doors!" she cried in alarm. "Don't mention those blinking Doors to me! They're not with you, are they?"

Robert shook his head.

"Thank goodness!" Her face turned shriveled and suspicious. "Why you looking for them anyway, boy? Don't you know they're nothing but trouble?"

"Selena Door's my mother," Robert explained. "I need to get a message to her as soon as possible. About Jack—he's after her. After both of us."

"JACK!" The woman's voice took on a strangled edge. "You've seen Jack Door?"

167

"Twice in the last two days," Robert said.

"Lord love a duck!" The woman slid back the locks on the door. "Quickly!" she said, motioning to him, and then to Lily, Malkin, and Tolly at the end of the path. "You'd best come in, all of you."

The interior of the house was almost as dirty as the outside, if not worse. The woman's shallow breathing echoed down the length of the hallway, making the space seem like some sort of giant lung, as slowly, one by one, she replaced all of the chains on the door, pulled across two bolts, and locked five locks.

"This place has got more security than the Royal Mint," Malkin muttered.

"But we don't want *him* getting in, do we?" the woman explained. "He broke out of Pentonville Prison—and they said *that* was impossible."

She led them wheezily up five flights of stairs to the top floor of the house, where she turned a key in a door and threw it open.

There was a single bed, in a tiny, squalid room, and a sash window with thick gauzy curtains drawn aside to let in the light. On a narrow chest beside the bed were various framed old lobby cards from the Door Family Show.

"You kept all their stuff?" Lily asked the woman incredulously.

"Well, I'd sell it if I could," she snapped. "But it's damaged."

Lily looked closer and saw she was right. A figure had been ripped from each framed lobby card, their name erased from the line-up and from family history.

"Besides," said the landlady. "I can't leave the house."

"Why can't you?"

"I'm cursed. The old woman cursed me before she died."

"What woman?"

"Artemisia, of course. Artemisia Door!"

Tolly examined the lobby cards. "These are old London theaters," he said. "Some of these gaffs don't even exist no more."

"How highbrow," Malkin sneered. He was snuffling around a stack of loose drawers, filled with interesting-looking pieces of theatrical junk.

"The Doors must've tread the boards in all these places," Robert said, peering closely at the family pictures. In the ones where Selena couldn't be ripped away her face had been scratched out, making her look like some sort of half-materialized ghost. "They really did disown her!" he whispered, shocked. "Why would she go back to theater after that?"

"Maybe she loved it despite her family," Lily suggested. "The inspector said he thought she was probably still a stage performer in London."

The old woman shrugged. "Who knows."

But Robert thought Lily might be right. He remembered Da saying Selena was an actress when they'd met—wasn't it likely that she'd returned to her old life?

The damaged lobby cards were all sorts of varied designs. But each had the Doors with a scrolled banner above their heads displaying the name of their show. Robert felt flabbergasted. Somehow they had stumbled upon a shrine to his family, a family that until this week he hadn't even known existed.

In the first card, the Jack of Diamonds appeared to be flying in the air, leaping between two grand buildings.

"Blimey," Tolly exclaimed. "He looks proper like old Spring-heeled Jack in this one."

In the second card, Jack had his arms out in a dynamic pose and was making Finlo and a scratched-out Selena levitate live onstage. In a third, he stood behind his wife, Artemisia, who was sitting on a chair with both hands at her temples and appeared to be summoning ghosts from the ether. The final card showed Jack bursting free from heavy chains and riding on the back of the giant mechanical Elephanta, a red diamond glinting in her forehead.

See Jack make the Elephanta disappear! said the caption.

"That one's from the show where he robbed the Queen," the landlady explained. "After that the police crawled all over this house searching for clues. Jack tried to make one of his famous escapes, but they caught him. And his wife and children were left here alone. Then it was just his wife, Artemisia." She pointed at a large iron bed, pushed against the wall in the corner of the room. On it was a bare mattress, with a big gray stain. "She died right there. Penniless—despite that priceless diamond, which everyone reckoned she had stashed. I'd been wanting to kick her out for years—since the day the police came and turned over my house and threw her husband in jail—but I couldn't."

"Why not?" Lily asked.

"They were a dark family," the woman explained. "Artemisia especially. She was full of black magic—could call spirits from the dead lands. She said if I threw her out she'd put a curse on the house and summon them to haunt me. Forever. So I let her be. But I reckon the place is cursed anyway, on account of her dying in it."

The woman gave a little shiver. "Those Doors brought ill repute here. I should've never rented to theater folk. Not the likes of them—magic ones. Nowadays no one comes for a room. No one! Not even overnighters."

"You don't know anything more about Selena?" Robert interrupted.

"That I don't. Sorry. She last came the day Artemisia died. I didn't recognize her at first. Then the son, Finlo, came an' all. Searched through everything, looking for something—ten years ago that was, but it's all still such a mess." She waved a hand at the room. "Nobody took the body, and her husband was in jail, his funds confiscated, so I had to send her to a pauper's grave. But then, as I recall, she didn't have many folks she called friends. Crossed a lot of people, or her husband did." She ran a finger thoughtfully through the dust on a side table, and wiped it on her pinny.

"Why don't you have a look through their things?" she advised, pushing open the door. As she shuffled off down the passage, she called back, "Take a keepsake if you want!"

"Thank you." Robert stared numbly at the wealth of Door family memorabilia scattered around the room. This would be his one opportunity to examine it thoroughly, he realized, without creating more trouble. He took a deep breath.

"Come on," he told the others. "Let's get started."

They set to, turning the room over from top to bottom; rooting through the various drawers and boxes shoved in corners and under the bed. They discovered all kinds of magical paraphernalia; crystal balls, Ouija boards, rune stones and yarrow sticks, tarot decks and stacks of playing cards with the jacks missing. They even found a suitcase filled with tangled ropes and chains, and a bag of oddly designed padlocks and keys that must've been part of Jack's act.

Despite these many interesting things, Robert was disappointed to realize that their search had uncovered neither the other half of the Moonlocket, nor any clue to Selena's whereabouts. The only thing they did find that must have once belonged to her was a children's book:

THE
Girl's ~~BOY'S~~ OWN BOOK

of

GAMES AND TRICKS

Codes and Cyphers
The Secrets of Ventriloquism
Card Tricks to Fool and Amaze

~~Finlo Door~~
Selena Door

For Jack

This book had obviously, at one time, been Finlo's and then was handed on to Selena. But why did it then say *For Jack*? Robert wondered. It was another strange find to go with the locket. He closed the book and put it under his arm, then nodded to Tolly and to Lily, who shooed Malkin off down the corridor to find the landlady to let them out.

As they walked away from Queen's Crescent, Lily's stomach began grumbling terribly. It was almost breakfast time, she realized, and she hadn't eaten anything since yesterday's lunch. "Can we get some food, please?" she asked Tolly. "I'm starving."

They stopped at a street stall and Tolly bought a meat pie with some of the coins from Lily's purse to share between the three of them. As soon as the seller had handed the steaming pie over, wrapped in newspaper, Tolly broke it into three, passing one crumbly piece to each of them.

When he'd finished his share, Tolly wiped his mouth with the back of his hand. "What now?" he asked.

Robert didn't know. As far as the investigation was concerned, they seemed to have come to some sort of dead end. They'd found neither Selena nor the other half of the locket, and most of what they'd discovered about the theaters, and so forth, they had already known.

The theaters—that was it!

"We could visit some of the theaters the Doors played, and ask about Selena," he proposed.

"Good idea!" Malkin said. "I've a good nose, I'll guide us."

"Maybe not," Robert replied. "You said that last time we were in London and look how far that got us. Where are all these theaters, anyway?" he asked Tolly.

"In the West End," Tolly explained. "It's not too hard to get to on the Underground. I'll take you if you like."

"We've never been on the Underground," said Lily.

Tolly grinned and shifted his satchel across his back. "Oh, you'll love it. Follow me and I'll show you."

The tiled lobby of the Underground station was thick with crowds. Morning commuters, hustling along in gray suits and black bowlers, thrust Robert, Lily, Tolly, and Malkin through a turnstile, where a mechanical man in the uniform of the Metropolitan Railway took money for tickets.

Malkin's clockwork echoed loudly as they walked along a tunnel and down a set of winding spiral stairs that descended into the earth. Robert laughed at the strangeness of it all, and glanced at Lily, whose eyes were lit up with intrigue.

When they thought they could get no deeper, they were spat out at the base of the stairs onto a railway platform crammed with people, jostling and squashing against one another to keep back from the edge.

A railway line ran in the recess beneath the platform, entering pitch-black, sooty tunnels at either end of the cavern. There was a tooting blast of a horn and a steam train chugged out of the farthest tunnel, slowly screeching to a stop alongside the platform. Smoke belched from its engine stacks, pluming off the arched roof of the chamber and covering everything in thick fog.

"It truly is an underground railway!" Lily said breathlessly.

"Just as I told you." Tolly snatched open a door. "Climb aboard!"

Robert looked at crowds of people doing the same. It was a bunfight of shoving and he thought that there would barely be room for them. They crammed in behind a large group of ladies in bustles, and Malkin gave a squealing yap: "Someone's stepped on my tail!"

"Mind the gap!" called a porter from farther down the train, and blew his whistle as he hopped onto the rear platform.

Then they were off. The train picked up speed and coasted away, and Robert saw the crowds and the station blur into the distance. There was a flash of sudden blackness as they sped into the tunnel, but the few blinking lamps down the length of the carriage were enough to see by.

No seats were available, so Tolly grasped a small leather strap that hung from the ceiling. Lily and Robert copied him. Malkin settled between their feet, crouching in the small space between Lily's legs. He grumbled softly to himself, examining his tail and poking at the injured appendage with his nose.

"It definitely looks less fluffy than before." He glared at the gaggle of ladies opposite. "Some people should watch where they're putting their feet. Could've pulled it right off my backside."

"Be quiet," Lily told him. For there seemed to be some sort of rule that everyone had to sit on the train in deathly silence, staring dead ahead and not speaking to one another, or anyone at all.

The dingy black tunnels were scary and a little disorienting, and the carriage rather stuffy. You couldn't open a window, Lily realized, as they all appeared to be locked. Anyway that would've let the smoke in, which seemed to waft constantly down the side of the trains, smearing the windows and the surfaces with soot; because of this, she didn't much want to touch anything.

As the train stopped at each station, more and more people got on, and soon they were hemmed in by bodies. The passengers swayed with every jerk and jostle of the carriage until Lily, squeezed in among them, thought she might topple over. But then a man in a bowler hat stood up, leaving a space. Lily grabbed the seat and, settling onto the wooden bench, caught her breath.

Some stops later they finally disembarked in a blaze of people and were thrust, in a tumbling rush, along another platform and up flights and flights of stairs, until they arrived back in the world above in an entirely different part of London. And not a moment too soon, Lily felt—for to be underground away from the light for so long had been rather horrible!

Tolly led them along a street filled with theaters. Lily, Robert, and Malkin followed him, their faces tilted up, taking in the colorful hand-painted billboards. Each hoarding advertised a unique show that could be seen beyond the gaslit porches and gold-painted entrance lobbies.

"Ignore all this," Tolly said. "We need the stage doors."

They stepped down a side alley, and came out in Drury Lane. Robert thought he caught a glimpse of a short dark-haired figure in a suit and dusty bowler hat, a little like Finlo, following them at a distance. But when he looked again the fellow was gone.

"Where should we try first?" Robert asked.

"The Adelphi," Tolly proposed. "It's right 'round the corner. I know the door hand and he's acquainted with everybody in theaterland. Maybe he can give us a clue to where your ma is."

The Adelphi had a long brick wall and a columned portico at the back. Actors and flower girls clustered in doorways and leaned against the tall grooved columns, smoking and gossiping. Tolly pushed his way past them, guiding Lily, Robert, and Malkin to the stage entrance, where an old mechanical was working.

When the mechanical man saw Tolly, his eyes lit up like new-fangled light bulbs. "Master Mudlark, how are you? And who's this?"

"Morning, Mr. Snapchance," Tolly said. "These are my friends Lily, Robert, and Malkin." He shoved Robert to the front of the group. "Robert is looking for his ma, Selena Door. She used to be an actress. And we thought you might know something about her."

"The Door family, eh?" Mr. Snapchance gave a racking cough that made his body shake and looked around nervously, as if even to mention that name might make them suddenly appear out of thin air. He scratched at a line in the scuffed paint on his chiseled chin. "They never worked here. Never."

"But we've seen a poster for them with this establishment's name on it," Tolly told him.

"That's as maybe, but I know nothing about it. They blackened the name of theater. Not only this one, but all the playhouses that put on their show." The old mechanical shooed them away and began closing the stage door behind him.

When there was barely a crack of an opening left, he paused and pointed a finger through it at them. "I'll tell you something else for nothing," he said. "You won't find any performer, actor, or sideshow magician in the whole of the city who's got anything good to say about the Doors. And if you want my advice, you won't go looking for them—Jack especially, but the rest too. They're a cursed lot and they'll bring you nothing but trouble."

And with that he slammed the door in their face.

Robert thrust his fists angrily into his pockets. He noticed that as they walked away from the theater, the actors under the archways distanced themselves from him, disappearing. It was as if they'd let off a firecracker in a flock of pigeons. The name Door seemed to scare off the possibility of any clue. Robert's downheartedness must've shown on his face, for Tolly placed a hand lightly on his back.

"Don't give up," the paper boy said. "There's plenty more theaters we can try." He glanced down at Malkin. "You'd best tell your mechanimal not to walk in the gutter," he warned Lily. "He'll get run down by a steam-wagon if he's not careful."

"I will not!" Malkin huffed. "I am perfectly capable of looking out for myself!"

Just then a blare of a horn made him jump from the road and skitter across the pavement into the shade of the nearest building.

Robert laughed for the first time in days.

"See?" Tolly said to the mechanimal.

"The steam-wagons should watch out for pedestrians," Malkin said, "not the other way 'round." But still, he was a lot more careful after that than he'd been before.

At each auditorium, they showed the photograph of Selena to the actors and stagehands who hung out there, but every single time they got the same response: scared, angry expressions and slamming stage doors.

As the morning trickled into the afternoon, Lily really had given up hope. "Let's go find Papa," she said. "He can organize us a room for the night. We should show him the locket too—he might be able to help us decode the message on the back and then, tomorrow, we can take it to Inspector Fisk, or Anna, for assistance."

"Who's Anna?" Tolly asked.

"She's an investigative reporter on *The Daily Cog*," Robert said.

"A friend of ours," Malkin explained.

"Anna Quinn," Tolly said. "Why didn't you say? I know her!"

"You do?" Lily asked, amazed.

"Of course. I see her sometimes at *The Daily Cog* offices. She's not just a reporter, you know? She writes for the penny dreadfuls as well, under a pen name. She did that series, *The Zep Pirates Versus the Kraken*—filled with gore, it was. One of my favorites."

Lily nodded. She remembered it well.

"Tell you what," he continued, "after I've finished selling my papers tomorrow morning, I'll meet you outside wherever you're staying and take you to see her."

"I suppose we'll be staying at the guild, with Papa," Lily said. And then she remembered: "But we don't have the address. It was in our bag, which we lost."

"It's all right," Tolly said, "we can ask a cabbie." He walked them to a cab stand a little farther down the road, where a line of hansoms, pulled by mechanical horses, were lined up. Tolly tapped on the side of the first one. "If you have a few coins he can take you there," he explained.

"Aren't you coming with us?" Lily asked, getting out her purse and checking her money, while Tolly helped them all up into the cab.

He shook his head. "I've got to get back to the mission, but I'll come see you first thing tomorrow." He shut the hansom's door behind them and Lily heard him speak to the cabbie.

"The Mechanists' Guild."

"On Fenchurch Street?" the cabbie asked.

"That'll be it," Tolly said. "Quick as you like. See you tomorrow then!" he called up to Robert and Lily. Malkin stuck his head out the window as the cabbie stirred the horse to action and the cab pulled off down the street.

CHAPTER 12

The Mechanists' Guild was the grandest building Robert had ever seen. Lily paid their hansom fare and they climbed the stone steps that led up to the arched entrance, hidden beneath a three-story-high classical pediment of finest marble. A single gold cog hung above the entrance—the insignia of the guild.

Robert and Lily pushed open the front door and entered, while Malkin gave one last glare at the cabbie's horse and slunk in behind them.

At the end of the long foyer, a mechanical man in a porter's uniform sat behind a big mahogany desk. His squashed-tin-can of a head was bent over a large ruled ledger and he was softly muttering sequences of binary numbers. "O-one-zero, z-zero-one, one-one-zero-one."

Lily approached the desk, grateful that this time she didn't have to ask after Selena, or the Doors. "Excuse me, Sir," she said.

The porter looked up, his irises whirring as they focused in on her.

"We wondered if you could help us? We're looking for our father, Professor John Hartman."

"Lily's father," Robert added. "He's working on a project for the Queen's Jubilee."

The porter shut his ledger with a snap. "I know the professor. He's been in and out. Using one of our labs, as a matter of fact, the biggest one…z-z-zero-one. Shall I take you there?"

Lily nodded and gave him a relieved smile.

"What is wrong with your voice?" Robert asked the mechanical man as he led them along a ground-floor corridor.

"I w-was attacked in the s-street by Luddites," the porter said, "and n-now I have a b-binary stutter."

"How horrible!" Robert exclaimed.

"We're so glad you're all right," Lily added. "But what are Luddites?" she whispered to Malkin.

"People who are against new technology—who want

to destroy mechanicals." Malkin shivered to the tips of his ears. "To wipe us from existence."

"Why would anyone want to do that?"

"Because they think we take their jobs. But mostly because we're different," Malkin replied.

"And t-to make us scared," the porter added.

"Oh." Lily put a hand to her heart. She knew what being different felt like.

"H-here we are then! One-zero!" the porter exclaimed, stopping at a door at the end of a long passageway.

The room did indeed have a number ten painted on its double doors. The porter opened them and ushered Robert and Lily inside.

They stepped into a hall that was almost the size of an airship hangar. A tall sliding screen door at the far end was rolled aside to reveal a courtyard beyond. Floor-to-ceiling shelves ran down one side of the room, filled with arms, legs, and torsos—spare parts for mechanicals.

But the most amazing thing about the hangar-sized space wasn't any of this. Instead it was the creature that stood at the room's center: the Elephanta—the world's largest mechanical elephant.

Lily had only seen a real elephant once before, when, as a young girl, her mama and papa had taken her to the Zoological Gardens in Regent's Park to show her the two Indian and the one African elephant kept there. The

Elephanta was larger than any of those. Her legs looked to be the height of two men, and the round body, towering way above them, was as big as a small house. Lily reckoned her to be about three times the size of her real-life counterparts.

The Elephanta's skin was sculpted from wood and covered in hand-etched scars and wrinkles. Her ears were made of big flat leather hides, bound together with rivets, and her eyes were made of blue crystals. Rusty iron tusks sat on either side of her trunk, which was made up of hundreds of wedge-shaped segments of wood that fitted together in a snaking shape. A ladder leaned against the far side of the Elephanta, and a panel in her flank had been flipped open, rather like the hood of a steam-wagon.

An iron figure with bow legs and wearing a leather belt of tools was standing on the top step of the ladder, leaning forward and fiddling around deep inside the cogged stomach of the Elephanta. The figure was simultaneously humming and hammering loudly.

The porter's jaw creaked as he opened his mouth wide and called up, "Captain Springer, there's some human children belonging to z-z-zero-John to see you!"

The figure straightened and there was a clang of metal against metal as it banged its head on the Elephanta's hood. Then there was a *prink-pronk-clank!* that sounded like something being dropped and tumbling down into the workings, and then a jittery shout. "Curse these jangling interruptions! And curse this clunking thing! Why won't it work?"

"Oh zero-dear!" the porter muttered. "Have we caught you at a bad time?"

"No, no, Mr. Porter!" came the echo from above. "It's a perfectly acceptable hour, according to my clockwork!" Captain Springer emerged from inside the Elephanta's interior and as he climbed down the ladder toward them his face broke into a bolt-filled grin.

"Well, grind my gaskets!" he cried. "If it isn't the tiddlers and Malkin! By all that ticks," he continued, "what the deviled kidneys are you doing in London?"

He stepped from the ladder and gave Lily and Robert a big creaky hug, ruffled Malkin's fur, and gave Mr. Porter a friendly slap on the back, which produced a loud bang like a bell.

"We came to find Papa," Lily explained, when Captain Springer had quite finished greeting everyone.

"I'm in trouble," Robert added, "and we need his help."

Captain Springer tapped a hand absent-mindedly against the Elephanta's stilled leg. "Your father went back to Brackenbridge this morning," he explained. "He sent a telegram to Mrs. Rust to check everything was in order, because he was so worried about the news he had been getting. Then, when he sent a second telegram and didn't receive a reply, he thought it best if he went back home—straight away tickety-tock!—to find out what had been going on. But it sounds as if he's gone off on a bit of a wild moose chase!"

"Oh dear," Lily said, "I feel rather guilty." She stared up at the gray flank of the Elephanta. "And we've interrupted his work for the Queen's Jubilee parade."

"Bilge pumps and brake levers!" Captain Springer gave a shuffling shrug. "Don't you worry about that, young madam. There's no way on this green earth that we could have this clattering mech-elephant up and running in two days, no matter how much we tinkered with it. Not even for the Queen and her jamboree parade!"

Robert peered up at the massive breastplate of the beast. Its side was open and he could make out an interior filled with cogs the size of cartwheels and ratchets and springs as big as his head. The Elephanta was one of the most impressive mechanical engines he'd ever seen—the workings were almost as grand and complex as those in the Big Ben clock tower. To his inexperienced eye they looked all present and correct—there didn't seem anything particularly wrong with it.

"How is she damaged exactly?" he asked. "Maybe Lily and I can help?"

Captain Springer shook his head. "Oh no, no, nope! If John can't fix the blessed thing then—sure as eggs is chickens—you won't be able to. You see, there's a part missing." He beckoned them around to the front of the beast and they stared up at its still head. In the center of the forehead was a massive dimple.

Captain Springer pointed it out. "That space used to house the Blood Moon Diamond… People think the diamond's ornamental. But it's what makes the creature run, what makes her clockwork turn, her insides jigger. Same as for every mechanical. No, she won't take a single step without it. She hasn't moved a cog since it was stolen fifteen years ago. I don't know what Professor Hartman was thinking when he took on this repair job. Even with all the time in the world, it would be an impossible task."

"The same for every mechanical?" Lily said. "What is? What do you mean?"

"Crenellated clockwork! Did John never explain that part?" Captain Springer asked. "Us mechanicals—" and here he gave Lily a nudge with his elbow—"we've all got fragments of Blood Diamonds in our hearts. They've a special energy that makes our motors turn, keeps our little synaptic-springs snapping!"

Lily put a hand to her chest. Blood Diamond…inside her? Occasionally she felt as if there was something alien in there—perhaps it wasn't just the Cogheart, but the lump of diamond at its center?

"The gemstones mined in the Red Caves," Captain Springer continued, "like the Blood Moon Diamond, they contain life-energy. They're what you might call living-diamonds, and they power us. But the Blood Moon Diamond was the biggest of them all, found in 1815, on the date of the century's shortest total lunar eclipse—so they say. It was gifted by Prince Albert to Queen Victoria on her birthday. She wanted to use the stone to power a mechanical, so she had the Elephanta built, and set the jewel in her forehead. It was perhaps the greatest mechanimal of all time—until Jack Door stole the Blood Moon Diamond and it stopped working!" Captain Springer wrung his hands together. "Anyway, enough of all that. You still haven't told me what you're doing here."

"We're searching for my ma. She's in grave danger," Robert said. "But all this stuff about the Blood Moon Diamond—it ties in with that too."

Captain Springer looked confused. "What d'you mean?"

"He means we've had a few run-ins with the Jack of Diamonds himself," Lily explained, flourishing the card Mrs. Rust had found.

"Gridirons and girders!" clucked Captain Springer. "Did you get this from Jack?"

Lily nodded. Admittedly it had sounded a little too casual the way she'd put it.

"We think Jack Door is looking for my ma," Robert explained. "And for this…" He pulled the locket out from beneath his shirt.

"By my iron britches, that's a most marvelous thing!" Captain Springer examined the locket. "What is it?"

"A locket," Malkin said dourly.

"What's it do?"

"It's some sort of map," Lily said. "To what, we don't know. There's a code but we can't translate it. Robert's ma would know the answer, we believe, but we haven't been able to find her."

"Yet…" Malkin added.

"Your father would be the person to ask, when he returns," Captain Springer advised. "He's an expert on cryptographs and cyphers."

"Then we should get word to him immediately," Lily replied.

"We have a telegraph office in the guild," Captain Springer said. "We'll wheel 'round there and you can send a wire. Let John know you're safe and sound. Meanwhile, Mr. Porter will find you a room where you can rest tonight."

"Z-z-zer-oh-dear! Of course, of course!" Mr. Porter said. "I shall see to it right away."

Captain Springer led them to a small musty room with a glass door that stood ajar, on which were etched the words: *Mechanists' Guild Telegraph Office*.

He nodded to the woman behind the counter, who sat beside the telegraph machine. "This is our telegraphist—Miss Dash," he explained to Lily. "She'll help you send your telegram."

Miss Dash gave a shaky nod of her head. "Call me Dot, please—Miss Dash is so formal, don't you think?"

She wore a visor hat bolted onto her forehead, and held a bunch of telegrams in one hand, reading them and then tapping out the letter codes at super-fast speed with the other using the telegraph key in front of her. Wires splayed from the machine out across the ceiling and through a hole in the back wall, and on, Robert imagined, to telegraph stations all around the country.

Lily opened her mouth to speak to Dot, but the telegraphist pointed at a wooden shelf that ran along the far side of the room holding a row of blotters and ink stands and dockets of telegraph forms.

"Fill out a telegraph form, please," Dot said.

Lily did as she was told. Picking up a pencil, she stared at the docket.

So much had happened in the last two days, she didn't know how to fit it into such a brief message; plus she was mindful of the fact she didn't want to upset Papa with stories of danger and derring-do—best to keep her sentences short and calm in tone.

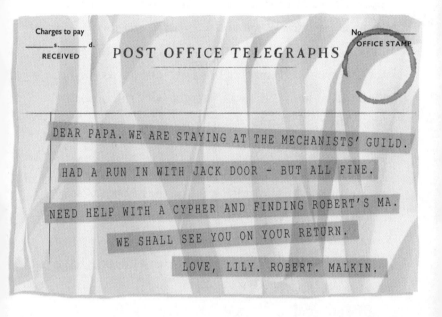

POST OFFICE TELEGRAPHS

Charges to pay
s. d.
RECEIVED

No.
OFFICE STAMP

DEAR PAPA. WE ARE STAYING AT THE MECHANISTS' GUILD.

HAD A RUN IN WITH JACK DOOR - BUT ALL FINE.

NEED HELP WITH A CYPHER AND FINDING ROBERT'S MA.

WE SHALL SEE YOU ON YOUR RETURN.

LOVE, LILY. ROBERT. MALKIN.

When she'd finished, she tore the page from the pad and headed back to the counter.

Dot had disappeared somewhere in the office out back, but Lily rang the bell on the desk and handed her the message when she reappeared.

"Dot, this wire is for Professor Hartman at Brackenbridge Manor," Lily told her. "It is to be delivered directly to his hand; no one else must receive it in his stead."

"Certainly, Miss," Dot said. Lily watched as she tapped the coded words into the machine by her side, her fingers a blur. When she'd finished, she looked up and smiled at Lily. "Your father should get the telegram later this evening. I imagine he's only just arrived home, so even if he makes his way straight back, he probably won't return until tomorrow."

"Zero-oh-dear-oh-dear, there you are!" Mr. Porter had reappeared. "The guild's accommodation is rather full, I'm afraid. All the professors and the mechanists are arriving for the Queen's Jubilee. But I've given you both your father's room until he gets back. There's a camp bed for one of you to use. I suggest whoever's joints are the least rusted."

"Thank you," Lily said. "I'm sure we'll be most comfortable."

The room itself was in a separate wing at the end of a long corridor filled with odd glass cases, each containing strange inventions.

"These are some of the earliest mechanicals," Mr. Porter explained, pointing them out as they passed. He indicated a scruffy-looking duck in a case: "That's

Vaucanson's famous pooping-duck."

Waving at another case: "This is James Cox's singing peacock clock." And nodding at a third: "That's Whisty, the first card-playing mechanical. He was a bit of a gambler, but he had a good poker face, as you can see, because he couldn't change his expression."

Robert noticed that Whisty, though run-down, had laid the Jack of Diamonds on the green baize table in front of him. It made him think of Jack Door, and he shuddered at the thought that the criminal was still looking for him and his ma.

Suddenly he felt rather downhearted. They couldn't just wait around for Lily's papa to return—that would be a whole extra day. They needed to find his ma as soon as possible, before Jack got to her.

They had arrived at their room. Mr. Porter showed them in. A long tapestry of cogs filled one wall, a big four-poster bed another, and beneath the large picture window, a camp bed had been set up. The furniture was practical and sparse and dotted with Papa's things, and the floor was filled with his cases and trunks.

As they made themselves at home, Lily realized they hadn't eaten since the meat pie at breakfast, so she asked Mr. Porter to bring them some jam sandwiches and a glass of milk each before they went to bed.

"We should go tomorrow and ask Anna for help,"

Robert said, after Mr. Porter had left. "In the meantime, I'm going to try my best to decode the message on the back of Selena's locket."

"Good idea," Lily said. "And I shall look through her book."

When the tray of food arrived, they sat on the floor amongst Lily's papa's trunks and ate with gusto. The night was muggy and humid; with the city's closeness, the air felt completely different from the freshness of summer in the countryside. As they ate, Malkin crawled down the end of the four-poster bed, settled himself on a cushion and promptly fell asleep, his cogs fizzing slower and slower as they wound down.

When Robert and Lily had finished their milk and sandwiches, Robert took the Moonlocket from around his neck and stared at the back of it. He was still trying to work out what the map and the message meant.

Lily had been flicking through Selena's book, *The Boy's Own Book of Games and Tricks*, when she noticed a chapter on cyphers. There was one called the Triangle Cypher. Suddenly she remembered the triangle at the end of the two-word code on the locket. This book had belonged to the Doors once…could that be it then?

She pointed at the page of the book. "Robert, I think I might have worked out how to solve the Moonlocket code!"

Robert leaned closer, peering at the page as Lily read the instructions. "You draw a right-angled triangle and place your word down the straight side, see? Then add letters to fill the space of the triangle after it; with each line you add one more letter." She wrote a word down the page to demonstrate:

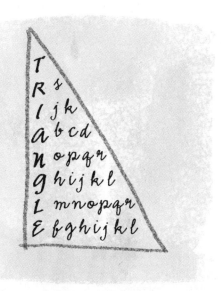

"When you've finished, you read the code off the angled side, so *triangle* becomes *tskdrlrl*—understand?"

Robert nodded. "And if we reverse that method with the locket code words," he said, "we'll get their translation."

So Robert took the locket off and they looked at the two words:

fmqzw uofhvlxvcwn △

    They took one word each and set to work on separate sheets of paper decoding them. When they'd finished they put the two sheets together, and this is what they had:

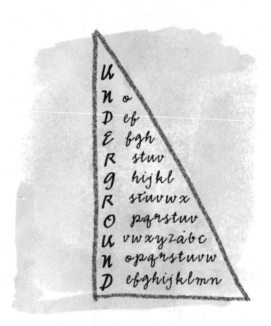

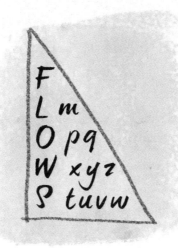

Robert's word was: *flows*.

And Lily's was: *underground*.

"Flows underground," said Robert. "What does that even mean?"

"It must mean something." Lily gave a big yawn. "But I'm too tired to try and work it out this evening. It's getting late, we should probably call it a night."

Lily found two fresh nightshirts in Papa's trunk; one she handed to Robert and one she kept for herself.

"Why don't I take the camp bed?" Robert said.

"You're sure?" Lily asked.

He nodded. "Of course."

Shyly, they turned away from each other and began to change. Lily hunched her shoulders as she put on her nightshirt. She was self-conscious of the vivid white scars on her chest and back—the lasting evidence of the steam-wagon crash from that winter's night seven years ago that had killed Mama. Some of the scars had healed since then, until they were barely visible, but others—like the cuts on her chest from the Cogheart transplant Papa had done to save her—were still evident. Tonight those scars throbbed painfully at the sudden memory of her loss. She felt for Mama's ammonite in the pocket of her folded pinafore, and held the gift tight against her chest.

Robert was distracted too. He put the Moonlocket back around his neck. He didn't even like to take it off to sleep anymore—he was so scared that someone might sneak in and steal it from him.

When he turned to face Lily, she was in her nightshirt and climbing into bed. Malkin was curled up tight in a ball at her feet. Lily pressed a button on the wall above the big four-poster bed, and they heard a clicking of clockwork in the walls as the curtains drew themselves around her.

"Goodnight!" she called out to Robert.

"Night!" he whispered back.

CHAPTER 13

Lily's breathing sounded soft in sleep, and Malkin's clockwork was ticking to a standstill as he ran down for the night. Robert tried to settle on the camp bed in the corner of the room, but he couldn't nod off; he kept thinking about his ma. It felt like today they had gotten a lot nearer to finding her, and yet she felt still so far away…

The two words, *flows underground*, kept floating through his mind. What did they mean? And why did it even matter to him? It wasn't only the thought that they might recover the Blood Moon Diamond, or even the possibility of getting the reward, he admitted to himself. It was also the thrill of the adventure…and the horror of being part of the notorious criminal Door family. The chance of maybe seeing his ma again… But why did he still care about her, when he could have become part of Lily and John's family? After all, the Hartmans had never rejected him.

He tried to put such concerns from his mind. But sleep wouldn't come. His blanket was itchy. He'd been lying in the dark on the camp bed with his eyes open for a good hour.

There was just too much to think about. Finally he got up and opened the window to look at the moon. He couldn't see it. It was lost behind a bank of smog and fluffy clouds.

He watched the sky for a long while, his thoughts drifting in and out of the blackness, waiting for the moon to reappear, but the clouds did not shift, and it seemed as if a deep well of nervous anger was gathering with them, inside him.

The truth was, he was worried sick about how he might react if he finally managed to reunite with Selena. What would he say to her after so many years? He probably wouldn't even recognize her. To know someone when you're a baby or a small child was not—he realized—the same as knowing them when you're nearly grown. They would have to forge their relationship anew—that is, if she wanted to see him. Maybe she didn't, and that was why she left.

Why had she abandoned him? Her only child? He would start by asking her that. As soon as he'd told her the news about Jack, he'd demand an answer. And she'd better tell the truth, because, if not, he'd no idea what he might do.

With every question filling his head he became more unsure about what tomorrow might bring. Then a hand touched his shoulder, and he turned to find Lily; she'd woken and had sneaked into the window alcove beside him.

She cupped her ammonite in her hand. "The riddle's keeping you awake?" she asked.

"Yes," Robert said. "But not that one…the other. Why she left, I mean."

"Well," said Lily, "when you find her, you can ask."

"How could she have done such a thing, Lily? Leave her only child?"

"Maybe to protect you from Jack?" Lily suggested.

"That can't be the only reason." He gave a deep sigh. "Because shouldn't it have hurt her as much as it did us…" He shook his head. "Never mind. You don't have answers, I know that." He pursed his lips and stared up at the sky. "The moon's gone. The cloud's blocking her."

Lily nodded. "But she's still out there, Robert. The clouds are only passing and when the wind pushes them away, you'll be able to see her right as rain."

"Will I though?" Robert asked. "How can you tell?"

"Now you're being silly," Lily said. "What do you mean?"

"It's something Da used to say: 'How can you be sure the moon shines if there's no one to see it?'"

Lily looked puzzled.

"It's a philosophical question," Robert explained. "I don't think there's supposed to be an answer. It means, can a thing exist if there's no one to experience it?"

"I see," Lily said. Although she didn't quite. She pressed her palm around her ammonite stone. "Maybe she's there if you believe in her enough?"

Robert leaned against the window frame. "Sometimes the fact she's gone, like my da, makes me feel so alone."

"You're never alone," Lily said. "You've got us."

Robert smiled at her, and glanced at the fox asleep on the end of the bed. "You and Malkin are good friends. I'm glad you're both here."

"Listen, when I was in trouble, you helped me. That's what friends are for. And now things are the other way around…I promise I'll look after you."

"You don't have to make that promise. And I wouldn't blame your father if he didn't either. After all he's given me, I feel bad to hanker after my own family—but it's as if something's still missing for me at your house."

"I feel the same sometimes," Lily admitted. "It's too closed off. Too quiet. Papa doesn't let us into the world

206

enough." She bit her lip and stared at her stone, thinking for a moment of Mama. "You always miss those who are gone. No one can truly take their place. Not friends, or family."

"Or," Robert replied, "you long for what you never had. I wish I'd had more time with my ma. I've only a few memories of her and what Da's told me... I remember once he told me she talked to spirits, but she didn't like to tell people in case they thought she was crazy." He wiped a tear from his eye. "You went to the other side, didn't you, Lily? And you saw...people?"

"I was never sure that it wasn't all a dream," Lily said, "but I like to think it was real. That Mama's spirit is watching over me. And your da's too," she added. "I've dreamed of them on occasion. Maybe that means they're present."

Robert shook his head. "Da didn't believe in such things. He called it mumbo jumbo, said there was no magic in the world but what you make for yourself. And maybe he was right. Or maybe she was."

Lily nodded. Her father didn't believe in spirits either—everything had to be scientific and fact-based, even though, to Lily, there had always been a large dose of mystery and magic in the work he did.

The clouds had drifted farther into the distance. Robert could barely see them now as they melded with the smog of the London night. He shifted on his feet. "Let's talk about this in the morning. I should probably try to get some sleep. We don't know what tomorrow will bring." He turned from the window, but Lily took his arm.

"Look!" she cried.

And he looked.

The sky had cleared suddenly and there was the moon—one day from full, with the thinnest, tiniest sliver missing—peering down at them from among the stars.

"It's a good omen," Lily said. "It means that what you're searching for is still out there. Waiting for you, when the clouds pass."

While Lily returned to bed, Robert stayed staring at the moon for a bit. Soon he could hear her breathing, slow and steady; she'd fallen asleep the moment her head hit the pillow.

He felt better for his talk with her, he reflected, as he climbed into his own bed. It helped to share the weight sometimes. Friends could give good advice, set you back on the right path when you got lost in the fog of worry, but only if you told them the truth of what you were thinking.

Gradually Robert's limbs grew heavy and his thoughts settled like dust in a glass of water, until he felt himself dropping off to sleep.

They woke early the next morning and dressed silently. Their clothes were creased and covered in splatters of yesterday's dried pond slime, but they had forgotten to ask Mr. Porter if he had any spares and all of Papa's things were too big, so for now they would have to do.

On their way out, they looked in on Miss Dash. She had received a reply from Papa, which read:

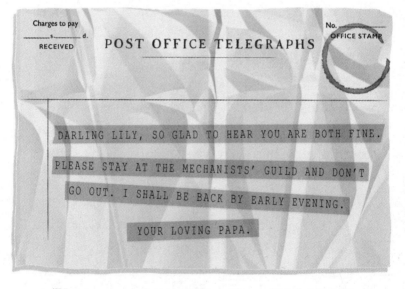

Charges to pay		No.
____ s. ____ d. **RECEIVED**	**POST OFFICE TELEGRAPHS**	OFFICE STAMP

DARLING LILY, SO GLAD TO HEAR YOU ARE BOTH FINE.

PLEASE STAY AT THE MECHANISTS' GUILD AND DON'T

GO OUT. I SHALL BE BACK BY EARLY EVENING.

YOUR LOVING PAPA.

"You can wait in my office, if you like." Miss Dash suggested. "And help me with my work."

But Robert shook his head—he wanted to get going and see Anna to show her the locket and code. They couldn't give up on finding Selena, not yet, not with the progress they'd made, and not with Jack back in town.

They left Miss Dash and sneaked out of the building, to find Tolly stood waiting in the shadows of the columned entrance, sheltering from an already blazing sun. "Ready to visit *The Daily Cog*?" he asked. "Someone else is doing my paper route for me, so I can spend the whole day traipsing around with you lot. We'll be like The Baker Street Irregulars."

"Who are they?" Robert asked.

"Only the gang of street urchins who helped Sherlock Holmes with his investigations," Tolly said.

"Couldn't he have employed some grown-ups? Or mechanicals?" Malkin asked.

"I think he found the Irregulars made better investigators," Tolly said. "They went everywhere, saw everything, overheard everyone; just like the majority of us guttersnipes."

He scampered down the steps and led their party across the road, dodging the horse-drawn hackneys and steam-wagons that trundled in both directions.

It was a short walk to Fleet Street. Despite the closeness of the river, London was humid and hot. Robert rolled up the sleeves of his shirt and adjusted his collar, which was itchy with sweat and dust.

Everywhere they looked, triangular flags and red, white, and blue bunting were draped between the houses, and wooden barriers were being set up along the edges of the pavement in readiness for tomorrow's parade.

They crossed under a high metal railway bridge that swept over the road between two tall blocks of terraces. Behind it, in the glaring sunlight, Lily could make out the dome of St. Paul's Cathedral, where the parade would end. She hoped that when Papa got back to the guild later, he would let them stay another day to see it.

Finally they arrived at a tall red-brick building with a porticoed entrance. On the roof of the building were six-foot-high letters that spelled out the words:

THE DAILY COG

Tolly grinned and pointed at the sign. "Here we are then—the place that inks all the news that's fit to print! Investigation's their middle name. They've covered all the big stuff—the Mechanical Mysteries, the Lost Arctic Airship, the Secrets of the Stolen Steam-Engines, the Behemoth and Big Ben Zep-Crash Disaster—they broke all those stories wide open!"

Lily nodded. She and Robert knew quite a bit about that last one themselves, since they'd given Anna the scoop. She felt the excitement rising in her chest. Tolly was right, this was the center of the newspaper world. And now she was standing outside its head office, going to see a friend who not only worked there, but was a lead investigative reporter on the news desk. It was exciting to think she knew such people! She had come so far in the last eight months from the sheltered childhood existence Papa had imposed on her since Mama's death, and she felt much happier for it, despite the dangers the outside world had flung at her.

They pushed their way around the side of the building and arrived at the wooden gates to a yard. Tolly knocked on a small door set into the main gate and, after a minute's wait, a man in printer's overalls answered.

The man wiped his nose with a hairy-backed hand. "Late again, Tolly? Or come to collect more papers? And who are these? New recruits? You know we can't take on any more street-sellers."

Tolly shook his head. "These are friends of Anna Quinn's, Charlie."

Charlie tutted and pointed with his thumb over his shoulder toward the rear of the main building. "She's up on the roof as usual."

"What's she doing on the roof?" Lily asked.

"Don't you know?" Tolly looked surprised. "That's where she moors her airship, *Ladybird*, when she's on this side of town."

Lily carried Malkin draped around her neck as she, Robert, and Tolly ascended a rope ladder that ran up the side of the *Daily Cog* building. Sweat poured down her back and her neck itched against Malkin's fur. It was far too hot to be wearing a fox shawl, especially a live one whose fidgeting paws kept scratching at her bare arms.

The ladder was beginning to slope irregularly to one side. Robert didn't dare look down. A few of the wooden rungs were missing, and the whole thing felt alarmingly unstable.

"Mind your step," Tolly said, as he ducked under the massive letter G at the end of the *Daily Cog* sign.

Lily and Robert scrambled off the ladder and followed, finding themselves standing on a flat tiled roof that stretched out before them like a patched runway, curving up at an angle into the smoggy sky.

At the far end, *Ladybird*'s gondola was wedged between a set of chimney stacks, tied to the largest one like it was a mooring post. The airship's gas balloon trailed off to one side, its patched silks deflated and encrusted with dirt and bird guano. Behind it, ramshackle spires and gray rooftops spread along the river.

Lily put two fingers in her mouth and whistled loudly across the rooftop toward the open door of the airship's gondola.

A moment later, a stout figure in a bulky aviator's

jacket appeared in the doorway. She swept back a fringe of brown hair from a pair of blue twinkling eyes and gave them all a ruddy-cheeked grin. Anna!

"Ahoy!" she shouted. "It's my old cabin boys! And I see you've brought a friend with you. Tolly, how splendid to see you again." She waved at them across the rooftop. "Well, what are you waiting for? A royal invitation? Come aboard, all of you, and mind the loose tiles on the way over!"

CHAPTER 14

With its low sloped ceiling and oddly angled cupboards, *Ladybird* was just as Lily remembered. Anna showed them into the starboard compartment, where the porthole window was open, letting in a nice, cooling breeze. In the center of the tiny space stood a wooden chair and a small fold-out table with a typewriter perched on it. Beside the typewriter was a pile of magazines and papers, topped with a loaf of bread and a knife.

Squeezed in behind all that, a miniature clockwork propulsion engine and a tiny stove were wedged snugly into the stern.

A frying pan hissed on the stovetop, wafting out a

strong scent of sausage, eggs, and bacon that made Lily's mouth water. She felt a pang of hunger and her stomach rumbled as loud as a steam engine when she realized that once again this morning they hadn't eaten.

Anna raised an amused eyebrow. "You caught me at an opportune moment. I was just taking a break from cooking up a few dreadful stories to enjoy some elevenses."

She picked up the frying pan and gave the contents a good shake. "Extra-breakfast, I like to call it. It wasn't meant to feed the five thousand, but there's enough for a butty each if I divide it up between us."

Tolly, who seemed right at home, cut four slices of bread from a loaf on the sideboard at the other end of the cabin, and began buttering them.

Anna glanced worriedly at Robert, Lily, and Malkin. Lily expected her to ask what was going on. But instead she said, "Do you like my new mooring?"

Lily squeezed round the table to peer out the porthole. "I love it," she exclaimed. "You can see the whole of London from up here!"

"You certainly can," Tolly said, pausing in his task as if he'd had a thought. "Here, Anna, this'd be an excellent place to watch the Jubilee parade from. Mind if I stick around till tomorrow afternoon to check it out?"

"Course not," Anna replied. "Long as you're prepared to kip down for the night on the floor in the passage."

"Excellent." Tolly handed Lily and Robert each a slice of bread and butter and gave them a confidential nod. "Anna's hiding from the bailiffs. She's in a spot of financial bother and *The Cog* hasn't paid her for her last piece, so she can't get a mooring at a proper airdock."

"Been nosing again, have you?" Anna scooped up the contents of her frying pan. "You're a proper little Sherlock Holmes!" She doled out a sausage each to Lily and Robert, rashers of bacon to Tolly, and kept the egg for herself. "I'm sure you'll make a lead reporter in no time."

Tolly bit into his bread and bacon. "I will when you hear the big scoop we've got for you about Jack Door."

"Oh, and what might that be?" Anna asked.

"We're searching for my ma, Selena," Robert explained. "She's Jack's daughter, you see, which means he's my grandfather, and Finlo's my uncle." He took a bite of his sausage butty, but a shiver ran down his spine—his story sounded odder and more frightening each time he told it out loud.

"Finlo's Jack's son, who broke him out of jail," Lily explained.

"And we think they're both after Selena," Robert continued, "because she has the key to the whereabouts of the Blood Moon Diamond."

Anna's eyes widened. "Your mother…" she said, and she seemed a bit lost for words. Malkin even thought for a moment that she might drop the rest of her butty, and he wished that he was a real animal so he might snatch it from her and eat it.

But she soon found her voice again. "Have you seen Jack Door then?" she asked. "We'd a few sightings reported at the paper, but none turned out to be real!"

"Jack's as real as the nose on my face," Robert said.

"And twice as scary," Malkin added.

"So he's after the diamond?" Anna asked. "And revenge?"

Robert shook his head. "Not only that. There's something else. They need…" He took a deep breath; should he mention the locket to Anna in front of Tolly, who they barely knew? "We have part of a map," he explained. "And we think my ma has the other half and the key to what it means. That's why Jack's looking for her…and for me."

"Where is this map then?" Anna asked. "Let's see it."

Hesitantly, Robert reached for the Moonlocket around his neck. He still wasn't sure about revealing it. It was the only thing he had of his ma's and he'd rather

218

not give it away, not even for a second. But Anna would help them.

"Blimey! Will you look at that!" Tolly's eyes went wide as coins as the Moonlocket was revealed. Robert felt a flash of awkwardness handing it over to Anna, but she seemed to sense his reluctance.

She took it delicately and inspected the curved ivory face with its unsettling facial features. "A crescent moon," she said, turning the locket over and examining the map. "This may be a place marker." She tapped the single red jewel.

"That's what we thought," Lily said. "A starting point."

"Or an end point," Robert added. "Like X marks the spot."

"You mean it could be the location of the Blood Moon Diamond?" Tolly asked excitedly.

"These two words," Anna said, "and the triangle—they're some sort of code. Perhaps it's a place name? Except there are no capital letters…"

"We've solved the cypher," Robert explained. "It says: *flows underground*."

"Very cryptic!" Anna muttered.

"Isn't it?" Lily replied. "But there's another part of the locket—we think Selena might have it. A gibbous moon that we're guessing makes a whole map and the rest of the riddle."

"I see," Anna said.

"And that's why we have to find her before Jack does," Robert added.

Anna opened the locket and looked at the picture of Robert's family inside. "Is this the only picture you have of your mother, Robert?" she asked.

"No, we've this as well." Lily took out the inspector's theater poster and unfolded it, revealing the picture of the Doors.

"This picture won't do you any good," Anna said. "It's too old. Selena's only a girl."

"We've already been 'round the theaters with it," Malkin added. "And everyone's so clinking scared of the Doors, they don't want to give us information."

"That's no good." Anna tutted. "We shouldn't make assumptions about the message or the map until we know more. But lucky you came to me with this; we should be able to dig up something more about the Doors and Selena in the records of *The Daily Cog.*"

She closed the locket and handed it carefully back to Robert. "Now, eat up, there's work to be done! I find I think better on a full stomach. Soon as we're finished, we'll head to the records office and start our investigation."

"Our investigation—you mean we can *all* help?" Tolly asked hopefully, finishing his butty.

Anna patted his shoulder. "Course, Tolly! We need every brain we can get. And you're the best detective I know... Apart from Robert and Lily, that is."

"And me!" piped a voice from under the table. "I'm the best investigative nose I know." Malkin gave a loud sniff.

"And you, Malkin, yes." Anna patted his head and took a bite of her fried egg.

Anna directed them across a factory floor filled with the most enormous printing press. The noise was deafening. Loud clanks and bangs emanated from the machine as a big roll of newspaper was dragged through it to produce the daily edition.

At the far end of the production line, where men and mechanicals took the printed pages from the machine and stacked them in piles to be bundled and sent out, she led them through a door and into an office room. It was filled with dusty shelves stacked floor to ceiling with yellowing newspapers. Above the door was a clock embossed round the edges with the emblem of *The Daily Cog*.

"This is the records room," Anna explained, pulling out the drawer of a card catalog in the center of the space. "We'll start by going through the theater ads, reviews, and classifieds for the last six months. If your ma's been performing in London, Robert, we're bound to find some evidence of her somewhere amongst those pages."

Anna took down stacks of papers and she, Lily, Robert, and Tolly took a pile each and began to leaf through them. Malkin they kept out of the way; he was too impulsive and they didn't want him shredding any important documents before they'd had a chance to read them.

It took nearly two hours to go through the papers from the last six months, and still Lily could find nothing that might be a clue to the whereabouts of Selena Door.

Finally, in despair, she picked up the newest issue of the paper, hot off the press, with the ink still wet, and turned to the advertisements.

A line-drawn portrait of a woman with her eyes shut and her fingers pressed to her temples caught Lily's attention. Behind her head was a large white circle that looked like a halo or crystal ball, or...yes, Lily realized, a moon! Underneath the picture was a headline. She read on.

CELINE D'ORE

THE REVELATORY MEDIUM WHO SUMMONS SPIRITS USING DARK LUNAR POWERS!

World-famous medium extraordinaire
CELINE D'ORE will communicate with her
astral spirit guide! With the loan of a single
personal item she'll tell your fortune live onstage!

Shows twice nightly, **seven** and **nine p.m.**
Special grand matinee performance, in honor
of the Jubilee, this Saturday at **four p.m.**

TICKETS AVAILABLE AT THE BOX OFFICE
*The Magnificent Theatre of Curiosities,
Valentine Street*

Lily rushed over to show Robert, Tolly, and Anna, who were sitting at another desk.

"Look!" she cried. "This can't be a coincidence, surely?"

Robert peered closely at the picture, trying to decide

if the portrait resembled Selena or not. "I can't be certain," he said finally.

"Lunar powers sound promising though…" Lily said. "You did tell me that Selena means moon, which also sounds like Celine, and if you think about it, Door and D'Ore are the same name too."

"D'Ore also means gold in French," Malkin added.

"Golden Moon," said Tolly.

Robert pushed his cap back on his head, and examined the poster again. "Maybe it is my ma," he said. "But if it is, she must know Jack's out of prison and desperate to find her. Why take such a risk…?"

He stood and consulted the clock above the door. "Today's Saturday. Matinee day—which means the next show is in less than an hour. We should go and see if it is her, and warn her immediately."

"Anna, will you come with us?" Lily asked. She was feeling rather anxious about everything all of a sudden.

Anna shook her head. "I don't agree with spiritualist shows. They're hokum. Besides, I want to find out a little more about this Moonlocket—there must be some mention of it in the archives somewhere. But Tolly will take you, he knows Valentine Street. I'll meet you outside afterwards."

"Please," Robert begged. "We need your help."

Anna shook her head. "I've far too much work to do," she said.

"Can't you leave some of it until later?" Lily asked.

"All right," she finally relented. "If you're both nagging me, how can I refuse...? Let me finish up here first. You go on ahead and buy some tickets, but don't go in without me. I shall see you there in a short while, I promise."

They crossed the River Thames at Blackfriars Bridge then followed the railway line behind terraced cottages down toward the riverbank. All along the back streets, people were decorating their windows and front doors with ribbons and pictures of the Queen in preparation for the parade tomorrow.

As they turned into Valentine Street they heard the lap of the river up ahead. A cool breeze with a mossy stink floated up from the water, banishing the muggy gray June heat. The smell of coal dust and smoke from the fires burning in the braziers along the front made Lily's nose and eyes itch. Gray smog floated across the cobbles and Robert covered his mouth and coughed.

Malkin, unaffected, trotted along beside them. Because he didn't breathe, the city air didn't clog him up the way it did humans.

Tolly too seemed fine. "Pea-souper of a London smog," he said. "People get ill from the fumes sometimes, but not me. I'm used to it."

They followed Tolly along Valentine Street, brushing past people lugging crates and barrels. The road bent around a corner, passing rows of little shacks clustered on the quayside.

Out on the river, boats were moored three deep. Tethered airships of various shapes and sizes floated above the water, grazing the clouds. The quay was buzzing with people bringing in last-minute provisions for the Jubilee celebrations.

Farther on, they reached the insalubrious end of the docks, where scuttled wrecks lay like beached whales in the shallows of the Thames. Strange spiderwebs of metal, the ribs of rusting airships, were swarming with scavengers, mudlarks, and beachcombers—hunched figures in torn coats and britches, who crawled about on those skeletal surfaces trying to pry free a likely looking dongle or screw from the carcass—anything that might be sellable.

Tolly led Lily, Robert, and Malkin past these wrecks and along the wharf, to where a sailor was stowing ropes. Tolly stopped and spoke to him.

"We're looking for The Magnificent Theatre of Curiosities."

The sailor nodded. "At the end of the dock. Be careful! It's a dangerous place—a house of spirits, so they say."

Lily felt a queasy sense of foreboding.

They thanked the man and scurried along the dockside, toward the place he had pointed out.

It was a small building with a wooden porch. The bricks had been painted in gray colors, and ghostly faces were faintly visible, chalked onto the shutters. The shadow of a zeppelin drifted over the roof, scaring up a murder of crows. The birds cawed and took flight, flapping past a faded white sign painted on the building's brickwork, whose six-foot-high letters proclaimed the place was indeed: The Magnificent Theatre of Curiosities.

CHAPTER 15

Despite what the sign said, there was truly nothing magnificent about The Magnificent Theatre of Curiosities. From the outside it had the feel of a dilapidated saloon rather than a reputable venue. They stepped from the muggy heat of the dockside into the shabby cool of a small lobby.

A box office booth filled the space. Behind it, through an archway, Robert could make out a large entrance hall, teeming with people, all chattering nervously as they waited to enter the auditorium. A horrible sense of trepidation bubbled through him as he and Lily approached the ticket counter.

A young girl sat behind its open window, humming softly to herself, deeply engrossed in a penny dreadful.

Her dark hair hung over her face like a tangle of twigs, and her head dipped close to the page as she read what Lily felt sure was *Murderous Mysteries Magazine*. If she could engage the girl in conversation, she might be able to glean some information.

Tolly, who'd entered last, shut the street door with a clang and the girl finally looked up, twitching them a smile. She'd a pale face and heavy brows, and something about her seemed awfully familiar.

"We're looking for Miss Celine D'Ore—we need to speak with her," Lily told the girl.

The girl shrugged. "She's getting ready for the matinee. She won't see anyone before that—says it disturbs the balance of her aura."

"I'll disturb the balance of her aura," Malkin snarled, "if she doesn't agree to see us."

"Shush," Robert told him. He turned to the girl. "Do you reckon we could meet her after the show? We can wait."

The girl shook her head. "'Fraid she's not doing personal readings anymore, on account of a family matter."

Lily leaned an arm on the counter. "Is that *Murderous Mysteries Magazine* you're reading?"

The girl closed the penny dreadful. "Why, yes, it is!"

"Our friend writes for that," Lily said.

"Really?" The girl seemed impressed.

"Yes," said Lily, "she'll be along shortly." She peered closely at the cover. "Issue fifty-two. That's the one with Sweeney Todd, isn't it?"

The girl's eyes brightened. "It's my personal favorite… I've read it at least a dozen times. What are your names?"

"I'm Lily Hartman," Lily said. "And this is my brother Robert. These are our friends, Tolly and Malkin."

The girl opened a side door to the box office and stepped out. Standing between them, she looked much smaller than she had behind the window. She was perhaps only nine or ten. Through the gap in the door, Lily noticed a stack of cushions on her chair and a biscuit tin on the floor to stand on—little tricks to make her seem taller in the box office window.

"I'm Caddy." The girl crouched down beside Malkin and petted him under the chin.

The fox purred, and nipped delightedly at the straggly ends of Caddy's hair. He was far more friendly than Lily had seen him with other strangers; she wondered what it was about the girl that put him at ease.

Caddy took up Malkin's winder, which hung on the chain around his neck. On the head of the key was the old logo for Hartman and Silverfish mechanicals, and she smiled as she examined it. "Your fox is a Hartman's mechanical! How marvelous!" Caddy let the key go and stood up abruptly. "What did you want with Miss D'Ore anyway?"

"It's a personal matter," Robert cut in. "But it is very important that we speak with her."

Caddy became rather brusque. "Well, I'll be sure to tell her that you called. If you're lucky, she might agree to see you after the show. Though private readings are usually three pounds."

"We don't have enough for that," Lily said.

"Well, the show's only sixpence," Caddy told her. "It's pretty spectacular. There's ghostly manifestations and all sorts—that is, when the stars are aligned..."

"Sounds fun," said Tolly.

"Sound tacky," said Malkin huffily; he was rather cross that the girl had stopped tickling him.

"If we buy tickets, can you persuade Miss D'Ore to meet us afterwards?" Robert asked.

"I'll try my best," Caddy replied. "But I can't promise anything. As I said, she's refused all visitors this past week."

Lily took her purse out from her pinafore. "Four for the show then, please."

"That'll be two shillings." Caddy ripped four tickets from a roll, while Lily counted out the last of her coins onto the desk.

"There," she said, when she'd finished. "That's the end of our money, Robert. I hope this Celine D'Ore's the one we're looking for."

"Just so you know," Caddy said, as she scooped up their change. "I would've let the fox in for nothing."

"Oh, the fourth ticket's not for him," Robert said. "It's for our friend Anna; she'll be along soon, I expect."

"There's no late admittance after the performance starts," Caddy said.

"And when's that exactly?" Lily asked. This was beginning to seem like a bad idea. Anna had told them not to go in without her.

"Why, right now, of course." Caddy snapped down the shutter on the box office. "Come on," she said blithely. "I'll show you into the theater myself."

"Oughtn't we wait for her?" Lily asked. But the others were already following Caddy through a crowd of what Lily guessed to be nearly a hundred people that filled the immense entrance hall. They were all slightly down at heel compared to the West End theatergoers she'd seen milling about the Strand the day before, and they were all clamoring impatiently to be let in for the show.

Malkin sniffed at everyone's shoes. Lumps of gilt and plaster had flaked from the ceiling and lay scattered about their feet. "Smells of mold and theater frippery in here," he declared. "Let's find this Celine D'Ore and get out of this place before I suffocate."

Lily ignored him. Her attention had been distracted by someone in the throng, a face she thought she recognized—it wasn't Jack, or Finlo, but someone else who she couldn't quite place. He was clean-shaven except for a neat mustache. She peered closer at him, but he turned away to talk to a friend—a tall, stately, official-looking man with a white beard—and then Caddy had ushered her past.

They had reached the far end of the room. Beneath a gold-leafed sign for the stalls stood two magnificent smoked-glass doors. Caddy threw them open.

"Ladies and gentlemen," she said, "could you kindly take your seats, the show is about to begin!"

The crowds began shuffling into the stalls. Lily lagged behind, clutching her ticket in her sweaty palm. The inky words on the cheap gray paper had already rubbed off against her skin. She searched through the passing faces for the strange men among the congregation, but they seemed to have entirely disappeared. "Shouldn't we wait for Anna?" she called out again to the others. But they weren't listening, they were already filtering into the auditorium, among the sea of heads. Lily soon found herself being jostled along with them.

The twenty or thirty rows of the smallish auditorium were filling up fast. There were only a few threadbare seats left at the front, beneath the gas footlights of the stage, whose proscenium arch Lily thought must've been rather grand at one time, but today looked faded, the figures in its designs all rather pale and flaky.

Robert squeezed into the front row with the others, grasping the locket chain around his neck to check it was still there. If this Celine *was* Selena and could look to the other side, then she would surely know his da had passed on, and would've realized Robert was trying to find her. How could he possibly face someone who knew all that and yet hadn't got in contact? As the last few people shuffled in, and began filling up the corners at the back, Robert began to feel faintly sick.

Lily gazed over the heads of the crowd searching for Anna, but it was too late. Caddy was already leaving, closing the exit doors behind her. She tried not to worry and settled herself beside Robert. Malkin crawled beneath her feet and gave a disinterested yawn. Tolly took a few monkey nuts from his pocket and began to crack them open, dropping the shells on the floor around the fox.

"Watch it!" Malkin yapped, giving him a look.

"Well?" Tolly said. "It's a theater, ain't it?"

Lily was about to tell them both to be quiet when, with a noise like the creak of an old set of bellows, the fire curtain rose to reveal a worn red velvet theater drape, brocaded in gold.

With a fizzing hiss, the house lights dimmed. The crowd murmured as a spotlight picked out a moon-white circle on the curtains. Lily clasped her hands together, shivering at the sight of such an omen. Then the spot went out and the footlights dimmed to nothing, plunging the stage into darkness.

A long time passed; Robert gripped the locket. A cold dread fell upon him that seemed to seep into his very bones. Something wasn't right. This wasn't how he'd imagined reconnecting with his ma. Fear filled him up like water in a glass… He shifted in his seat. He dearly wanted to leave, but suddenly…

POP!

The spotlight flashed back on. Standing in the center of the stage was a woman in a white silk cloak and a bejeweled blue velvet dress with a tall collar that framed her hair, which was piled high on her head like an inky thundercloud.

She raised her hands in the air and pressed her palms

together in front of her, before giving a small bow. When she rose, the flickering spotlight illuminated her face. She had a strong nose, sculpted cheekbones, and inquisitive hazel eyes—just like Robert's—that were highlighted in thick lines of kohl. She frowned, taking in the full auditorium, and her eyebrows slashed across her forehead like two charcoal dashes. For a moment it seemed as if she was struck with stage fright. Lily meant to say as much to Robert, but his mouth was open and his white knuckles clutched the seat of the chair.

"D'you think—" she asked.

"It's her," Robert interrupted. "My ma."

Celine smiled briefly and motioned with her hands. The red curtains behind her opened to reveal an indigo backcloth, covered with stars made from glass beads that matched the ones on her dress. They flickered in the footlights until it seemed as if astrological patterns were floating between them, picking out signs of the zodiac and other celestial formations.

"Behold, the spirit cabinet," Celine said.

The spotlight shifted from her face to reveal a black lacquered wooden cabinet about the size of a person that stood upstage. A white circle shone in its center like a mother-of-pearl moon. A thin line split the moon down the middle. It must've been the edge of two panel doors that made up the front of the box. And indeed, as Lily looked closer, she saw a small glass handle on either side of the line.

Celine stepped over and, grasping the handles, opened the two doors to reveal the inside of the cabinet. Dark as death itself, it seemed to suck away the light.

"This is a portal into another world..." Celine's voice was loud and authoritative, but it contained an edge of melodious mystery. She waved a hand around the inside of the box. "At the moment the space is empty, but with a few words I shall summon my astral spirit guide to appear."

Celine clapped her hands together. "Usually she takes the form of a harmless girl, but the truth is she's a dangerous foe. Don't cross her, or make her angry, or she may lash out with her powers.

"Luckily we have ways to protect ourselves." Celine walked to the front of the stage, where a wooden chair and a table with a glass of water had appeared. She took a small object from the table, and held it up so it glinted white in the light. It was a piece of chalk.

"Before I make the summoning, I must draw a pentagram to stop others entering into our world from the land of the dead."

Celine crouched then and drew a circle around the

entire four sides of the box. She made a second circuit of the cabinet and chalked a strange-looking star symbol inside the circumference of the circle.

Then she returned to the front of the stage, took a short drink of water, and sat down on the wooden chair.

A soon as she was comfortably seated, she closed her eyes, put her fingers to her temples, and began to hum a tune softly to herself. Slowly, gradually, she added in words, getting louder and louder, until the echoes of the song filled the whole space.

The song seemed nonsense at first, but soon it echoed and morphed into real phrases that Robert could understand.

"*I invoke thee, spirits of the furthest places,*" Selena sang, her voice shifting and quaking with the odd rhythm of the words.

"*Leave your graves, and wing your way, from lost eternal starless spaces.*

I call you forth, from breathless, sleepless, deathless slumber.
Down winding paths; bright guided by the moon.
Follow her gibbous face.
We await your presence…
Bring knowledge everlasting, and awake…
NOW!*"

A loud *KERRrraAACcCraaaCK!* echoed around the theater.

238

Robert's gaze leaped to the spirit cabinet, and his heart skipped a beat, for it was no longer empty. There, in its dark confines stood a ghostly figure with a pale, cadaverous face.

CHAPTER 16

Inside the cabinet the deathly figure with the pale face hovered in mid-air. Her white gown and long blonde hair billowed behind her in the blackness, as if she was deep underwater. The room had grown colder. It seemed the spirit-girl had brought a winter chill with her. Celine shivered, and wrapped her shawl tighter around her shoulders; the light about her dampened and discolored.

With a loud hiss, the ghost-girl awakened. Lily caught her breath. The spirit's eyes were rolled back in her head, but still it seemed as if she was staring deep down into everyone's hearts.

Even Malkin, who was normally scared of nothing,

was shaking beneath the seat—Lily could feel his tail trembling beside her leg. She wished Anna was with them, to pour scorn on the whole occasion. Why had the aeronaut not arrived? Had Caddy the lobby girl refused to let her in?

"Please welcome my spirit guide," Celine was saying. "I call her No-name. She's been dead nigh on forty years. She passed over when she was young and has been lost in the underworld ever since, treading broken, misty paths. In that time she's gathered to her many dark and supernatural arts…"

Celine stood up from her seat and spoke directly to the floating spirit. Her voice sounded slow and calm, but a slight tremor of panic danced through her words, as if she wasn't entirely sure what the ghost might do.

"No-name, I invoke thee to bring forth the lost loved ones of these people present so we may commune with them. Are you ready to make that calling, No-name?"

The ghostly figure in the cabinet nodded slowly in assent. "I am ready," she rasped, and her voice, loud and brash, carried across the theater, then faded slowly like dispersing smoke.

Celine walked toward the footlight and descended some steps into the auditorium. She wandered along the far aisle and the spotlight followed, sending inky shadows flickering across her skin. Robert, Tolly, and Lily had to crane their necks to see her, as she flitted between the packed rows.

She stopped beside an elderly gentleman, and took something from his outstretched arm.

"No-name, what is it I hold in my hand?" Celine asked. She had her back to the stage and Lily could see that her eyes were glazed over. In her trance she appeared not to see anyone in the room.

A long second passed and then the spirit answered in its hissing raspy tone. "This is Mr. McNally," it said. "And you hold a ruby ring in a clasp of silver he gave to his wife on her thirty-fifth birthday. Precious Amelia, who died three years ago this June."

The man's face turned red with shock. "Yes! I want to know...I-I want to know if she's all right?"

"She's with you, isn't she, No-name?" Celine's eyes were watery with tears.

The spirit nodded. "Her hair is knotted and white, and she has fierce green eyes."

"That's her," the man sobbed, brushing his hand across his eyes.

"She wants you to know everything is fine. She's at peace, and she's watching over you. She'd like me to tell you that you may sell the ring, if needs be. And she says to give away the rest of her things, the old clothes that you kept in the chest of drawers. It is time, she says, for you to move on with your life."

The man took a deep breath, and gave the spirit a little bow of thanks.

Celine placed the ring back in his hand and moved on. She was coming closer, but she turned aside and halted beside a well-dressed lady, who held up a jeweled moth hatpin.

Celine took it from her and seemed to focus afresh on something far off in the distance. "Do you know this, No-name?" she asked the spirit.

The spirit answered with surety. "A French hatpin with a polished amber stone set in a silver decorative moth design, bought in Paris by Miss Lomax's mother... Ida was her name." The spirit shifted and bowed its head; its long blonde hair hung bedraggled across the scorched rings of its eye sockets. Then it continued. "You found the pin last week, Miss Lomax, when it fell from a box on the shelf at the back of the wardrobe. Your mother wants you to know she's with me. She hid the pin there for you. She wants you to have it. To keep it by you always as a reminder of her..."

Celine turned and walked back up the aisle then came along the front of the stage. Ignoring the other patrons, she wandered toward them. She was barely three steps away now. She stopped at Tolly's seat, but he had nothing to give, merely some monkey-nut shells, and the stub of a pencil, which Celine rejected.

And then, she was at Lily's side. Lily felt in her pocket for something. But all she could find was Mama's fossil. She handed it over and Celine grasped it in her palm and closed her eyes.

"What manner of thing have I been given, spirit?"

"It is an ammonite," the spirit replied. "It belonged to the girl's mama, Grace Hartman. She's by my side at this very moment. A handsome, clever woman with a big smile. She says that she found this fossil in Braklesham Bay, where you were all three together on holiday, long ago, Lily, when you were barely six years old. She loved fossil hunting, especially with you. She misses you always, but she's glad you still have the rosewood box with her gifts in, and your purse, with the many treasures inside that once belonged to her. And the heart, Lily, she's glad you've a good heart! She says you must forgive your father, he'll come around eventually to knowing what you are capable of, and realize you're not an invalid, but a strong-hearted girl who can look after herself. And that strength you have will last forever."

Lily dug her nails into her arms to stop herself shaking.

She hadn't been thinking of Mama when they set foot in this place. It hadn't even occurred to her that No-name might be able to speak with her.

"She loves you, Lily," the spirit continued. "And she wants you to remember what she told you in that moment when you last spoke. Whatever your problem is, whatever the question, you must trust your heart. It will make the right choices."

Lily's hand jumped to her chest; the Cogheart fluttered beneath it. How could the spirit know such things? Could it be true that she was speaking from the other side? And yet, there was something familiar about her, even hidden within the deep shadowy interior of the cabinet…

Celine placed the stone back in Lily's hand—it felt warm from her touch but heavier somehow. Heavy as a rock. Lily clutched it hard in her palm and turned to Robert to say something, but his face was filled with dread.

Celine had stepped away from Lily and was standing right beside him.

She brushed her hair behind her ear and moved closer, her eye landing on the chain glinting around Robert's neck. She indicated it. "You've lost someone too," Celine said. "I can feel that loss leeching from you. Did this belong to them once upon a time?"

Robert nodded.

"It won't take but a moment," Celine whispered. "No-name can't call forth anyone for you unless you let me hold the keepsake."

Robert felt a twinge of worry as he undid the clasp and slipped the Moonlocket from around his neck. What if she didn't recognize it? He wanted to say something, to ask her, but the words dried in his throat and lodged there like a misshapen cog that had come loose inside him.

Celine took the Moonlocket lightly in her hand, barely glancing at it as she closed her fist around it. She was about to turn and speak to the spirit, as she had done with the others, when something—perhaps the feel of the crescent shape in her palm—made her glance down, and she let out a low moan.

She stared hard at Robert, then fell back heavily against the edge of the stage.

"It's the Moonlocket—the other half of the Moonlocket!" she cried, stumbling over her words. "That means…you're Robert…the son I left behind!"

"And you're my ma?" Robert stood, and tentatively held out a hand. "You're Selena Townsend?"

Selena nodded. Then she threw her arms around him and hugged him close. Robert put his head against her chest; he could hear her heart beating hard, and her shawl against his cheek smelled of smoke and dry wool.

"It's been such a long time," she whispered tearfully, brushing the hair from his face. "How on earth did you find me?"

THUUUD!

Something had fallen to the floor.

Lily looked around.

In the spirit-cabinet, No-name, who had been floating impossibly in the shadowed aperture, now stood upright on its floor, with her bare white feet visible.

No-name walked toward the threshold of the cabinet and paused…then stepped out onto the stage. The audience gasped in unison as the spirit scuffed the complex chalk pentagram, then opened its mouth and made a deep wailing sound, before running, hair straggling and arms outstretched, toward Selena and Robert.

Lily held her breath, choking back the terror as the wailing No-name spirit clawed toward them. It reached the edge of the stage and jumped down among the onlookers who froze and shrank back in their seats, and it seemed as if the spirit might attack them all. Selena, Robert, or anyone nearby.

But then it paused, and wiped a tiny hand across its brow. Smudging its ghostly pallor. And Lily realized it was just stage make-up. The spirit was much shorter than it seemed in the cabinet, almost the size of…

The spirit pulled away the thatch of blonde hair. It was a wig, and beneath it was a black twiggy tangle. Lily breathed a sigh of relief. No-name was Caddy, the girl from the box office.

"My brother!" Caddy whispered softly in her own voice. She dropped her wig on the floor, where it was immediately pounced on by Malkin, who ripped it to shreds. From inside the neck of her dress, she produced a locket on a chain that matched Robert's. Lily saw it was the opposite piece to his—a fuller and fairer moon.

It had been Caddy then, not Selena, who'd had the other half of the Moonlocket. She was Robert's sister. The lost piece that made up the whole. Lily wondered why she hadn't guessed when they'd spoken with her in the lobby—she and Robert looked so alike.

Caddy handed her locket to Selena, who held up both halves and examined them, and her two children, as one for the first time.

By now the poor confused audience was on its feet, muttering, and peering from all angles, trying to see around the heads of other onlookers to the small gaggle of people in the front row. They hadn't a clue what to make of things. The whole outrageous act had been revealed as a fraud, but was this now part of the show? No one was entirely sure.

No one except Lily and her friends. She wiped a tear from her eye. She wanted to embrace them all. She'd helped Robert do this—find his ma. And it seemed in that very moment that was what Selena became. Her tall and foreboding performance persona had disappeared and she'd blossomed into a softer, friendlier figure. She barely noticed the reaction of the crowd. Nor did she take in Lily, Tolly, and Malkin, standing beside her. She only had eyes for Robert and Caddy and the Moonlocket she'd gifted them.

Selena took the two pieces and fitted them together with a click and the whole Moonlocket glinted in the spotlight. The crescent face and the gibbous face together made a perfect whole moon. For a second, Selena scanned the auditorium, as if she was worried about something else, but then she looked back at her children and smiled. "Finally," she said, her voice hoarse and cracking, "we're together again. A family."

"Not quite!" growled a gravelly voice from the gods. "There are still a few more specters to arrive at the feast."

Selena tensed against Robert, as if she was ready to

spring like a cat, and her gaze darted around the shadowy theater. "Who's that?" she called out.

There was no answer. Only silence.

And her words echoed away into the darkness.

The audience shifted uncomfortably, wondering what was going on. This show was getting stranger and stranger. If it was a show at all. A few of them stood and put on their coats, readying themselves to leave. But their quiet flutterings were interrupted by the disembodied voice breaking into song.

It was a low harsh tune, very different to Selena's singing. To Lily it seemed like it came from nowhere and everywhere in unison, as if someone was whispering the words into her ear, but also shouting them across the heads of the whole room.

"*See-saw, Jack Door,*
Selena shall have a new master;
She shall earn but a penny a day,
Because she can't work any faster."

The audience whispered among themselves. At the back, Lily saw the tall, official-looking figure with the white beard from the lobby and his mustachioed friend, squeezing past people, making for the aisle. At last she realized who they were—Inspector Fisk and Constable Jenkins! They must've been following the same lead.

The last note of the song sounded and the owner of the dark voice stepped to the front of the highest balcony. The spotlight swung toward him and he leered, his face hidden under the brim of a hat. As he tipped his head back, Robert's breath caught in his throat, for he saw straight away that it was Jack. Jack broke into a silky laugh, and then sang a different tune:

"Jack of Diamonds,

Jack of Diamonds,

I know you of old.

For you've robbed my poor pocket of its silver and gold…

Of its silver and goooooooooold!"

The inspector and the constable were making their way toward the stage now, but the rest of the audience were pushing against them, rushing toward the exit—for Jack Door, the most infamous criminal in all of England, was in the theater!

"Remember that one, Selena?" Jack said, as his song ended.

Lily looked to Selena. She was frozen, like a rabbit in headlights.

Quick as a flash, Jack jumped over the balcony's buttress and shimmied down a rope tied to the wall. The spotlight lost him for a second, and when it found him again he had reached the bottom. He jumped onto a seat back, and with his arms out for balance, he leaped acrobatically from seat to seat. It was almost as if he had springs in his heels.

The last few stragglers in the audience pushed out the ends of each row, clogging the gangways, as Jack passed them by. They knew something bad was about to happen. Inspector Fisk and Constable Jenkins grappled through the throng, Jenkins reaching for something beneath his trench coat.

Meanwhile Jack was closing in on Selena, step by step.

Lily wrenched Tolly closer, and they positioned themselves in front of Selena, Robert, and Caddy. Malkin dropped the wig he'd been chewing on and arched his back, curling his lips to show his razor-sharp teeth.

Selena shook her head, and came to her senses.

"All of you, come with me!" she cried and, clasping the Moonlocket, she ran up the steps and onto the stage. Caddy took Robert's hand in hers, and dragged him after their ma. Lily, Tolly, and Malkin quickly followed, just as Jack reached where they'd been.

They rushed through the red velvet curtains, which closed behind them, leaving only the wells of light from the wings to illuminate their path. Ropes and panels of painted scenery hung in the theater's proscenium, like fragments of floating buildings, and the jeweled stars of the backcloth and the moon on the spirit cabinet twinkled in the dark.

"Is there another way out?" Tolly asked.

"The back exit." Selena hitched up her skirt and ran toward it, but as she brushed past the cabinet, a hand shot out of its pitch-dark interior and grabbed her.

Tanned brown fingers held Selena tight in their grip. Caddy screamed and Lily felt her insides drop away as the bowler-hatted figure who the fingers belonged to stepped out of the cabinet.

"Finlo!" Selena croaked.

"The very same," he said. "A bit taller, granted, but I still fit through the cabinet trapdoor." He turned to Caddy. "Your daughter makes a good No-name, sis. Such a realistic dead spirit—you'd almost think she was one."

"Don't you threaten her," Selena shouted. "Let go of me, right now!" She struggled against his grip. "What are you doing? Why are you helping Jack? He always treated you like dirt!"

Finlo laughed and prized the Moonlocket from her hand. "Pa's not like that anymore, jail's changed him. Besides, we have a deal to split the diamond fifty-fifty."

"Idiot," Caddy said. "You can't split a perfect diamond."

"She's right," Selena said. "Don't think he'll play fair, Fin. He'll trick you."

Finlo shook her. "No, you're the trickster, Selena. And don't imagine you can wangle your way out of this one. You'll get what's coming to you."

Selena looked desperately at Robert and Caddy, and then at Malkin, Tolly, and Lily. "Run," she whispered.

Robert shook his head. "Not this time. I've lost one parent. I won't lose another."

"A grand sentiment, boy." Jack smirked, stepping through the red velvet drapes, as the heavy safety curtain dropped with a clang behind him.

Finlo threw Jack the locket and, still grappling with Selena, inched out of the box to cover the other exit upstage. With a start, Robert realized they were well and truly surrounded.

Jack fastened the locket around his own neck. "I heard you trying to turn him against me, Selena. Perhaps you should look to your own children first, or should I see to them for you?"

He strode toward Caddy, but was interrupted by a noise from the auditorium.

"Jack? Can you hear me?" a voice shouted. "This is Inspector Fisk, Jack."

Thank goodness! Lily thought.

"We have you surrounded. Let your hostages go. And surrender, like a good fellow."

"You set me up?" Jack glanced over her shoulder. Lily

254

followed his stare and saw more shadowy figures in helmets arriving in the wings. "This whole performance was put on to catch me?"

Selena smiled, but it was a weak, fearful smile.

"I knew it was too good to be true!" Jack seemed almost pleased at her cleverness. "One joker in the pack though, wasn't there, Selena? You didn't know your son would be here. That really was a surprise!" He nodded to Lily, Malkin, and Tolly. "You three may go. Tell the inspector his show's over. This is how it ends, with a big finale—the disappearing act!" He smashed a vial against the side of the cabinet and an explosion of gray fumes billowed about him, engulfing everyone.

Lily's eyes watered as she convulsed in a coughing fit. At her feet Malkin barked in agitation, while beside her Tolly waved an arm, trying to disperse the clouds of smoke. But it was no use, everything was a gray fog. She could feel people being plucked away around her one by one. And then, suddenly, the smoke cleared, and only she, Tolly, and Malkin remained.

Seconds later, the gaggle of policemen spilled onto the stage along with a pair of stagehands, all rubbing their eyes and hacking to clear their throats. They were closely followed by Inspector Fisk and Constable Jenkins, who'd finally managed to fight their way past the safety curtain.

"Where is he?" the inspector shouted. "Where's Jack?"

A last plume of smoke billowed from the spirit cabinet. Lily waved it away, and peered inside.

The box was empty. The entire Door family, including Robert, was gone. The only evidence they'd ever existed was a small white playing card pinned to the center of the black lacquered back, that depicted the Jack of Diamonds.

CHAPTER 17

Lily, Tolly, and Malkin rode from the theater with Anna and Constable Jenkins in the back of the police wagon. It turned out Anna had arrived a few minutes after the show had started and found the theater doors locked. When she couldn't get in, she'd tried to break them down, but she wasn't strong enough on her own.

Then, she told them, she'd heard some kind of ruckus, and a great crowd of people had smashed their way out from the inside, pouring into the daylight and dispersing almost at once. She'd tried to find her friends among them, but they weren't there, and it had been another few heartstopping minutes before they finally emerged with Constable Jenkins…and without Robert.

Lily listened distractedly to this story and stared out

at the sunny streets of London. Decked in their bright Jubilee bunting, they were at odds with the somber mood inside the cab. She couldn't quite believe the darkness they'd encountered at the theater. If someone had told her that morning she would be part of such an unnerving turn of events, she could not have imagined it.

Things hadn't become any less scary after the Doors disappeared. The inspector had turned red-faced with anger, and started kicking at the spirit cabinet, searching for the secret door. The rest of his men had swarmed the theater, shining lamps into odd corners of the stage and pouncing on the final few confused members of the audience trying to leave.

Lily, Tolly, and Malkin had stood shocked in the center of the stage, ignored by everyone. Finally Constable Jenkins had offered to take them back to the guild in the police wagon.

Lily shifted agitatedly in her seat. Anna put an arm around her, but soon they arrived at *The Daily Cog* and it was time for her to get out.

"If you need anything," Anna said, "anything at all, we'll be here waiting, both of us. I hope they find Robert and his ma and sister, Lily. And I hope you get back to your papa safely. Send him good wishes from me, and tell him I'll do everything within my power to help. But in the meantime we'll keep looking into your riddle."

258

"What riddle?" the constable asked as Lily waved Anna and Tolly goodbye.

She ignored him. As the police steam-wagon pulled away, she and Malkin watched their friends disappear around the side of the *Daily Cog* building. Suddenly Lily felt quite upset. "Why didn't you tell us you were setting a trap for Jack?" she demanded of Constable Jenkins.

"The same reason you didn't tell us that you'd found the locket," he replied. "We didn't want you getting involved."

"Didn't Robert deserve to see his ma?"

"We would've put them in touch after our undercover operation was over."

"Seems to me you've made a right mess of things," Malkin admonished the constable.

Lily was inclined to agree. The police had failed to capture Jack or Selena, and she'd lost Robert, after she'd made a promise to look after him.

"I'm sorry," Constable Jenkins said, apologizing to Lily rather than the fox. "You should've trusted us. And we you. We can only try and make amends. You'd better tell me everything you know about the Moonlocket. And the riddle Miss Quinn mentioned, whatever it is. It may be our only clue to finding Robert and the Doors again."

So Lily described the map and the two mysterious

code words she and Robert had translated: *flows underground*.

The constable wrote them down in his notebook.

"They're the end part of a sentence," she explained. "I caught a glimpse of the rest of it on the other half of the locket when Selena had it. Something-something-something, flows underground. Do you know what it means?"

Constable Jenkins shook his head. "Not yet," he said. "It's a strange one, I'll grant you that, but I'm sure we'll solve it."

Lily wondered when that would be. Soon, she hoped. Jack was a criminal on the run, willing to do whatever it took to find the Blood Moon Diamond. For Robert and his ma and sister, those kinds of odds weren't good.

The police wagon jerked to a stop outside the Mechanists' Guild. As she and Malkin jumped down from the passenger compartment to join Constable Jenkins on the pavement, Lily tried to shake the horrible feeling that everything was lost.

Constable Jenkins paused outside the guild workshop, letting Malkin and Lily enter first. There was Lily's papa, standing before the Elephanta. He turned to stare at her, his hands clasped behind his back. It was a posture he only adopted when he was exceedingly cross. Beside him was Captain Springer, his arms tight across his chest, bow legs jittering.

Lily averted her eyes from them. She felt guilty that she had run away from home, and then the guild too, and got into so much trouble. She was about to explain to Papa what had happened when he rushed forward and hugged her to his skinny frame. "Lily," he cried. "Where've you been? And where's Robert? We were so worried about you both. I'd no idea what's been going on."

Constable Jenkins coughed, awkwardly. Papa spotted him and then Malkin, hiding behind his legs. "Malkin, you moth-eaten mongrel!" he cried. "You were supposed to look after Lily *and* Robert! Keep them out of trouble."

"I did my best," Malkin muttered.

"What happened?" Papa asked the constable.

"Your daughter and Robert decided to visit The Magnificent Theatre of Curiosities," the Constable explained. "To make contact with Robert's mother, Selena, and his sister Caddy. Unfortunately they then interrupted a rather delicate sting operation, and, I'm afraid, Sir, Robert and his entire family were taken by Jack Door."

"Taken where?"

"At this time, we don't know." The constable sounded rather embarrassed. "But we're working on it."

"They all just disappeared," Lily said. "In a puff of smoke."

"Good grief!" Papa adjusted his half-moon glasses, which had become skewed on the bridge of his nose. "I told them both to stay at home..." he admitted to Constable Jenkins.

"So did we, Sir," the constable advised.

Papa's hands shook against Lily's back. "I wish I'd left someone sensible to keep an eye on them. After the telegram from Mrs. Rust I was distraught with worry... then I didn't hear a thing... But whatever kind of trouble Robert was in, he would've been safe at the manor, surely? At least, that's what I thought. It was in such a state yesterday, when I got there..." He trailed off, hugging Lily closer to him and gazing distractedly around the room.

Lily pushed free from his grasp. "We *weren't* safe at home, Papa. We found Jack at the shop and then he came looking for us. All we could think to do was to try and find Selena, and then come and see you. But you'd gone. And now that you're back, we need to look for Robert at once."

Papa seemed to come round then. "Best leave everything to the police, Lily." He looked to Constable Jenkins.

"That's right," Constable Jenkins said. "This whole situation is far too dangerous for you to be involved in,

Miss. We can deal with things now. You should probably just stay here and get some rest."

"What about Robert?" Lily said. "I have to find him. I made a promise to help."

"No, Lily," Papa said. "With this Jack Door…anything could happen—"

"I'm not at risk from him, Papa; Jack let me go." She turned and appealed to the constable. "I know Robert best. I'm the one who understands him. Robert and I, we've been investigating the Doors for days, I've got as much of a clue about them as anyone."

"I don't think so, Miss… Besides, London's too big. The Doors and your friend could be anywhere. Best leave it with us—we'll lay hands on them soon enough."

"Listen to him, Lily." Papa gripped her arm. "He's right. I'm responsible for your safety. Remember what we talked about at home, before I left? You've a good heart, but I can't let you get involved in this anymore. If anyone should be out there searching for Robert, it should be me." He smiled at the constable. "Thank you for bringing her back, Sir. I'll see that she stays out of trouble. Now, if you wait down here, I shall come to join the search with you when I return."

Lily, Papa, and Malkin climbed the stairs of the guild's accommodation wing, then walked past the frozen automatons she and Robert had noticed last night. To Lily that already seemed a lifetime ago.

"But we do have a clue," Lily said suddenly.

"What's that?" Papa asked.

"You said we didn't have a clue, but we do: *flows underground*. The words Robert and I translated from the locket. They have something to do with where the diamond's hidden."

"And you told the constable this?" Papa asked.

She nodded.

"Well then, he'll probably be able to work out what that means." Papa unlocked the door to his quarters. "Why don't you take it easy for a bit?" he said, escorting her and Malkin in. "You've had a strenuous couple of days. I'll get one of the mechanicals to bring you up some food later this evening. A plate of something soothing. Plus, I brought a case from home, for you and Robert." Papa indicated a travel trunk among the others in the center of the room that hadn't been there last night. "By the time you've changed into some fresh clothes, had some dinner and a nap, I'm sure the police will have solved everything, and Robert will be back with us."

"It's not even dark," Lily said as she watched him step around the camp bed and draw the curtains to block out the afternoon light.

The truth was, she did feel rather tired. She wondered if a rest was actually a good idea.

"It's better this way," Papa said as he closed the door. "Try to sleep for a bit. I'll let you know at once if there's news."

After he was gone, Lily took Mama's ammonite from her pocket and placed it on the bedside table. Then she lay down on the bed.

Papa was right, she did need to rest briefly. Later, when her mind was clear, she would be far more capable of helping Robert. And hopefully, by then, the police or Anna or even Papa would have discovered something new. Malkin nuzzled her ear and she rubbed woozily at her face and put her head on the pillow, shutting her eyes for a brief moment…

Flows underground.

The phrase jolted her awake, tumbling around inside her head like the locket twisting on its chain. If only she could figure out what it meant.

Blearily, she reached over and wound Malkin with the winder key on the chain around his neck. Then she got up and went to the window, throwing back the curtains.

The room was on the top floor of the guild and she

could see the whole of the city. Behind the spire of St. Paul's Cathedral the sun was setting, bathing everything in a bright orange light. She must've slept for a good few hours. Was it really only last night she and Robert had stood here waiting for the clouds to pass, so they might see the moon and stars? She'd thought that all clouds would pass with time...but maybe she was wrong.

Robert was lost somewhere out there with Selena and Caddy. She gave a deep sigh.

"What are we to do, Malkin?" she cried. "It feels like time is running out."

She put her head in her hands and thought about how angry Jack was, and how hotheaded he'd been about the locket. "Maybe I'm wrong. Maybe Jack will let Robert go? He got what he wanted. And they are family."

Malkin jumped up on the window ledge beside her, and licked her face. "I don't think so, Lily. Jack doesn't seem the sort to forgive a grudge. But don't you worry," he said, "we'll find Robert. I'm sure of it. We'll leave and look for him as soon as it's light. Perhaps Tolly will assist us? He's a good sort. Seems to know London."

Lily nodded. She'd been wondering about Tolly. Scraping around alone on the streets gave him a kind of freedom. She remembered the joyful feeling of walking with him yesterday morning, how he knew every landmark. He'd even told her about…

"Of course!" she shouted. "Malkin, it's the Fleet River that flows underground."

"What?" Malkin said.

"The map on the locket showing where the diamond's hidden, it's of the Fleet River. Tolly told me it ran underground through the sewers, right beneath Queen's Crescent, where the Doors used to live."

"You think Jack will have worked that out?"

"Robert will—he has to!" Lily said. "And Jack will want to get the diamond as soon as possible, so they'll probably go there straight away."

"Then we should tell someone right now." Malkin jumped down from the window ledge.

"Good idea," Lily said. "We'll go back to Anna. She'll know what to do." She ran to the door and tried the handle, but it wouldn't turn. And with shock she realized that Papa had locked them in.

CHAPTER 18

Robert shifted on his feet. He, Selena, and Caddy were imprisoned in a room with a bare mattress, a broken cupboard, and a table with a single chair shoved against the far wall. Beside the door was a tiny fireplace, with a dying fire hissing and flickering in the grate. In the slanted ceiling a skylight looked out on a purple sky—the last moment of sunset.

It'd been quite the journey getting here, Jack and Finlo hustling the three of them down a long dark tunnel beneath the theater, that led out into a number of other underground passages. They'd twisted this way and that, passing brick columns and clanging pipes, until Robert was sure they were no longer under the theater, but in a completely different part of town.

When they'd finally come up through a trapdoor into this derelict house, Jack and Finlo had marched them up the stairs and straight into this room. Finlo had searched them, before Jack locked them in. That had been hours ago.

At first, after Jack and Finlo had gone, they'd hammered on the solid metal door and screamed, hoping someone in the house might hear them. But their voices grew hoarse and no one came.

Eventually Selena gave up and told them it wasn't worth it; the place must be empty. Now, to Robert's annoyance, she was dozing on the bare mattress, her shawl wrapped tight around her shoulders.

Caddy was sitting beside her, shifting her bare feet on the wooden floorboards and anxiously rubbing her arms. She was still in her No-name costume—the ragged white spirit-dress from the stage show.

Robert stared angrily at Selena. It was frustrating not to be able to talk with her, after all his searching. He was desperate to find out why she left, to get everything off his chest, and yet here she was…dozing.

"I don't know how she can sleep in such a terrible situation," he complained.

Caddy smiled and placed a hand gently on Selena's back. "That's Ma's way sometimes," she said. "When the nerves get the better of her she falls asleep, even in the middle of the day; then she'll be up at odd hours at night."

"Never mind. I should try and work out where we are."

Robert dragged the chair from the corner of the room. He climbed onto it and stood on tiptoes to peer out through the barred skylight.

Outside, in the pink gloaming, airships floated along the air lanes, and the dark silhouetted buildings were pinpricked with squares of soft yellow light. He tried to spot Jack and Finlo in the cuts and alleyways down below, but it was a fruitless task. The shadows had grown long, and the street lamps were not yet lit.

He gave up, and jumped off the chair to sit down beside Caddy.

His sister.

Those words echoed in his brain, making him feel giddy, almost faint.

He had a sister. A real one. Strange to discover something so big about himself that he never knew. She'd appeared out of thin air today, like a…magic trick! That's right, that's what she was! He let out a laugh, and covered his mouth in embarrassment. He was feeling a little hysterical about everything.

Caddy gave him an odd look and furrowed her eyebrows in that serious way his da used to. It was almost like seeing a younger version of himself. Truly, they were more alike than he could have ever imagined. Why hadn't he noticed it before?

"Your hair and eyes…" he said. "They look like Selena's, but your face…the shape…it's Da's, Thaddeus's."

Caddy sat up, interested. "Thaddeus? That was my da's name too." She looked confused. "But do you live with him?" she asked. "Because Ma told me he was far, far away."

"We weren't that far away," Robert said, and then he looked sad. "Well, Da is…Da's…dead."

"Oh," she said. And then it seemed as if she didn't know what to say. "What was he like?" she asked eventually.

"He was a kind man," Robert began. "Clever, like you. He knew practically everything about watches and locks, lockets and miniatures, but stars and clocks were his specialty."

"I wish I'd known him," Caddy said.

Robert bit his lip to hold back the tears. Nowadays, he didn't like talking about his da…about *their* da. An awkward silence spread like glue, gumming up the other things he wanted to say. He wasn't ready to ask Caddy about their ma. Not yet. It was too nerve-racking.

He was dying to understand more about her disappearance, but a part of him worried the reasons might make him hate her. He tried to think of something else to ask that wasn't a question about his past, or Caddy's... Finally, he hit upon her role in the show. That was a safe subject.

"How do they work?" he asked, quietly. "The spirit readings?"

Caddy smiled. "You mean you don't think they're real?"

He shook his head. "No. So what are they?"

"It's a code." Caddy looked down at Selena. "Ma knows lots of secret codes."

Robert scratched his head. "But how does it actually work?"

"Like this..." Caddy sat up straight and closed her eyes, waving her arms about. Robert laughed because she was doing an almost uncanny imitation of Selena's trance. She opened her eyes and gave him a conspiratorial sideways glance.

"Right... Imagine you're the medium and I'm the spirit in the box, and you say to me: 'Tell me what it is'— that means the object you're holding is a coat. If you say: 'What is this, please?'—that means a needle case. 'Do you know this?' means an umbrella."

"So you use different phrases, different code words, with different emphasis, to mean different things?" Robert asked.

"Exactly!" Caddy looked pleased at how quickly he'd got it. "And if you know what thing belongs to what person—because you've had a conversation with them before the show, when they bought their ticket—then you know a bit of their story to go with your guess. After that you just embellish the rest according to their reaction."

"I see," Robert said. "So how did you know about Lily's past?"

"Do you know, that's the strange thing, I'm not entirely sure. Perhaps I'd read about her somewhere. But I recognized her face in the lobby and, when I was in the spirit cabinet, it truly did feel as if I had a message for her from her ma on the other side. A real message."

"Maybe sometimes the spirits *are* real," Robert said.

"Yes," she said. "Maybe sometimes they are."

She was shivering. He took off his coat and draped it around her. "'Tell me what it is,'" he said softly, looking at the coat. "That's the right phrase, isn't it?"

She nodded and smiled. "It is," she said. "And if I had to guess, I'd say the coat belonged to Da?"

She was a good reader of people, Robert could see. She could sense the details of their past that they carried with them. He was about to tell her so, when Selena woke up.

Selena yawned and looked around the disheveled space. "This must be Finlo's lodgings," she said. "He always did keep a scruffy room." Then she noticed a scratch on Caddy's arm.

"You've cut yourself." Selena held Caddy close and dabbed at the mark with a handkerchief from her pocket. "Don't scratch it, you'll infect the wound."

Robert wished jealously that she'd been around when he was younger to do that for him. "Ma?" he asked softly. "Ma?" he tried again.

That name felt strange in his mouth. Wrong.

Selena looked up and smiled widely, and he could see in her eyes that she was listening. He wanted to say he'd missed her, but he couldn't quite bring himself to. The words were too knotted and tangled together inside him. He drew back and tried to shake them free, but they wouldn't come.

"Do you know what the map on the back of the Moonlocket is?" he asked her instead.

Selena seemed to be expecting a different question; she pursed her lips and stared thoughtfully at him. "Not entirely," she said, "but I know that it leads to a secret room that contains something Jack stole years ago."

"The Blood Moon Diamond?" he asked, relieved that the awkwardness had passed.

She nodded. "It's the only thing Jack cares about. He wouldn't have come to the theater today otherwise. He didn't come for me, or for you, or Caddy. He came for the Moonlocket and its treasure map. He cares for nothing but that diamond, not even his family. Not anymore."

"I didn't know you were his family until recently," Robert said.

"Why did you fall out?" Caddy asked.

"Because I gave him up to the police," Selena said. "Afterwards he disowned me forever. Scratched me out of his life as if I'd never existed… Can you imagine doing that to your own kin?"

Robert could well imagine. It was exactly what she'd done to him—left him behind with Da, never to return. He bit his tongue and choked back an irritation in his throat, but before he could say anything, his thoughts were interrupted by footsteps in the hall.

Jack and Finlo had returned.

They unlocked the door and stepped into the room.

"Enjoying your new home, Selena?" Finlo took his bowler hat off and hung it on the hook behind the door, then smoothed back the dark curls atop his head.

275

Jack swung the conjoined locket back and forth on its two chains. "I think it's time you told me what Artemisia had to say about the Moonlocket on the day she died."

Selena pursed her lips, then gave a defiant laugh. "You mean to tell me, after fifteen years, you don't have a clue what it means? You, the expert—the one who knows everything!"

Jack's features were icy calm, betraying nothing, but his fingers snapped around the locket. Stopping it mid swing, he grasped it tight. "You were the one who spoke with her about it. What were her last words? There must be some clue as to what this means?" He pointed at the locket's back.

Robert saw, for the first time, that the two halves together made a larger map and a whole coded sentence. Suddenly, he remembered the part he and Lily had translated—*flows underground*.

Selena lowered her head to avoid Jack's gaze. "Ma didn't tell me anything about her secret codes," she said. "I haven't a clue what it means."

"You're bluffing," Jack said. "I don't believe you." Jack grasped Robert and shook him roughly. Then he clamped his hands down on Robert's shoulders, stopping him from standing. "Make her tell us, Fin," he said nodding to his son.

Finlo took Caddy by the arm and dragged her from

her seat toward the fire.

"Please, Fin!" Selena was up like a shot, pulling at her brother, trying to free Caddy. But Finlo didn't let go. He threw Selena aside and held Caddy's hand closer to the flames.

"Stop it, you'll burn her," Selena shouted.

"Then tell us," Jack said.

"Fin!" Selena begged.

Finlo wavered for a moment. He looked to Jack.

"You worm," Jack said. "Are you going to let a woman tell you what to do?"

Finlo held Caddy's hand closer to the fire.

Caddy's body shook; she bit her lip to stop the tears, and clenched her fist, trying to keep her fingers away from the flames.

Robert smelled the acrid scent of the hairs on her hand singeing in the heat.

"Please, stop!" Selena screamed. "I've told you, I don't know what it means!"

"You're lying," Jack said. "I can see it in your eyes."

Robert felt sick. Caddy's fingers were almost in the fire. He wanted to end this but Jack was still holding him down by the shoulders; he could do nothing.

"Wait," he cried. "I-I know part of it… *Flows underground*—that's the last two words. That's what they say! The Moonlocket code's from a book of games and tricks. I remember it. I can translate the rest, if you show me."

"Finlo! Enough!" Jack barked, and Finlo jerked Caddy's hand back before it touched the flames.

Caddy was sobbing. Finlo threw her into Selena's shaking arms.

Robert felt a fresh pang of jealousy and then a wave of guilt. Jack let go of him and pulled a piece of chalk from his pocket, slamming it on the table along with the locket.

"Do it then. Translate the words. You've got five minutes."

Robert pulled out a chair from the table and sat down. He picked up the locket and regarded it. Now it was complete he could see the whole map, on Caddy's half was a small symbol like a house, with the number forty-five inside it. Beneath it was the rest of the map, and the rest of the sentence...

Fmghx it tig rjxhv ticw fmqzw uofhvlxvcwn ◺

He stared at this gibberish. Suddenly he could barely remember how the code worked. His mind was racing and his scalp itched, his back was wet with sweat, and his heart beat raggedly in his chest. He had to think.

"Go on, Robert, you can do it," Selena whispered to him.

He took a deep breath, and leaned in closer to the locket, peering at each word in turn. The strange letters shone and for a second a vague face appeared beneath them, reflected roundly in the locket's silvery surface.

For a moment, he thought it was his da. He'd such a strong image of Thaddeus bent over his workbench, intense in his concentration, studying the broken springs of a watch or engraving a locket like this one. *No one conquers fear easily, Robert. It takes a brave heart to win great battles.*

A shadow interrupted his thoughts. It was Jack, looming over him with arms folded. Robert's eyes flicked back to the locket, and the reflection on its surface.

It was not his da's face but his own.

Robert closed his eyes briefly.

Then he opened them again and drew five right-angled triangles on the table, one for each unknown part of the cypher. After those he added the last two known words—*flows underground*. Finally, he set to work.

Soon, the translation was appearing. As Robert uncovered the last few letters, Jack pushed him out of the way and read the entire sentence out loud.

"Fleet is the river that flows underground."

"What does that mean?" Finlo asked. "Is it some kind of riddle? Fleet means fast…fast is the river that flows underground…?"

But Robert understood what it meant. It was the Fleet River; the map was of the Fleet River. The river Tolly had told them about that ran through the sewers under North London.

"You clattering idiot!" Jack hit Finlo across the back of his head. "Fleet is the river that flows underground," he shouted. "It means the sewers." He tapped the back of the locket. "This here's a map of the Fleet River that runs through the London sewers, from Hampstead down to the Thames at Blackfriars. And this"—he pointed at the marking on Caddy's half of the locket with the number 45 inside it—"is where it runs right under Queen's Crescent. That's where Artemisia hid the diamond after my arrest, when the police were watching our lodgings. And that's where we have to go to get it back."

"Hadn't we better stake out the house first, check that the police aren't snooping around?" Finlo said.

"Yes," said Jack, putting on the locket. "We'll go right away."

"Both of us? But I only just got back. I haven't even had my dinner yet."

"I said NOW!" Jack shouted.

Finlo got up and, mumbling under his breath as he pulled his hat from the hook, followed Jack out.

Robert heard the key turn. As soon as their voices had faded away, he got up and shook the door handle.

"Can you open this?" he asked, pointing at the lock.

Selena shook her head. "Jack never taught me those skills, I'm afraid. He was too scared that if he did I would use them to escape him."

She finished tending to Caddy's hand, and dried her tears. "There," she said, kissing the girl's fingers. "It's not so bad. Just a few singed hairs." She reached out and squeezed Robert's arm. "Tell you what, let's see if we can't find something to make a brew. That'll make us feel better."

They opened the cupboard in the corner, and had a rifle through it. Caddy found an old tin kettle and a bottle of water, and Robert a jar of tea leaves, two cups, and a small bowl.

Selena poured the water into the kettle and set it to heat on the hearth. When it was finally boiling she stirred in some leaves with a spoon.

"Pity we've no milk." She poured the tea, keeping the bowl for herself, and handing Robert and Caddy a cup each. Robert's had a delicate Chinese pattern.

"Must be stolen," Caddy said.

They sat in silence, drinking their tea. Robert clasped his hands around the warm cup and sipped his slowly to calm the knot in his stomach. "Who made the Moonlocket?" he asked.

Selena smiled. "Your grandma, Artemisia Door. It

was a map to let Jack know where she'd hidden the Blood Moon Diamond. But when I first got it from her I couldn't break the code. How did you do it?"

"It's from a book you used to own," Robert said. "We found it at Queen's Crescent."

"I thought so," Selena said. "After I left home I could barely remember any of that stuff. I must've blocked it from my mind along with everything else." She patted his hand. "I wish I could have worked it out. I would've returned the diamond to its rightful owner years ago. In the end, the best I could do was leave half the locket for each of you, hoping that one day—when the rest of us Doors were gone—you'd be able to solve the mystery together. The last thing I wanted was for Jack or Finlo to get their hands on it."

"But how did you get the locket if it was meant for Jack?" Caddy asked.

"It's rather complicated," Selena said. "And you must know this: I never liked Jack's thievery, always found it difficult to accept. Finlo, on the other hand, had no problem with it. And neither did your grandma. They went along with whatever Jack did. But I felt differently.

"The things Jack stole, his bullying and deceitfulness—they came about because fame wasn't enough for him. He wasn't always that way, not when we were young. But when the acclaim for his act got stale, he became hectoring and imperious. To Fin and me especially he was a bullying despot. Eventually, he turned to grander, more outrageous tricks, and robbery and destruction became his downfall. That's why I chose not to give him the locket when I received it by mistake…"

CHAPTER 19

"Let me tell you the whole story…" Selena said it like a proper mother would, and shifted on the mattress to put an arm around both her children.

Caddy curled up against her like a kitten, and Robert tried to do the same. It felt strange to be held so close by his ma at first, but something about it was also achingly familiar. Smoke scented her hair, her breath was warm on his face, and as she spoke he could almost feel every word.

"In the old days," Selena was saying, "the Door family was part of a troupe that toured theaters. Jack was a famous escapologist and magician, like his father before him, and my ma, Artemisia, was a psychic. My brother Finlo and I helped with their acts.

"Jack's show was always first, and involved a startling

bit of escapology or magic. Then, after the interval, it was Ma's turn. That's what the audience came for. They would bring the valuable jewelry of lost loved ones to help them commune with that loved one's spirit.

"What they didn't know was Ma and Jack were using this part of the performance as a means to gather treasures. During the show, Artemisia would find out as much as she could about the jewels and their worth, then later, as the audience left the theater, Jack would pick their pockets.

"Over the years his own show faded from the limelight somewhat, and Ma's grew more successful, so he began using his escapology skills to break into the houses of the rich and famous.

"Things really came to a head fifteen years ago, when Artemisia and Jack were both to take part in a royal command performance for Queen Victoria, onstage at the Egyptian Theatre. Also appearing in the show was the mechanical Elephanta.

"Ma knew from her knowledge of precious things that the forehead of the Elephanta contained the most valuable jewel ever mined: the Blood Moon Diamond— given to the Queen by her husband Prince Albert. So Ma and Jack set about making a plan to steal it.

"Jack told everyone that for his part of the show he would be chained in the path of the Elephanta and he would escape and ride the beast before she trampled him to death.

"During the performance, with everyone watching, Ma shackled Jack to a frame at the center of the stage. The Elephanta was wound up and she set off walking toward him. Jack seemed to struggle in his chains— for the very first time it seemed as if he might not escape. As the Elephanta was about to crush him beneath her feet, the lights in the theater flashed off, and when they came on again, Jack had vanished. The Elephanta was stilled, frozen in the center of the stage, and the Queen's Blood Moon Diamond, which had sat in the Elephanta's forehead since the day it was made, was gone. Disappeared.

"An Inspector Fisk from Scotland Yard visited Queen's Crescent and questioned us, but Finlo and Ma told him nothing. As for me, when I heard what Jack had done, I wanted no part of it, but I kept my own counsel.

"Then the police began watching the house. We sat there for weeks, brewing and stewing, being followed wherever we went, Ma issuing veiled threats. Eventually, I'd had enough. I couldn't take any more. I contacted the inspector and revealed where Jack was hiding."

"Where was he hiding?" Robert asked.

Selena bit her lip. "By the docks, at The Magnificent Theatre of Curiosities. The plan was, as soon as the brouhaha blew over, he and Ma would take a boat out to sea with the diamond and leave Britain forever. But that never happened, of course. As soon as the police knew where he was, they went to arrest him. And they did a better job of it, that time.

"At the trial, Jack took the blame for the whole plot, claimed my mother knew nothing of his plans. The judge sent him down for life, but the Blood Moon Diamond was never found. The police couldn't work out where it was, though they'd eyes on us constantly while he was in court." She shook her head. "Obviously they never thought to look under the house."

"Fleet is the river," Robert repeated. "It runs beneath Queen's Crescent, like Jack said."

"It does." Selena smiled. "I don't know why I didn't think of that."

"I never heard any of this!" Caddy's mouth was an O of amazement.

Selena brushed a hand through her daughter's hair. "Ma planned to wait for Jack to escape jail, so they could collect the diamond together, then they would sell it and escape Britain on the proceeds."

"But how did she manage to keep it a secret?" Caddy asked.

"By trusting no one," Selena said. "Not even Finlo knew where the diamond was hidden.

"Instead she drew a map of its hiding place and commissioned someone to engrave it on the back of a locket she had. A Moonlocket—of two halves. The first half was a crescent moon, which my father had given her when I was born—to celebrate, see, because I was named Selena. He gave her the second half—the gibbous moon—when my brother Finlo was born, and the two fitted together, as one, to create a whole moon. She couldn't have got the map engraved on only one half because it didn't fit, so she had the map engraved across both parts, and added a clue in code. I suppose it was an extra precaution, a final trick to obscure the diamond's secret location.

"On the day she had to collect the locket from the engravers, she couldn't go for some reason, so she gave me the jeweler's ticket and sent me to collect it instead. The apprentice boy behind the counter at the clockmaker's, he was so handsome. He told me his name was Thaddeus and asked what I was called. When I told him my name was Selena, he asked if the locket was mine—because, he added, I was named for the moon and it was as beautiful as I was. I think that was the moment I fell in love with him. After that we started courting in secret.

"I took both halves of the Moonlocket back to Ma, and everything was fine for a time. But Finlo was so angry. He'd started digging around, asking questions, wanting to find out who'd betrayed our father to the police.

"One day he came home and told Ma it was me, that I was the one who'd given Jack up. She threatened to kick me out of the house. I'd nowhere to go. I went to Thaddeus, and he couldn't take me in where he was working, but he said he'd a family who kept a shop in a little village called Brackenbridge. It was a proper clock shop that served the whole county, repairing people's clockwork and mechanicals. We could escape together and work for his da, who was getting on and would soon retire."

Robert remembered Townsend's as it had once been—a gleaming family shop. It was true what his ma said, it *had* belonged to generations of his family, but today his da was gone, and it was an empty, burned-out shell of its former self.

Selena seemed to sense his melancholy. She touched the ring on her left hand. "So I ran away with your father, Thaddeus, to Brackenbridge. We were married in the village church and began a life there. None of the Doors knew where I was, and in that way I hoped to keep safe from my family. To forget their bullying and my unhappy youth.

"In the back of my mind, I thought that when things had quietened down we'd return to London. But then we had you, Robert. You were such a bonny baby, and we all loved you, and your grandparents—Thaddeus's parents, I mean—loved you the most. They were very old, and died within a year of each other, leaving Thaddeus and me in charge of the shop, and I realized that this was to be my life. There'd be no going back."

She paused and took a deep breath.

"I loved you both dearly, of course, but in those few years at Brackenbridge I never truly felt comfortable. It was always at the back of my mind that none of us were safe because of Jack and what I'd done." She wiped a tear from her eye, studiously avoiding Robert's gaze as she continued.

"Then I saw in the paper that my brother had returned to England, after five years away—traveling in a circus 'round America. At the bottom of the article was one extra line about why he'd come back: his mother was very ill—dying—and he needed to see her one last time.

"When I read that, I knew I had to do the same. I'd seen Thaddeus lose his parents and I knew I couldn't let my mother go without saying goodbye, even though she'd said she never wanted to see me again.

"I set off post-haste to our old house on Queen's Crescent, where she'd rented rooms for years. When I arrived, the landlady mistook me for a boy, for I was dressed in traveling clothes, with my hair pinned back, wearing an old jacket and a bowler hat like Fin's—a disguise so I wouldn't be harassed on the road. I told her who I was and she showed me up to my ma's room, though she warned me that the old lady cursed my name daily for putting Da in jail.

"I knocked and went in. A single bed filled the tiny, squalid room. Above it was a sash window with thick gauzy curtains partly drawn to keep out the light. On a narrow chest beside the bed were various framed lobby cards from the Door Family Show—advertising our act together. Except, when I looked closer, I could see I'd been ripped from each one, my name scratched out of the line-up. I'd been erased from the family history. A no-name girl, who'd disappeared."

"That's horrible." Caddy's voice was choked with tears.

Robert felt a pang as he remembered the cards in the room they'd visited. Caddy knew nothing of this, he realized. "Go on," he whispered to his ma.

"The room smelled of camphor and candle wax," Selena continued. "Your grandma was lying in bed with the covers pulled up to her chin. Her head nestled on an old grimy pillow, her arms resting by her sides. The skin on her hands was so thin, you could see the delicate veins and bones beneath. I'd been scared of her forever, almost as frightened as I was of Jack, but here she was, on the way out. And she looked like if you stood her up she'd blow away with the wind.

"Consumption, it was. She was so weak she couldn't even sit to receive me. I perched on the end of her bed, for there were no chairs.

"The room was filled with a lampless evening gloom, so that I could hardly see, and her eyes were barely open, but she smiled at me.

"'Hello, Finlo,' she croaked, mistaking me for my brother.

"Her voice sounded rough as a coal shovel scraped across macadam. I was about to open my mouth and correct her when I remembered the pictures on the chest. So I played along. I knew if she realized it was me she would refuse to speak, tell me to leave, and I wanted a few moments with her to call my own. I still loved her, you see.

"I tried to make my voice deeper, more manly.

"'Hello, Ma,' I said, taking off my bowler hat and placing it on the end of the bed.

"'I'm glad you came.' The words dropped slowly from her mouth onto the bedspread. 'There's something I want you to do for me.' She reached around her neck and her hand shook as she took off a necklace—the Moonlocket—and handed it to me. I thought somehow she knew who I was, and this was an act of forgiveness.

"She took a jagged breath. 'I want you to have this, Fin,' she said. 'One last thing… Live the life you choose. Good or bad. No regrets. Like your father…like Jack.' She peered closer at me. 'You're his spit, you know? His double. Just like him.'

"She closed my hand around the locket. 'When Jack's finally out of solitary and they're no longer keeping an eye on him, go visit him in jail, help him break free, and give this to him with my love. Tell him he'll need games and tricks to solve its code.' She laughed wheezily."

"She meant the book!" Robert said.

Selena nodded. "Precisely. But I didn't know that. Not until you mentioned it just now to Jack. I thought she was talking gibberish, or in some garbled riddle.

"I clasped her hand and asked no questions. And soon she closed her eyes and was gone. I sat for a long time then, stroking her hair in silence, and when I finally let go of her hand, I sobbed so hard I thought I might choke.

"I put the locket 'round my neck, tucking it into my shirt. Then I kissed Ma on the forehead, and left.

"It was three flights down from her rooms to the ground floor, and as I walked those stairs a figure brushed past me in the gloom. I knew from the set of his shoulders and hat that matched mine that it was Finlo. He'd a key in his hand and must be going to let himself in.

"I realized, soon as he saw Ma, and spoke with the landlady, he'd clock what'd happened. I needed to leave right away. I turned my face to the wall and continued on downstairs, kept walking—through the hallway and out the door. And I never looked back."

Selena took a deep breath.

"That afternoon I caught the first zep back to Brackenbridge. Soon as I arrived, your father saw from my face that I'd had a terrible shock. I filled him in as much as I could on what had happened and gave him half of the Moonlocket. It was a gift for you—it was mine, after all, to do with as I pleased. Artemisia had told me to live my own life. I didn't know what the locket was then—or, at least, didn't suspect. If I had, I might've thrown it in the river. I just wanted you to have a legacy, a connection to me and the past you'd never know.

"I told Thaddeus I had to go, and to keep the locket safe somewhere. To hide it where no one would find it. Then, when you were fully grown, he was to give it to you and tell you the whole story. And if you decided you wanted to see me again, given all the risks, you would be able to come and find me."

"He must've been the one who hid my half of the locket in the fireplace," Robert said. "He always kept his promises."

Selena nodded. "That night, he comforted me, tried to change my mind about going, but it was no use, the next morning I knew I had to leave. Brackenbridge wasn't safe. Finlo could easily find out where I was. And one day Jack would escape from jail and come looking for me. After all, no lock had ever held him...

"Thaddeus was still sleeping when I made my final decision, and so were you. I packed my things and visited the church to say a prayer for you both and, before I left, I ripped our marriage certificate from their book of records. So that Jack could never ever discover we were connected."

"Somehow he found that out anyway," Robert said.

Selena wiped at her puffy eyes. "He always does... After that, I returned to my old world of the stage. Not in this country—I didn't want to be found so easily... Instead, I crossed the channel. Not as Finlo once had to America, but to Europe. And I joined the traveling shows there.

"It was only when I got to France I discovered I was pregnant again. I named her Cadence—it means the rhythm of things." She smiled at her daughter.

"I kept Caddy with me, while I tried to make a new life. And I knew you'd be all right. Safe with your da."

"Da's dead," Robert said. "This six months gone."

"I thought as much," Selena said sadly. "I felt it somehow—deep inside. But I wasn't sure. And I couldn't risk returning, the way things were. I'm sorry."

Beside her, Caddy was in tears, crying softly to herself.

Selena was silent, waiting for him to say more. But Robert found he had no words with which to ease her pain.

CHAPTER 20

The trouble with hairpins was sometimes they took an awfully long time to pick a lock. Lily had been at it a good hour when she finally heard the mechanism *click*. She tried the handle and the door swung open.

She and Malkin peered around its edge, before slinking out into the guild's corridor.

"Claptraptions!" cried a voice behind them. "Where do you think you're going?" It was Captain Springer.

"Nowhere," Lily tried.

"I should think not." The captain folded his arms in front of his chest. "London's a very dangerous place, tiddler! Your papa told me to stand on guard outside your room all night if I have to, while he joins the search for Robert and the rest of them."

"But don't you see?" Lily said. "That's exactly why you must let Malkin and me go. We've worked out where Jack's going, and we can get Robert back."

"I don't know." Captain Springer tutted and clucked like a cooling engine. "Better to leave things to the police."

"They don't have a clue, Captain. And neither does Papa. He wouldn't listen!"

"Sometimes adults don't."

Lily wrung her hands together. "What can we do? We need to save Robert. It's down to us. We're the only ones who can do it—you have to let us go!"

"Sprocket-springs!" Captain Springer said. "What a decision…" He thought about it for a long time. "I'm afraid I can't disobey specific instructions," he said finally. "It goes against all my clockwork. But, perhaps, if I wasn't paying attention… I'm only a clueless mechanical. If you ran away, I probably wouldn't be able to find you. You and Malkin could probably sneak down the stairs, while I was looking the other way, and I wouldn't even notice. Or perhaps I ran down during the night and you got past me that way." He turned and stared hard the other way, as if he hadn't even been looking for them.

"Thank you, Captain." Lily patted his hand, then nodded to Malkin. " Come on, Malkin, we need to go to *The Daily Cog* to get Anna—we have to save Robert."

They ran down the corridor, past the retired

mechanicals in their cases, and down the stairs of the guild. As they sneaked past the large workroom, Lily saw that the door was ajar. She peered in, but there was only the elephant in the room. Lily was glad Papa wasn't around—if he'd caught her loitering in the corridor, he would've sent her back to bed at once, and this time he would've made sure to double-lock the door.

Quickly, she signaled to Malkin and they sneaked onward into the lobby of the guild…where Mr. Porter—the mechanical porter—was wide awake and guarding the entrance to the building.

They hid behind an archway and peered out. To get to the main door, they would have to get past Mr. Porter's desk.

"Malkin," Lily whispered. "You're going to have to create a distraction."

"What sort of distraction?" Malkin mumbled.

"I don't know, do I?" Lily said. "A distracting one."

"You want me to create a distracting distraction?"

"Yes!" she hissed.

"Fine. Then that is what I'll do."

Malkin raced out from their hiding place, barking as he did so. And when he reached Mr. Porter, he pulled the paperwork off the mechanical's desk and ran off with it down the corridor in the other direction.

Mr. Porter gave a yelp of alarm that quickly turned to

anger, and he stood and chased after Malkin, waving a metal fist.

Quick as you like, Lily sneaked out of the guild, leaving the door ajar for Malkin.

Once outside, she hid in the dark behind the Doric column farthest from the entrance lamp, and waited cautiously for Malkin to catch up. And a few minutes later he darted out the door in a streak of orange, and paused on the steps, snuffling about. Lily poked her head out from behind the column and whistled to get his attention.

"You managed to lose Mr. Porter then?" she asked as he wound toward her.

"He slipped on the polished parquet floor," Malkin said with a spiky yellow-toothed grin. "We'd best get going before any guild member comes to see what the commotion's about, and helps him to his feet."

Lily nodded. They crept across the courtyard, through the gate, and out into the main street. Then hurried through back alleys toward Fleet Street.

Lily climbed from the top of the ladder and ducked under the G of the *Daily Cog* sign. The rooftops of London glistened in the gaslight of street lamps. Behind the shadowy dome of St. Paul's Cathedral, the night sky was flecked with heavy clouds, jagged as broken roof shingles. It looked as if a big storm was on its way.

She unwound Malkin from around her neck and dropped him by his scruff on the rooftop. Then she knocked at the door of *Ladybird*'s gondola, and pushed it open and entered.

Tolly was sleeping on the floor of the engine room. Lily tried to shake him awake, and when the paper boy wouldn't get up, Malkin stuck his nose in Tolly's ear.

"Oy! Gerr'off!" Tolly shouted, opening his eyes and shooing the fox away. But when he saw Lily, he smiled wide with surprise. "Lily, what are you doing here in the middle of the night?"

"I've worked it out, Tolly!" Lily cried.

"Worked what out?" Anna asked, ambling in from her berth in the corridor, with a loud yawn.

"Everything!"

"You should be with your father."

"He's gone out searching with the police," Lily said. "But he doesn't know where to look, none of them do. The map on the back of the Moonlocket—where Jack's going—it's the Fleet River, the Fleet Sewer! And it goes right under Queen's Crescent, just as you said, Tolly, remember?"

Tolly rubbed his eyes wearily. "I think so…"

"So I'm sure that's where Jack'll be. He's headed to recover the diamond. But if we hurry, right away, we might just be able to catch him."

Anna shook her head. "No, Lily, I don't think that's a good idea."

Lily felt that sinking feeling once again. She knew what was coming next…

"You've been in enough trouble as is," Anna scolded. "It will be much safer if we let the police deal with this. I shall go and speak with them immediately. Tolly, why don't you take Malkin and Lily straight back to the guild? And make sure you don't dawdle or detour on the way. It's not safe to be wandering off to look for Jack."

Tolly held a lantern up high to light their way along Fleet Street as they walked toward the Mechanists' Guild.

"Don't take me back to my papa, Tolly," Lily protested. "He won't listen. He'll lock me up again as soon as he gets back. He doesn't understand Robert's my friend and I owe it to him to do all I can to save him. I made a promise to look after him. I can't just sit around and hope for the best."

"I don't know…" Tolly said. "Anna was very firm."

"*Please*," she begged.

"Remember, the longer we deliberate, the less time there is," Malkin added gravely. He gave Tolly a big puppy-eyed look, and made a little whimpering, whining noise for good effect.

Tolly ignored him. "Anna's only thinking of what's best. And, as for your father, he's probably just trying to look out for you too. This is a dangerous situation—"

"It's not just that," Lily replied. "He doesn't trust me to do things on my own, because I'm different."

"Different how? You look the same as anyone else."

Lily felt sick. She couldn't tell him about the Cogheart. He would think she wasn't right. Think there was something wrong with her. Would he ever speak to her again if he knew?

She needed to tell him, but it felt as if she had swallowed a boulder. It sat like a heavy cold lump in her chest beside her heart, blocking the words from coming out.

"What is it?" he asked.

"If I told you the truth about me, you might not want to be my friend."

"Why not?"

"It's...I'm...there's something unusual about me..." She put her hand to her chest. Her skin prickled with an electric discomfort. She wanted to reach out and take his hand, but her arm was shaking so badly she thought she might not be able to lift it.

"Papa thinks I can't cope with anything because I'm a hybrid. Because I have a mechanical heart."

Tolly stopped dead in his tracks and whistled. "Blimey, a mechanical heart—I ain't never heard of such a thing."

"It's called the Cogheart—it's made of clockwork and it might go on forever. People have tried to steal and possess it. That's why Papa worries so. But I want to take risks, do things. And today I need to rescue Robert. Despite the dangers, I have to prove Papa wrong. I need to show him that, just because I'm a hybrid, doesn't mean I need to be kept safe every moment of every day. The truth is, I'm as strong as anybody else."

Something about this chimed with Tolly; she could see it in his eyes. "I know what you mean," he said. "People are always judging me the same way. Calling me a guttersnipe, or a ragamuffin. They think I'm not as clever or capable as them because of who I am. But, the truth is, I'm more so. I only wish I didn't constantly have to prove it."

He stopped in his tracks. "All right," he relented. "I'll take you to Queen's Crescent. But, whatever happens, I'm sticking to you like glue."

"And me too," said Malkin, jumping up and nipping at Lily's dress.

CHAPTER 21

Robert couldn't sleep. He had too much to consider. It was like arriving at a fork in the path, and suddenly seeing ahead of you an alternative…a future where things could go differently. Another life with another family—one who'd never even existed before in his mind.

He watched Selena and Caddy dozing on the bare mattress. It was strange, he'd not only found a mother, but a sister too—two good people, who were both as alien to him as complete strangers, because his ma had chosen to leave him behind… She'd said it was to keep him safe from the Doors, but could he ever understand that? It hadn't even worked in the end… Could he possibly forgive her? Perhaps, in time…

Lily was somewhere out there. She was sort of a sister to him too, though he'd known her only eight months. He sat back down on the mattress, and listened to the night sounds of the city. Someone was singing somewhere in the street below, and there was a screech of fighting cats, or could it be a fox? With a sudden pang he thought of Malkin—he hoped his mechanimal friend was taking care of Lily, wherever she was.

Robert stifled a yawn. He'd better stay alert for Jack's return. He focused on the sound of his ma's soft breathing, and Caddy's occasional murmurs in her sleep. It was funny how she was his sister and yet her voice, her accent, sounded nothing like his. Her face seemed so calm and tranquil. Despite everything, he was beginning to feel a great deal of warmth toward her, and, in some ways, for Selena too.

The fear of what Jack might have in store for all of them—especially Selena and Caddy—filled him with anxiety. He only hoped that, whatever it was, it wouldn't split his new-found family apart.

He needed a plan to get them out and away, but he was so tired, so lost. His usual sharpness had leached out of him, and his thoughts were a mushy haze. Soon, though he tried to fight it, sleep crept up and pulled him through her dark doorway…

"Time to get up." Rough hands shook him awake.

"What's going on?" Robert asked, as he sat up and rubbed his eyes. This night wasn't over yet. The room was still black. Beside him Caddy and Selena lay asleep. Finlo stood over them, holding a lantern. Jack wasn't with him.

"You're coming with me, you scrawny runt." He reached out to grab Robert.

Robert balled a fist and hit at his uncle's face, but all that did was knock his bowler hat askew. Finlo laughed.

Robert trembled and looked down at his sister and Ma. Selena hugged Caddy, holding her close. She snorted and threw a hand over her face, twitching at the light, but she didn't wake up. The pair of them were cuddled together, spooning like slumbering angels. He was leaving them in the middle of the night, just as his ma left him all those years ago. If he went with Finlo, he might never return. "I don't want to go," he said, his voice quaking.

Finlo nodded at the sleepers. "You'll do as you're told. If you want them to wake and see another day."

Robert felt sick. "Where are you taking me?"

"Never you mind," Finlo spat back. "Put your jacket on quietly. Or it'll be worse for you later. And for them."

Carefully, Robert reached for his coat and cap on the

chair beside the mattress. He struggled into the coat and pushed the flat cap back into shape before wedging it jauntily on his head. He wished he felt that way inside. He hoped Selena and Caddy would be okay without him. What if he never saw them again? What if he never got the chance to say all he needed to say? He bent down to kiss them both goodbye but Finlo grasped his sleeve and jerked him away.

"None of that," he growled. "I warned you, didn't I? Now, come on, no time to dawdle, Jack's waiting!"

Finlo dragged Robert along murky streets filled with gray smog and a watery drizzle, which floated up from the cobbles and made Robert's eyes water and his throat itch.

In the distance, behind London's shadowy domes and turrets, a blanket of black clouds was rolling in across the night sky. The air was filled with a muggy, tingling tension that seemed to promise the coming of a great storm.

At one point, as they passed beneath the glistening spotlight of a gas street lamp, Robert thought he saw the tall helmets of two policeman coming toward them along the pavement in the fog. Finlo shielded the lantern and clasped a hand over Robert's mouth, steering him down a side alley.

"Why do you do as he says? Jack, I mean," Robert gasped, when Finlo finally removed his hand. "You don't need to, you know."

Finlo gritted his teeth. "I didn't ask your opinion."

"I just think—"

"Keep quiet, nephew, and do as I say," Finlo snapped, "or your ma and your sister'll never get out. You follow?"

Robert nodded, but didn't reply.

"Not so chatty now, are you? Speak up if you understand."

"Yes."

"Yes, Sir."

"Yes, Sir!"

"Good."

It started to rain heavily. The water splatted off them in drops. They had reached an area that looked vaguely familiar. Robert could hear a soft rustling from the drain covers they passed, as if water was running under the streets.

They turned another corner into a curving road lined with elms, and there, lurking beneath the tallest one, was a tramp in an old overcoat. His hands were thrust in his pockets and his collar was turned up against the foul weather. As they approached, he turned his head into the lantern light and Robert saw that it was Jack.

"What took you so long?" Jack asked Finlo.

"Problems." Finlo took off the bowler and scratched his head. "We ran into some peelers when I went to collect this one. But we got by unnoticed."

"You ought to be more careful. There's been none 'round here." Jack darted a look across the street. Robert followed his gaze and realized they were standing opposite the Doors' old rental house—number forty-five, Queen's Crescent.

Jack put a hand on Robert's shoulder. "You're going to get us in, boy. If you do as I say, and all goes well, then you'll see your ma and Caddy again. If not, well, it'll be the worse for you…"

Robert gulped back a wave of panic.

Jack looked around, then nodded to Finlo. "Coast is clear."

They dashed across the road and sneaked up the steps to the porch of the house, to shelter from the brewing storm.

Jack pointed out a small square window above the front door. "Loosen that transom," he whispered.

Finlo put down his lantern, took a crowbar from his coat, and jimmied open the tiny window. The dark space behind it was far too narrow for a man to squeeze through…but not, Robert realized, a skinny boy. Jack clenched his arm hard.

"You're to climb through that gap, son, and open the locks on the door, and be quick and quiet about it. Or else." He kneeled down. "Get onto my shoulders."

Robert did as he was told, and Jack stood up and thrust him upward, as if they were in some sort of acrobatic show.

Robert found himself soaring toward the dark window; he reached out and grabbed hold of the frame. The buttons on his coat scraped against the edges as Jack and Finlo shoved him through from behind.

Then he fell, tumbling into the hall. Luckily the doormat and some piles of newspapers broke his fall and muffled his landing. He worried that they might wake the landlady. Then he remembered the old woman had told him she slept like the dead. Lucky really, or Jack might have seen that she meant it for real. For a moment he considered refusing him entry, but the thought of his grandfather's rage and what he might do to Selena and Caddy made him change his mind.

He stood and took a deep breath. Then he undid the locks, one by one, and opened the door.

Outside he could make out the shapes of Jack and Finlo in the glow of their lantern's light.

"You did it!" Jack rubbed a callused hand through Robert's hair as they crept silently inside.

Robert felt a moment of strange pride, before remembering the many reasons to hate his grandfather.

"Let's go," said Finlo, closing the door softly. "We have to find the diamond and get out before daylight or else the police'll work out where we are for sure." He held up the lantern and they stumbled down the stairs, descending into the basement.

They found themselves in a long, narrow room with an earthen floor, which stretched out under the street. In its center was a large manhole cover.

Finlo took out his crowbar once more and forced it open. Air wafted from the hole, humid and claggy, and filled with a fecund stink. There it was: the Fleet Sewer. It ran all the way down to the Thames, and somewhere in its straggling maze of deep, dark tunnels it held the Blood Moon Diamond in its clutches.

Robert stared down into the hole. Iron rungs descended into a darkness deeper than he'd ever known.

"Get down there and wait at the bottom," Jack told him. "We're coming after you."

"Please..." Robert whispered but he tailed off. He coughed and felt a gritty dry emptiness in his mouth. He wanted to refuse. Wanted to tell them that he couldn't swim. He tried to push a reply from his throat, but when he thought of Selena and Caddy locked up, the words stuck there, wedged behind the great lumps of fear filling his chest, as scratchy and solid as tree bark.

"Don't think about being brave," Jack told him. "And don't think you can protect Selena from my retribution. Remember what I told you, boy, she's not worth saving. She doesn't want you. Doesn't care! Family means nothing to her."

Jack thrust the lantern into Robert's hand and pushed him into the hole.

Robert stumbled down the rusted ladder. As he reached the last rung, his feet dangled in noxious water. It slopped, cold and clingy, about the tops of his socks and he wished he was wearing stout boots rather than the thin leather shoes he had on. The turn-ups of his trousers soaked through and slapped heavily against his ankles. He was in a narrow arched passage of filthy yellow and red brick. The stench of sewage surrounded him, seeping into his every pore.

He held the lantern high above his head and glanced upward.

Jack and Finlo were descending. Jack had the Moonlocket around his neck, with the strange map Robert's da had engraved on it long ago at the request of Artemisia Door. It was the only guide they would have down in these underground ways beneath London.

Could the jewel on its back really mark the location of the Blood Moon Diamond? To think a part of the locket had been hidden in his house those many years…

At the top of the ladder, Finlo paused to pull the manhole cover across behind him.

"Come on!" Jack whispered angrily at him. "Hurry it up!"

Finlo's posture tightened for a moment, then he carried on.

Robert shoved his hands deep into his pockets, hoping to find something, anything, to help him thwart Jack's plan. Beneath his fingers was a thing the size of a bean, hard and crumbly. He took it out. It was the nub of chalk Jack had given him to complete the code.

Quietly, while Finlo and Jack weren't looking, he marked the wall beside him. At least if the police, or Lily for that matter, had worked out what the locket map meant, they might see this mark and be able to follow him. Though heaven knows how long that would take.

Robert glanced up one last time. Finlo was nearly at the base of the ladder. He'd left the cover open a chink— probably in case they had to return that way. Holding onto his hat, he jumped down the last few rungs into the water.

Jack had been reading the locket in his palm. Now he nodded, indicating the tunnel to the right and strode on ahead. Robert traipsed behind him and Finlo took up the rear, urging him onwards into the dark sewer, following the path of the Fleet.

CHAPTER 22

The rain grew heavier, rushing in rivers along the road before being swallowed up by drains and gutters. As Lily, Tolly, and Malkin approached number forty-five, Queen's Crescent, Lily saw at once that something was up—the small window above the door had been jimmied open. They climbed the steps to the porch and tried the door handle. It gave and the door swung inwards. They stepped quietly inside and tiptoed across the empty hall, dripping rainwater on the linoleum.

From somewhere deep in the cellar, they could hear voices. "Jack," Lily whispered. She'd recognize his gravelly tone anywhere. She put a hand across Tolly's chest to stop him going downstairs, and gave Malkin a warning look, to make sure he stayed quiet.

She could just make out Robert's voice. He sounded quiet and pleading, full of fear. Then there was the noise, of someone descending a ladder, and a clattering as if something heavy was being pulled closed across a gap.

When it finally fell silent, they slipped down the stairs and found themselves in a long dark room. No one made a sound. In the center of the floor was a round manhole cover, open a sliver. A crescent moon of light emanated from it, as if someone below was holding a flickering lantern.

The light disappeared; Lily guessed they were walking away from the manhole. "We have to get this open," she said, desperately pulling at the cover's edge—but it was too heavy for her to move.

Tolly and Malkin looked around the room for something to use as leverage.

"Will this do?" Tolly pulled the wooden pole of a mop from a pile of junk.

They wedged it under the edge of the cover and, with the three of them putting their weight on it, they managed to lever the grate aside.

A rusted metal ladder led deep underground. The aroma that wafted up from it was like rotten vegetables mixed with rubbish left out for days.

"Pooh-eee!" said Tolly, holding his nose.

"You don't have to come with me," Lily said. "You can wait for the police."

"I want to." He put a hand on her arm. "I've been thinking about what we talked about earlier, and you're right—when you're different, people don't believe you're as good as they are. I need to prove them wrong about that too. We can do this together, I know it. We can recapture Jack and the diamond, and rescue Robert!"

He reached for the ladder and climbed into the hole. Soon only the top of his head was visible, lit by the lantern hooked over his arm, and then he disappeared into darkness altogether.

"Come on, Malkin," Lily said. "Us next."

"Oh no," said Malkin. "I've already been dumped in a lake this week. I'm not setting paw in some rat-infested sewer, even if it is to save Robert. Water's not good for me. Besides, what kind of person buries a diamond in a pipe full of sewage anyway?"

"If you won't set foot in there, then I'll have to carry you." Lily picked Malkin up and threw him over her shoulder.

"This again! You make me feel like a fox-fur ruff!" Malkin complained. "And I wish you'd stop climbing up and down things! It's getting to be rather a habit."

Lily ignored him and clasped the rungs of the ladder with her free hand. The metal hoops were crusty with

318

rust and slippery with wet dirt and she could hear the chittering of bugs, cockroaches, and spiders as she descended. Light thrown by Tolly's lantern revealed their tiny dark shapes, crawling about the walls. He stood uneasily on a narrow promontory at the base of the ladder, barely as wide as his two feet.

"I can't see Jack," he hissed up to her. Then, mumbling softly to himself, "This place reeks. Still, better out than in I say—though I'd rather it wasn't wafting around us."

Malkin, round Lily's neck, turned up his nose in disgust. "Ugh, you're right," he whispered. "It does smell awful!"

The stench made Lily gag. She jumped down beside Tolly and lowered the fox to the ground.

"I said I *wouldn't* set foot in here!" Malkin groused, quietly.

"You're too heavy to ride on my shoulders," Lily answered under her breath. "If you don't like it you can climb back up."

Malkin looked up the rickety rungs. "You know that's not possible!"

"Then it looks like you're coming with us."

"Goody!" The fox gave a disgusted sniff and delicately stepped over what looked like a dead rat. He prodded at it with his nose. "I'm sure we can make umpteen new friends in this underground abyss."

Tolly lowered his lantern. On the wall at the edge of the tunnel, someone had made a small chalk mark at hip height: an arrow and an *R.T.*

"Robert Townsend," Lily said, rubbing at the goosebumps on her arms. "They did come this way, and he's left us a trail. All we have to do to find them is follow his marks. Come on!"

They set off walking along a shallow path that ran down the main tunnel, while a rushing torrent of water streamed alongside them—the Fleet River.

Lily had no idea what they would do when they caught up with Jack. How she was going to capture him and find the diamond, or how she was going to rescue Robert. She would just have to work all that out when she got to it.

Slushing gushes of rainwater and sewage spouted from the ceiling, spattering into the Fleet. As it ran down the central trough of the tunnel, Lily's dread flowed with it. She closed her ears to the distant plops and drips, the chitters and squeaks of rats and insects, and attempted to ignore the things floating past.

Tolly had spotted another chalk mark on the wall. A hastily scribbled arrow that pointed along the main tunnel. "They've gone this way," he said.

They turned a corner, and far ahead, in the murky distance, they could make out three silhouettes, one carrying a tiny flickering lantern. Their dim shapes, distorted in the viscous atmosphere, were each no bigger than burned matchsticks. Suddenly, the figures turned off the main drag and were gone in an instant.

The tunnel undulated as Lily, Tolly, and Malkin set off after them. It narrowed in places and widened in others. The rancid Fleet Sewer water gurgled over rocks and stones, pushing them along the trough, and making disgusting slurping noises as if it was being swallowed by some gulping gullet.

"Current's getting stronger," Tolly said. "If you slipped and fell now, you'd be carried away and drowned, heaven help you!"

"Or you'd inhale your own body weight in filth," Malkin added, turning his nose up.

Lily shuddered. She reached out carefully and brushed the side of the tunnel with her fingers, trying to steady herself. It was coated in a slimy thick mucus that sent a chill through her.

More water poured from rust-encrusted pipes in the ceiling, throwing down fragments of rock, brown mold, and soggy paper. The Fleet had started to slosh over the side of its trough. It frothed a dirty brown color in the lamplight.

Soon the route they were on ended abruptly in a weir. A metal handrail ran across its front to a footpath on the far side. Sewage flowed over its edge, pouring downward in a scum-filled waterfall that was becoming stronger by the minute.

Tolly went first, holding onto the railing and clambering across. Lily took Malkin on her shoulders once more and followed.

The Fleet water rushed and bubbled along the weir in a strengthening torrent. Lily waded through it, the scum breaking across her legs. Her dress was soaked through, clinging to her skin like a shroud.

Tolly had reached the weir's far side. He held out a hand to her and she stepped forward to reach for it, but with a cry, she felt her feet slip from under her.

Her arms failed to grab anything and she tipped back…

Tolly snatched her hand just in time, and yanked her and Malkin to the other side. Malkin twisted on Lily's shoulders, staring behind them. They'd been a hair's breadth from tumbling over the weir and being swept away.

Time passed; Lily couldn't tell how much. She only knew she could no longer feel the occasional blast of wind on the back of her neck. The muggy sour air was making her feel sick. She tried to breathe in less, throwing a handkerchief across her face. In the gloom, all she had to guide her was the tick-tock of the Cogheart—a heart that ached for her friend Robert, and that Mama had told her to follow, always.

Tolly was taking a turn carrying Malkin and had fallen a few feet behind. Lily heard voices echoing from a right-hand tunnel and paused at another chalk arrow on the wall. Should she wait for the others to catch her up, or investigate?

She inched down the side tunnel and was immediately engulfed in darkness. A shiver ran down her spine. She'd better wait for Tolly to catch her up. She could hear his heavy footsteps. He stepped from the tunnel mouth behind her. His breathing echoed off the walls.

It was too deep and loud.

A hand slapped hard over her mouth and a tall, broad figure grasped her. She swung at where she thought its face would be and knocked a bowler hat askew… Finlo Door!

"This way," he whispered. "Jack wants to see you."

They stumbled up a narrow set of stairs. Lily could feel rancid water frothing in a torrent over their feet. With Finlo just a step or two behind her, Lily had to pull herself physically upward using the rusty handrail set in the wall, which shifted and creaked ominously each time she struggled onto a new step.

Finally, as they reached the top, there was a faint light. In front of her was Jack Door. He stood on a rickety old platform holding a lantern over a square tank sunk into the floor level beneath them, like an empty swimming pool. Not that anyone would want to swim down here. Lily shivered at the thought of it.

Robert stood in the tank's base, up to his ankles in sewage. In front of him was a strange drawing and a nonsensical code scrawled on the wall, and beside that was the locked door of an ancient, rusty safe, embedded in the wall.

Jack turned angrily to Finlo. "What happened to you? I thought you were right behind us?"

"We were being followed," Finlo said. "By this one."

"Another meddler." Jack's gray eyes glared at Lily, and then he smiled. "But this is even better. You can help Robert retrieve my diamond!"

CHAPTER 23

"Have you solved the code yet, boy?" Jack shouted down at Robert in the tank.

"Not yet," Robert called back, "but I'm working on it."

"You! Help him!" Jack thrust Lily down a metal staircase from the platform, holding up the lantern so she could see her way down to Robert.

"Hurry," he told her. "Time and tide wait for no man!"

Lily staggered into the tank and splashed through the slurry, pulling Robert into an embrace, kissing his cheek in relief.

"Thank goodness you're fine," she whispered. "Hold steady, help's on the way."

She wondered where Tolly and Malkin had gone to. And the police? Surely Anna had told them where to look? She should've waited for them to deal with Jack, she knew that now. She hoped she would live long enough not to regret her constant impulsiveness.

Robert shivered in relief in Lily's arms and hugged her back as hard as he could. He had chalk in his hand and his clothes were damp with the humid stink of the tunnels.

"What have you been doing?" she asked.

"Puzzles."

He let go of her and Lily rubbed her arm where Finlo had been grasping it. She stared about the tank, trying to figure out what he meant. The front of the safe was a circular dial filled with numbers. Beside it was etched a diagram of sorts. Lily peered closer at it and strange markings and inscriptions leaped out at her from the dark...

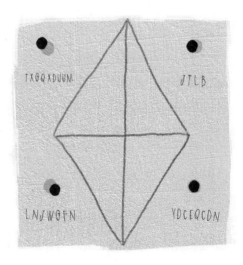

It was a pictogram of a diamond divided into a quadrant of separate chambers, like a heart, or the quarter hours of a clock. Around this were images of a lunar eclipse, and beneath each of those was a different code word.

"They're numbers," Robert whispered. "Because that's what's on the safe dial. You must have to read them clockwise, in the order of the eclipse."

Lily nodded. He had to be right... But what numbers? A date perhaps? Captain Springer had told them the Blood Moon Diamond was discovered during a lunar eclipse. Could it be that date? What had it been again? As she racked her brains, the water sloshed about her calves. With cold, creeping shock she realized it was rising. Jack was right—they had to solve this fast!

She gazed at the diagram. It was more like four right-angled triangles than a diamond. Maybe Artemisia had used the same code as on the Moonlocket?

"It's like the locket puzzle," she guessed. "Each word has a translation triangle."

"I started down that route," Robert told her. "But it doesn't work."

"What are you saying?" Jack shouted down at them from the platform.

"Leave them be, Da," Finlo said beside him. "They have to think."

"No," Jack said. "No secrets, remember, Fin!"

"It's a similar code to the locket." Lily's words echoed around the tank, sounding more forceful than she felt inside. "It must mean the date of a lunar eclipse."

"Did I ask you what it means?" Jack paced up and down the platform. "I don't care what it means! I just need you to find the numbers and dial them into the safe before high tide. So get on with it!"

The water was at Lily's shins now, soaking through the fringe of her already wet dress. She stared at Robert in shock. His eyes were wide with alarm.

"We should leave, before we're trapped," Lily called out to Jack. "The tide'll cut off your exit through the tunnels."

Finlo turned to Jack. "She's right, you know. If we stay too long we'll drown."

"No one's going anywhere!" Jack shouted. "Not until I get my diamond!"

"*Our* diamond," Finlo retorted. "And I don't understand why we can't come back another time?"

"I told you why." Jack bristled. "I want to stand on Tower Bridge today, with that diamond in my hand, and watch the Queen of England go by in her parade. I want everyone to know that I outwitted her. And the Crown Prosecution Service, the prison guards, the police inspectors, the bobbies; everyone. I shall stand there as they pass and my picture will make the front pages, alongside the Queen. It'll be the greatest trick ever pulled, the ultimate revenge—reappearing in public at the Jubilee with the very thing I stole fifteen years ago! Then afterwards, when I'm sure everyone has seen me with my diamond, I shall disappear in a flash of smoke before their very eyes, and get the hell out of this forsaken country forever!"

"You don't have to do those tricks, Da," Finlo said. "They're not important, they don't matter. This isn't a game. You're not the world's greatest showman anymore. You're a wanted criminal. What matters is getting the diamond out safely. We should go back into hiding and come for it another day, when things have quietened down."

Jack shook his head. "Don't you understand, you idiot? It'll be too late by then. The police are onto us— with the information they've got from Selena and these two here, how long d'you think they'll take to figure out where the diamond is? Then the only thing stopping them recovering it will be this code." He pointed at the marks on the wall. "These two obviously like cracking mysteries or they wouldn't have kept coming after me. It won't take them five minutes to work out the cypher."

While he'd been ranting, the water had risen above Lily's and Robert's knees. A dead mouse washed against the wall in the far corner, battering against a mess of leaves and twigs.

"We haven't got long," Robert whispered to Lily.

"Solve the code quicker or drown," Jack shouted from above. "The choice is yours."

Lily felt sick with fear. She could barely think straight. She had to get a grip. The only way they were going to get out of this alive was if they did as Jack asked. She stared hard at the diagram and the code.

"Wait," she said. "I think I've got it! What if it's the same system but reversed… The coded words go down the middle—along the straight edges of the diamond—then you fill the triangle with the preceding letters to get the translation along the slanted edge."

"How did you guess that?" Robert asked.

"It's the easiest possible variation on the cypher," she replied. "Now hurry, we have to work it out."

The freezing water was lapping their thighs. Robert began to write on the wall, filling in the gaps as Lily suggested with the wet chalk. It left sludgy white lines. His fingers shook so much he could barely write. After he'd done the first triangle, he passed the chalk to Lily and she took over, scrawling the other coded words down the straight sides of the triangles—and then adding the letters alphabetically before and after them to fill out each space.

The water had risen to their hips now. Lily filled in the last few parts of the code, and then she was done.

The pictogram diamond was a mess, but she read the words out clockwise from around its edges.

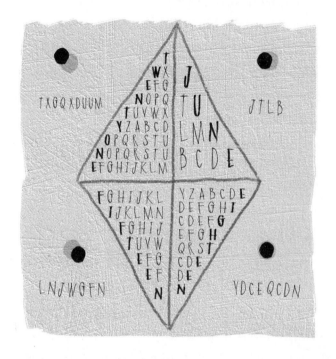

"Twenty-one, June, Eighteen, Fifteen."

"Ha!" cried Jack. "That's it! Open the safe, quick!"

Lily waded through the water, which was now level with her waist.

Robert held his arms out for balance and read the numbers aloud to Lily as she dialed them into the safe.

"Twenty-one," he said, "then June...June's letters, not numbers." Lily could hear the panic in his voice.

"It'll be six," she said, "June is the sixth month." And she turned the safe's dial to six.

"Then eighteen and fifteen," Robert said.

He felt himself shift along the floor as the current gamboled around his feet. He braced himself to stay upright.

Lily spun in the last two last digits on the wheel and the safe gave a loud *click!*

She hoped upon hope that the diamond was inside. Then they could get out of here before they drowned.

The lever on the safe turned, and she tugged the door open.

The shelves were scattered with old rings and trinkets…and in amongst them was a diamond bigger than all the rest. A perfectly cut red stone at least five times the size of all the others: the Blood Moon Diamond. It was the most impressive gemstone Lily had ever seen, red as wine and shifting in color. In the feeble glow of the lantern it twinkled bright as a star, reflecting the light back at her in fizzing red droplets that sparkled across her face.

What a wonder it was! And it would surely be even more radiant in daylight—if they were ever destined to see it in such conditions, for the water had almost reached their chests. Without further ado, she pulled the diamond from the safe and, holding it above her head, waded toward Jack, dragging Robert along behind her.

Jack held the lantern high and rushed down the metal steps of the platform to meet them. He snatched the diamond from her hand and was about to stuff it in his pocket when there came a clang from behind him.

Finlo rested his crowbar against the metal rails of the platform. "I think you'd better give me that, Da," he said. "I know the kind of tricks you're capable of pulling. I imagine you've no intention of splitting the diamond, and I'm afraid I can't let you walk away with it."

Jack grasped the stone tight in his fist. "I spent fifteen years inside waiting for this moment, boy, and I'm not going to let you take it from me. You'll get what's coming to you, if you do as I say."

"That," said Finlo, "is what I'm afraid of. But not this time."

"What're you going to do?" Jack asked. "Kill me? Your old dad?"

"I will if I have to. You can't bully me anymore, Jack." Finlo took a step toward him. "I'm my own man now."

"Are you?" Jack asked. "Or are you the same sniveling worm you've always been?"

"Don't underestimate me." Finlo's face turned purple with fury, he raised the crowbar over his head.

Lily braced herself for the thud.

But Jack laughed and, with a wave of his hand, the diamond vanished and a gun appeared in his grasp. A tiny pepperbox pistol.

"You know the difference between you and me, Fin?" he asked.

Finlo shook his head.

"I know when to keep my powder dry." Jack jerked back the trigger and a bullet exploded from the muzzle of his pistol. Finlo dropped the crowbar and it clattered to the floor of the platform. He clutched at his chest.

Lily blinked in shock as Finlo listed sideways and plunged over the rail with a splash. His body sunk for a second then drifted upward in the rising tide. His bowler hat bobbed from his head and bumped against the base of the metal staircase.

Robert gasped and scrambled up the steps away from it.

Jack had killed his son. And for what? A stone. He was no father, no grandfather either—just an evil, selfish man.

"Time to go." Jack raised the lantern and waved his pistol at them both. "I've a boat waiting in the Thames. I'm going to need someone to row me to Tower Bridge in time for the big finale. You two'll do fine for that, I think!" He grinned, patting at a bulge in his pocket. And, with a start, Lily realized that he'd hidden the diamond there during his sleight of hand.

Back in the main tunnel the Fleet River had engulfed the path. Here the water was fast-flowing and had already grown knee-deep. Lily felt queasy. Jack stopped to consult the engraved map on the locket around his neck, and used his fingers to trace a path. When he'd gotten a sense of where they were, they headed off again.

But soon they heard the echo of footsteps, and glimpsed a faint far-off light. Jack threw Lily and Robert against the edge of the passage and crowded in behind them, blowing out the flame in the lantern. "Keep quiet, both of you, or else," he said, raising the gun and resting it on Lily's shoulder.

Lily's legs shook. She leaned forward and narrowed her eyes, trying to see who was coming.

In the dimmest of dim lights, she could make out a silhouette holding a lantern. As it pushed through the waters, she saw a furry creature wound around its neck like a shawl. Tolly and Malkin!

Lily's heart ticked hard in her chest. Tolly couldn't see them in the dark; he didn't know Jack was armed.

Jack took aim and cocked the hammer, and with a lurch of horror Lily realized he actually intended to shoot again. "Tolly!" she cried. "Hide! Jack's got a gun!"

"Don't come any closer!" Robert added.

Tolly threw himself behind a narrow brick pier.

"Be quiet!" Jack shouted and pushed them both out of the way. Lily's head bounced off the bricks. In a haze of pain, she glanced at Jack. He waved the gun about, searching the tunnel for Tolly's light. There wasn't much time…

She barreled forward, throwing her weight against him, and pushed.

Jack slipped on the slime-coated floor, and tumbled. He yelled and threw out his hands to break his fall, and then plunged into the stream of sewage. Ripping the gun free, he raised it and fired—but it fizzled, wet and useless.

"Blasted thing!" he cried, tossing it away.

Robert rushed forward in a flash, smacking one hand against Jack's chest, and snatching the Moonlocket from around his neck with the other. While Robert had him distracted, Lily seized her chance and shot a hand into Jack's pocket, plucking out the diamond. "OY!" Jack grabbed wildly at them both, trying to get his treasures back, but he didn't know who to go for first.

Suddenly, with a lurch and a scream, he slipped, his feet teetering in the current, arms flailing about the air.

His face darkened as he opened his mouth to curse them all, but then fell into the raging water instead.

Instantly he was wrenched beneath the surface and swept away.

They waited for him to come up, but he did not.

Lily hugged Robert and stood there, breathing heavily, shocked and relieved. Jack was gone, and they had the diamond and the Moonlocket—their map to freedom. But they weren't safe yet.

Tolly bounded up the tunnel toward them, and embraced them both. "We heard a splash," he said. "Thank tock it wasn't you!"

Malkin, who was around Tolly's neck, sat up and licked their faces. "Yeuch! You're covered in sewage!"

"We could have done with your help half an hour ago," Lily said. "Where were you?"

The fox looked sheepish. "We got lost in the dark," he admitted.

"We couldn't find anything," Tolly added. "And then we heard a noise coming this way and thought it might be Anna arriving with the police at last. It's a good thing you shouted a warning to us or I never would've realized you were with Jack. Was that him falling in the water?"

Lily nodded. "He never came up."

"Well, good riddance," Tolly said. "I hope he washes

out to sea with the rest of the sewage. What happened to the other one—his son?"

"Jack killed him." Robert put a shaking hand to his temple; his head was spinning fast, as if the sound of the gunshot was still echoing inside him.

It was like his da's death all over again. Even though he hated Finlo and what he'd done, Robert did feel sorry for him. It seemed to him that Finlo had taken part in his father's plan not only for the money but also to please him. But you couldn't please a father like Jack; no one could. He was a cold-hearted killer who had valued a gem over his flesh and blood. How could Robert bear to be part of a family like that? Well, he didn't need to be. Not when he had Lily and John, who he loved and who loved him. His home was with them, and if he got out of this alive, he'd make sure they knew it. He only hoped his ma and Caddy would be fine together now that Jack and Finlo were gone.

"What on earth...?" Tolly said suddenly, glancing over their shoulders, up the tunnel, the way they'd come. The engorged Fleet raged in a torrent over the weir. "I don't think we can get back over that."

"We need to find another exit." Lily pointed at the locket in Robert's hand. "The opening to the Thames is marked on the Moonlocket. It's a storm drain under

Blackfriars Bridge. Jack told us he'd moored a rowing boat there. If we follow the map, we should make it."

"Thank goodness!" Malkin said. "And whatever happened to that clunking Blood Moon Diamond that everyone made such a fuss about?"

"I picked it from Jack's pocket." Lily opened her hand and it glistened.

"Played him at his own game, eh?" Malkin said. "Perhaps his book wasn't so useless."

Lily put the diamond away in her pocket. "When we get out of here," she said, "I shall return it to its rightful owner. Until then, at least we're alive and we have each other."

"Only if we get moving though!" Tolly said.

Robert nodded. He'd been consulting the Moonlocket. "It's this way, I think," he said, pointing a finger off into the distance, and they set off at once, following the map.

CHAPTER 24

As they walked the main tunnel, odd blasts of fresh air blustered toward them. Lily felt relieved that they were all in one piece. They had the Moonlocket and the diamond, and soon, very soon, they would be closing in on the exit.

"The longer I stay down here, the worse I whiff," Malkin groused from around Tolly's shoulders as they walked along. "I tell you, the whole place smells worse than a dog with no nose!"

"Why?" Tolly asked. "How's that smell?"

"Awful!"

Robert laughed half-heartedly, but he was starting to fade. Lily was slowing too, wary of slipping into the water that ran deep and fast beside their path. Malkin and

Tolly went ahead. Tolly held the lantern aloft, and Robert called out directions as he traced their path on the back of the Moonlocket.

They'd been following the main tunnel for a long time, but it felt as if it was finally nearing its end. When they came around a corner and glimpsed light in the distance, everyone breathed a sigh of relief. There was a large oval hole in the wall, filled with a cross-barred iron grate that let in checkered chinks of the outside. Water poured through the base of it and away into the river.

"Look how high the tide's got," Robert cried in despair as they got nearer.

"We'll have to step into that torrent to open the grate," Lily said.

"Not me," Malkin told her, as he hopped down off Tolly's back. "I can't get *that* wet."

"If we fall in," Robert said, "we'll be pulled under for sure."

"We'll link arms and I'll hold onto that," Lily said, pointing out a ring she'd spotted that was set in the side wall beneath their path.

With a determined breath, Lily locked arms with Robert and Tolly, and the three of them jumped into the water. The current tore at their legs, making it hard to stay upright. Lily grasped the brass ring and spread her feet wide apart to balance. The others did the same.

Carefully, each of them put a shoulder to the grate and braced against it.

"Three, two, one!" Tolly shouted, and they pushed.

The grate gave slightly, making a low groaning sound.

"Thank clank!" Lily cried. "It's opening!" The words tumbled out of her mouth as fast as the falling water.

She wished for a moment they'd more help—someone like Captain Springer or Mrs. Rust with them, someone who'd be strong enough to rip the grate away with ease and let them out. But they didn't, and with the torrent pounding against them, it was hard to have courage.

It took their combined strength, and one more go, to heave the grate aside fully.

With the barrier gone, the flume of rain and sewage plunged through the gap and over the precipice into the river. Lily, Robert, and Tolly clung onto the tunnel wall to stay upright.

Outside, the first light of sunrise bled around the edges of heavy clouds. The boats and steamers moored along the river, and garlanded with bunting in preparation for the Queen's Jubilee parade that afternoon, rocked to and fro in a raucous wind. Fog floated about their hulls, and electricity seemed to hang in the muggy air. The storm was gathering closer, but had not yet hit.

"When that squall breaks," Malkin yapped, "the tide'll rise as fast as a greased goose, and then we'll drown!"

342

"We have to row to the jetty," Tolly said, pointing at Jack's boat, which bobbed under Blackfriars Bridge, a few feet from the waterfall pouring from the tunnel. A rusty access ladder, screwed to the wall, led down to it.

"I'll go first," Tolly said. "Then I can help you across and down to the boat."

He reached out sideways from the entrance and gripped the ladder.

"Hurry!" Lily cried.

Water spattered across him and, as he swung onto the ladder, a flash of lightning illuminated the underside of the bridge.

"Quick!" Tolly called out. "Hand me Malkin, and I'll carry him down to—"

His voice was drowned out by a roll of thunder. The rain was strengthening, slashing spears of water into the river, breaking its black surface to shards. Lily grabbed Malkin from the narrow promontory and handed him quickly to Tolly, who climbed down the ladder one-handed and leaped into the boat.

"You next, Lil," he called. "Come across!"

Lily glared out into the storm and turned to Robert. "I can't do it. Lightning's attracted to metal. If it hits my heart, I might explode."

"We need to go!" Robert shouted. "Before the tunnel floods completely!"

Another fork of lightning flashed.

"This deluge will drag us in and I can't swim, remember!"

Lily took a deep breath. The air was damp with fear. She waited for it to ebb away. But it would not. "Right… fine…" she said at last. "We'll go together. Ready?"

Robert nodded.

She took a good look out of the tunnel entrance, gauging the distance to the ladder. Beside them, water thundered over the edge of the opening. But she didn't let it distract her. She let go of her handhold and reached across, stretching toward the top rung.

As Robert did the same, they heard a strange rumble coming toward them.

"Storm water!" Lily shouted.

They glanced upstream. A wall of sewage smashed toward them; something was swimming in it like a half-drowned rat.

"Jack!" Robert screamed. "He's alive!"

The water engulfed them with a loud whoosh, but somehow Jack caught them in his arms and held them as they were catapulted from the tunnel entrance and into the raging river below.

Lily struggled to pull her head above the waterline. She could see Robert battling beside her, kicking his legs to stay afloat, while Jack, whose eyes bulged wide with anger, grasped both of them.

Malkin and Tolly were remote figures now, the boat swept away in the distance. The Thames dragged Lily, Robert, and Jack along, spiraling them in currents and eddies, tugging them farther from the bank. The storm raged on above them, rain battering their heads.

A sudden rip tide forced Jack to let go of Robert, and he was swept away from them. Lily tried to reach out to him but Jack had her clasped firmly by the neck, the fat fingers of his other hand twitching through her pockets as he trod water.

"Give me my diamond!"

A shard of lightning illuminated the murky river.

Lily was choking for air. Over her shoulder, she could see Robert flailing. "Kick your legs, Robert," she cried. "Keep your head above water!" But her voice was hoarse and got lost in a sudden crack of thunder that sounded like the sky splitting in two.

Lily watched Robert drift farther and farther away. The river was engulfing him in its watery grip, and there was nothing she could do. Jack clutched her tight as they were swept farther downriver and into the eye of the storm.

A buoy! There was a buoy bobbing on the waves. Atop its tower, a bell clanged loudly. They slipped past it and, in a fit of strength, Jack reached out and snatched a metal hoop on its side, tugging them both from the water. Lily tried to escape, but Jack yanked her up beside him, her feet dangling over the river.

The storm was close. Lightning crackled in the sky above. A fork arced down a lightning rod on the tip of St. Paul's, and another hit the steel mast of a boat near the bank. It was flashing everywhere.

"Give me the diamond," Jack commanded.

"It doesn't belong to you." Lily clutched it in her fist.

"Says who?" Jack clamped his fingers round hers and squeezed hard, until the sharp edges of the stone cut into her hand.

The buoy rocked to and fro, the metal bell ringing out as she fought him off, but he was winning, slowly prying open her fist, until she could no longer grip the diamond. Finally it slipped through her cold wet fingers and she fell backwards, hitting the water with a splash.

"I have it at last!" Jack crowed, clasping the diamond to his chest.

Lily struggled in the water, gasping for breath, as a fork of lightning slid across the sky, undulating like a white snake...then it hit the buoy, fizzing through the structure and crackling through Jack himself. His

346

mouth writhed open and the lightning bloomed from his fingertips, refracting through the diamond and splintering away in a thousand beams of red light.

Jack stiffened. His face had become a grimacing mask. The diamond dropped from his rigid hand and rattled around the base of the buoy before coming to a stop. Jack's body clanged once against the bell, then plummeted into the river and was sucked down by the undertow of the Thames.

Lily trod water for a moment, almost unable to believe what she'd just seen. Then cautiously she swam closer to the buoy. The diamond glinted at her from where it had fallen. She snatched at it and it rolled and skittered around the base of the buoy, the glow inside it fading. She'd best be quick or she'd lose it altogether in the dark. She stretched out her hand and seized it. This time it wouldn't slip through her grasp. Now she just had to find Robert…

She swam hard, away from the buoy. She could see hands, flailing above the water twenty feet away…

Then thirty…

Then she lost sight of him.

She struck out for the spot where she thought he was turning, glancing about.

At the last moment, she spotted his fingers in the choppy waves, sinking beneath the surface.

347

She kicked against the current, and holding her breath, dived beneath the waters. It was murky and dark down there, and she could barely see. Then lightning flashed again and she caught sight of Robert floating beneath her feet, sinking into the abyss.

She swum down and grasped his waist, hauling him upward with all her might.

They hit the surface and Robert spewed water and spluttered out a choking scream. His face was pale, his hair plastered in a question mark across his forehead, and his eyes were wild and red with fear. He was alive! Lily's heart sang with relief.

"Hold on to me," she said. "I'll save you, I promise."

Robert put an arm around her shoulder, and together they swam for the shore. Lily could see a wharf; if they could get to that, it would just be a short step to dry land. "Kick harder!" Lily cried. "Together!"

Robert did his best, but somehow the weight of him was working against her strokes. The waves raged higher and higher. And the shore got no closer. In fact, it seemed to be receding…the river was lugging them farther away from it, toward the concrete piers of Tower Bridge.

Just as her hope was fading, Lily heard the sound of a long low howl. She looked around frantically and behind them saw a little boat. A tiny figure with scruffy black hair sat in its seat, pulling on the oars to navigate it over the hills and troughs of each wave. Malkin was standing at the stern, his head darting this way and that, searching for them.

"Over here!" Lily cried, and gasped with relief when Malkin pricked up his ears and barked to Tolly. "This way!" Tolly turned the prow of the boat toward her, and she called out again until her throat was raw, so they could keep track of where she was.

Finally the boat came alongside and Tolly and Malkin dragged them over the gunwale. They flopped down in the stern and lay on their backs, staring up at the sky.

Robert curled against Lily's side and coughed, sobs racking his body.

The boat tossed and turned in the storm, but somehow Tolly managed to row her onward, under Tower Bridge. By the time they came out the far side, the storm was drifting farther upriver. Lily sat up in the stern and stared wearily around. She could see white flashes over far steeples, illuminating the sky. Robert stretched an arm around her and gave her a hug.

"What happened?" Tolly asked.

"Jack sank down to Davy Jones's locker," Lily told him. "He was struck by lightning."

"I saw that bolt when I was struggling in the water," Robert said. "It was the biggest lightning storm I've ever seen. It lit up the whole sky. Then struck Jack and bounced in a thousand streams out through the diamond…" His face fell. "The diamond…" he said.

"I've still got it." Lily opened her fist to reveal the Blood Moon Diamond in the center of her palm.

"I can't believe it!" Tolly said.

Lily gazed out across the river. In the west the moon was fading like a ghostly penny, but in the east, behind the dissipating storm, a dawn light signaled that the day was about to break. "Somewhere," she said, "Papa and the police are looking for us; Anna too."

"I hope Caddy and my ma are all right," Robert said.

"They've every chance now," Lily said. "Don't worry, I'm sure they'll be fine."

"Let's get this boat ashore and go and find them," Malkin snapped. "We seem to have spent half this week soaking wet, and I've decided that's not my kind of adventure!"

"Right you are!" Tolly said. He took one oar, and Robert the other, and they rowed toward a rickety pier.

CHAPTER 25

London had always been a stinky city, what with the horse droppings, the rubbish, and the steam-wagon exhaust fumes; the flavor of it tended to embed itself in people. But no one there that day smelled as bad as Robert, Tolly, Malkin, and Lily—even their bath in the Thames and the heavy storm had failed to rid them of the foul aroma of sewage. It hung about them as they walked through the streets, and the morning crowds, gathering early for the Queen's Jubilee parade that afternoon, parted for them like the Red Sea.

As they approached the Mechanists' Guild, the nearby clock tower at St. Paul's was striking nine o'clock. Their stench arrived a few minutes before they did—in fact it was already inside and halfway up the stairs as they rang the bell, for the various professors with rooms off the main lobby were throwing open their windows and exclaiming in disgust at the loathsome odor.

When Mr. Porter opened the door for them he didn't know whether to let them in or run away. They barged past him and ran down the corridor, bursting into Papa's workshop, where the Elephanta stood. Papa was pacing around it, trying to think; one hand ran agitatedly through his hair, the other held his nose. Anna and Captain Springer milled around anxiously, but neither of them was as jittery as Papa.

As he came around the Elephanta's flank, he suddenly spotted them, and was confused, shocked, delighted, and amazed all at the same time to realize that they were the source of that incredibly strong odor.

"Lily and Robert, thank goodness you're fine!" Papa exclaimed. His arms shook as he embraced Lily, then gave Robert a bear hug. "And Malkin." He picked the fox up and kissed his furry forehead, and then was so pleased that he did the same to Tolly, who was standing to one side.

"I was worried sick. Especially about you, Lily. When I returned last night and found you'd run off, I searched everywhere. I knew you must have gone to find Robert."

"Then I arrived," Anna added, "and told him about

the clue you'd decoded, and how I had sent you back to the guild. But you never returned here."

"We were in the sewers," Lily began to explain. She stopped—there was too much to tell, and she didn't know where to begin.

"My ma?" Robert blurted out. "And Caddy? Did the police find them? Are they safe?"

John put a hand on his shoulder. "They're fine, son. Constable Jenkins called by first thing to say they'd rescued them. Caddy dropped a sheet out of the window and waved to alert people. The inspector should be bringing them here at any moment. He thought we might be able to pool our information to find you."

Robert was relieved, but he wondered how Selena would feel about losing Finlo, and Jack too. They were her family, no matter how horrible, and his as well—even though he barely knew any of them. But perhaps, now that Selena was free of her awful past, that might change over time? Perhaps the broken pieces of the family might start to come back together? Or maybe they wouldn't... He glanced at John and Lily, talking joyfully together— could he truly join their family?

As he was wondering this, Selena and Caddy burst into the room, along with Inspector Fisk.

"Robert, my darling, my dear one. My brave-hearted son!" Selena pulled him into a deep embrace.

"We're so happy to see you," Caddy said. "We've been fretting about you all night!"

"I was worried sick," Selena added. "When we woke up you'd disappeared. I told the inspector, they must have taken you to Queen's Crescent and the Fleet…"

"Miss Quinn here explained where you were too," the inspector nodded toward Anna, who smiled at them. "But when we got there, the place was empty. The property had been broken into, yet, according to the landlady—who seemed to have just woken up—nothing was taken. We found the entrance to the sewer beneath the house, but when we opened the drain cover the water was so high, we thought you couldn't possibly have… There wasn't even a Jack of Diamonds playing card as a clue!"

"We're all fine now," Robert said, and he kissed his ma's cheek. Then he took the Moonlocket off and hung it around her neck. "This is yours, I think?"

"Thank you," she mumbled, taking it up and turning it in her hand. "It really has caused us nothing but trouble. It's a legacy that's cursed the Door family almost as much as the legend of that diamond."

"The diamond, of course!" Lily took it from her pocket. It glinted and flickered in the sunlight, throwing bright red sparks about the room. "Now that we found it we should return it to its rightful owner at once."

"I'm sure the Queen will be delighted," Inspector Fisk said.

"I didn't mean the Queen. I meant the Elephanta."

Lily stepped toward the mechanimal. Her cogs and parts were no longer scattered around on the workbenches, but still she wasn't moving. That was because Lily had the final piece of the puzzle to make her tick.

Papa raised a hand to stop her climbing the ladder leaning against the Elephanta's side, but she brushed it aside. When she reached the top rung, she carefully placed the diamond in the Elephanta's forehead. Then she took the gigantic winding key hanging on a chain around the Elephanta's neck, put it in the hole beside the stone, and wound her.

As Lily descended the ladder and moved away, a noise like a thousand grandfather clocks ticking came from deep inside the Elephanta's chest.

The Elephanta blinked and opened her big wooden eyes. Her large leather ears, wrinkled as cabbage leaves, flapped about. The various segments in her trunk moved together as she waved it around and she trumpeted loud enough to shake every jar of cogs in the room.

The inspector put up his arms. "I say," he cried. "Step back, everyone, heaven knows what the beast will do."

Then the Elephanta turned and spoke to him in a

resonant, melodious tone. "I'm not a beast, I'm perfectly well behaved. If anyone is beastly, Sir, it is you. I was having such a nice sleep, but I thought I might carry on forever... Until this girl woke me, that is. I shall never forget that. Never." She smiled at Lily beneath her trunk. "What is your name, child?"

"Lily."

"A pleasure to meet you, Lily."

Papa spoke up then. "We needed to ask you if you might march in a parade for the Queen's Diamond Jubilee?"

"Still the same Queen?" asked the Elephanta.

"Yes, Victoria," Anna said.

"In that case," the Elephanta proclaimed, "I think I might, if Lily and her friends are allowed to attend."

Lily clapped her hands together in excitement and looked round at everyone. Malkin was sitting beside Papa, while Robert stood between his sister and ma, and Tolly with Anna.

"I think they need to answer a few questions before that," the inspector said. "About Mr. Door."

"Surely those can wait?" the Elephanta said. "When does this procession take place?"

"In about three hours' time," Papa told her.

From her place on the howdah on the back of the Elephanta, Lily could make out the squat figure of Queen Victoria, a hundred feet in front. She was sitting in her landau carriage, with its eight white horses, waiting patiently for the Diamond Jubilee celebration to start. She had on the traditional black mourning dress, which she always wore in memory of Albert, and was holding a white parasol to shield her from the noonday sun, which was shining like a jewel in the sky after the morning's ragged storm.

The Queen's carriage set off and, as soon as she'd left the courtyard, the rest of the parade began following behind her in a long snaking line, traipsing through the low-rise houses of Greenwich. The Elephanta, carrying Lily and Robert's families, plus Anna and Tolly, on her back, marched somewhere near the rear of the line.

Everyone ran to the edge rail of the howdah, leaning over it to watch the city go by. Malkin jumped up and poked his head between the lower bars to get the best view.

Down on the streets, people were decked out in red, white, and blue—the colors of the Union Flag. Arches had been built at various intervals along the route and were garlanded with bouquets of brightly colored flowers—red roses, bluebells, and white lilies. The crowd waved flags, shouting and cheering and generally enjoying themselves in the June heat.

Lily, Robert, Tolly, and Caddy waved back at them from their position on top of the Elephanta. But Malkin didn't agree with waving and claimed he couldn't manage it with his paws anyway.

Though they were near the end of the long procession, they discovered that the crowd of onlookers still gave loud hoorahs and waved their flags madly when the Elephanta walked by. Barring the Queen herself, the Elephanta was the next most popular attraction. Lily felt elated that she and Robert had found the diamond and brought her back to life, and she was so glad that the Elephanta had insisted they take part in the spectacle.

It'd been a comfort helping to prepare for it that morning, and had taken their minds off the terrors of their adventure. There'd been time to wash and tidy themselves up, and they'd found a marvelous spare set of tweeds for Tolly to wear. Then they'd scrubbed Malkin clean too, and—in deference to the happiness of the occasion—Lily had tied a huge blue bow around his neck. He'd complained to her most vociferously about that, but she'd just ignored him and changed into the fresh clothes Papa had brought her from home. She had to admit it had been a great relief to finally get rid of that awful sewer smell, and she felt extremely proud to be on show in her smart new green dress and bonnet, next to

Robert, who looked rather dashing in a fashionable black suit. In between the raucous shouts, flag-waving, and loud music, Lily made sure she hugged him and told him so.

"Thank you," he replied, grinning at her from ear to ear. He was about to say something else when the Elephanta interrupted him with a loud bellow and Papa, Malkin, Anna, Tolly, and his ma and sister all cheered.

Shadows drifted overhead as the procession approached the river. Robert and Lily glanced up to see the entire fleet of red zep balloons with the gold insignia of The Royal Dirigible Company on each, performing a synchronized fly-by over Tower Bridge. Their bulbous shapes were reflected in the Thames, where a long flotilla of barges, boats, and paddle steamers streamed along the river in a separate display.

As the Queen in her carriage crossed the bridge, she waved down to the boats and then at the onlookers crowding the walkways and towers. Lily thought her arm would probably be aching by now, but the Queen never lowered it, not for one moment.

Soon the whole cavalcade was passing the Tower of London. The Elephanta barely flinched when the cannons atop its walls fired off the twenty-one gun salute.

When they reached Blackfriars they turned and

headed up Farringdon Street. They were marching above the route of the Fleet River. Lily looked down at the road—it was hard to imagine they'd been deep under this very street last night!

The parade turned onto Ludgate Hill, marched past the Old Bailey and then on to St. Paul's Cathedral itself, which had been spruced up and shone as white as a wedding cake in the afternoon sun.

By the time the Elephanta arrived in front of the cathedral, a big cheer was rising for the Queen, who was being helped down from her carriage. In a moment she would make her way up the steps, through the grand double-doored entrance, and into St. Paul's.

Everyone was waiting. But instead of heading that way, the Queen turned and walked along the length of the procession. Finally she stopped beside the Elephanta. The Elephanta looked at the Queen, and the Queen looked at the Elephanta.

"Good afternoon," said the Elephanta.

"Good afternoon," said the Queen.

Lily thought they sounded quite alike.

Victoria's eyes alighted on the Elephanta's forehead and she smiled. "Albert's diamond," she said softly to herself, under her breath. Only Lily, leaning over the railings of the howdah, caught the words quite clearly.

It was then that the Queen glanced up and noticed her.

"You there," said the Queen. "Throw down a rope ladder!"

Lily did as she was bid and the Queen climbed up toward her and clambered onto the back of the gigantic mechanical elephant.

Papa quickly took the Queen's hand and helped her into the howdah. "Oughtn't you to be heading into the cathedral, Your Majesty? For the ceremony?" he asked.

"This will only take a moment," the Queen answered. She turned to Lily. "Are you the one who recovered my diamond and fixed the Elephanta?" she asked. "The one who deserves the reward?"

Lily dropped her best curtsy, at least as well as she could remember it from her lessons at Miss Scrimshaw's Academy last year.

"Yes, Your Majesty, but I had some help from my friends." She waved at them. "Master Robert Townsend, Mrs. Selena Townsend, Miss Caddy Townsend, Master Bartholomew Mudlark…and Malkin."

"A pleasure to meet you, Your Majesty," Robert said, bowing his head.

The others did the same, following his lead.

"And you," the Queen replied. "And what a marvelous cinnamon-colored cat!" she exclaimed, staring at Malkin. "I'm more of a dog person myself. I have ten of those, you know—spaniels and pomeranians mostly—

one's even a mechanimal—but I'm not averse to cats. A cat may look at a Queen, so they say, ha-ha!"

"I'm a fox," Malkin replied.

The Queen took a pince-nez on a chain from deep within a pocket of her voluminous dress and perched it on her imperious nose, peering at Malkin. "Good heavens! So you are! And a jolly fine fellow."

She smiled at each of them. "Thank you so much for repairing this marvelous creature. It is wonderful that the return of the diamond has allowed it to run again. But it's not only that...the Blood Moon Diamond is very valuable, and I don't mean monetarily, I mean emotionally. You see, my husband Albert gave it to me as a present, and it has strange and great powers, because it was found on a full moon, on the date of a lunar eclipse..."

"The twenty-first of June 1815," Lily interrupted.

The Queen's gaze softened. "Exactly right! How did you know that?"

"I discovered it today," Lily said.

"You certainly are a most remarkable child!" She turned to John then. "This is your daughter, Professor Hartman?"

John nodded. He was somewhat dumbstruck. "You don't know the half of it," he said.

"Anyway," the Queen continued, "it was discovered

that Moon Diamonds have life energy trapped in them. As your father will tell you, every mechanical has a smaller sliver of a similar Blood Moon Diamond inside them, for it contains such power that it's able to bring them to life."

Lily put a hand to her chest and felt the Cogheart beating and thought of the sliver of diamond inside it.

"When Albert commissioned the Elephanta from the Mechanists' Guild," the Queen continued, "he wanted her to be powered by the biggest diamond of all. But the creature took so long to build it was only completed after his death. Then, on its debut outing, as we all know, the diamond was stolen by Jack Door."

Selena curtsied. "Your Majesty, Jack was my father. I can only apologize for his behavior."

"For that, I thank you, Madam," the Queen replied. She turned to Lily and smiled. "You see, Lily, when you lose someone close, the gifts they gave you become keepsakes to remember them by—it's as if they magically contain a part of that person. And when you mislay such a gift, it is like losing that person all over again. But when you recover it, it is always a great and unexpected blessing."

Robert thought of his da's coat and its faint smell of tobacco, of Da; and Lily felt for the ammonite in her pocket—the last gift from her mother. They both knew exactly what the Queen meant, as did everyone standing there listening to her words, for they'd all lost someone dear to their hearts at one time or another.

"Shall I help you down the ladder, Your Majesty?" John suggested, and suddenly the Queen came out of her reverie and realized the world was watching.

The Queen leaned out over the edge of the howdah and peered down at the crowds of royal attendants who had gathered like ants beneath the Elephanta's bulk. They were wringing their hands together silently as they waited for her to descend and commence the very important state business of the afternoon. Business that mainly involved sitting still in a chair through unimaginably long and very dull speeches.

Victoria shook her head. "I've a better idea. A most amusing diversion that Albert would have adored, and one that will keep the crowds talking about my Jubilee for years to come."

She walked to the front of the howdah and put a hand on the Elephanta's head. "Elephanta," she commanded. "I want you to please ascend the steps of the cathedral and march through the main doors. I shall then disembark."

"As you wish," the Elephanta said, and she let out a deep mechanical bellow and marched toward the front of the parade.

The Queen's attendants and advisors cowered on the pavement, goggling in disbelief as the Elephanta's flat gray feet pounded past them. The Elephanta climbed the steps of St. Paul's and her big metal flanks brushed against the tall columns of the cathedral, shaking the Roman portico and the statues of the saints.

She paused for a moment in front of the enormous entrance. Though its doors had been thrown wide open, it still wasn't quite clear if she could make it through.

She sucked in her sides and stepped forward. The tented roof of the howdah brushed the lintel stone with a crunch, and Lily and everyone else held onto their hats, while the Queen held onto her diamond tiara.

Inside, the rows of European royalty waiting expectantly to take their seats for the service flinched in alarm and staggered away as the Elephanta galumphed down the central aisle of the cathedral.

When she reached the throne at the far end, she stopped. While a long set of stairs was pushed up to her side so that the Queen could descend, the Elephanta let out a booming roar, which echoed through the space from end to end; blasting dust from every archway that dissipated up into the great vaulted dome above.

Afterward, people claimed that they'd heard the Elephanta down the length and breadth of Fleet Street. Lily wasn't entirely sure that could be true, but it was certainly a great trumpet, loud enough to fill the whole cathedral, and she knew it was a memory she would long recall, and treasure forever.

CHAPTER 26

In the week following the Queen's Jubilee, Selena and Caddy stayed with the Hartmans at Brackenbridge. At first it felt strange to Lily to have other people around the house, but they were pleasant company.

Since their arrival she had found herself dreaming more vividly of Mama at night. It was almost as if another mother and daughter being there had brought the visions of her own mother to the light once more.

In tonight's dream, Mama stood opposite her, holding the rosewood box that had once contained all the memories and mementoes of her. She opened it to reveal a sky spiraling with moons and constellations. Then, just like Robert when he and Lily first met, Mama explained how each star was a billion years old, and how their light was shining from every moment in history.

"Keep me in your heart," she told Lily, "and the memory of me will burn as sweet and strong as these stars."

Mama bent down to kiss Lily, and she woke up.

She was rewarded by a lick on the face from Malkin, who had slowed down in the night and was nearly out of ticks. Lily wound him up with his winder key and he jumped down from the bed and ran to the door, mewing to be let out.

Lily got up and let him into the hall. Everything was worryingly quiet. Wasn't today the day that Caddy and Selena were supposed to be leaving? Surely they hadn't set off yet? She went to her window and drew back her curtains.

The sun was almost up and the real stars had long since disappeared, but the waning moon was still visible faintly in the distance. Soon it would be gone completely and then it would gradually return night by night— marking the start of a new month.

Until then, there were things to do. Lily could hear Mrs. Rust clanging about downstairs. She put on her green summer dress and her pinafore, and tugged on some slippers. Then she called for Malkin and, together, they went to see if she could scour up any breakfast.

Robert's empty plate and mug were standing on the

draining board when Lily arrived in the kitchen. "Where's Robert?" she asked Mrs. Rust, who was busily washing the crockery. "Is he up already?"

"He went with his sister and Ma," Mrs. Rust replied. "To the airstation. The pair of them are catching the early commuter zep to London."

"They've departed already?" Lily's heart leaped. "He's not taking off with them, is he?"

"Cogs and chronometers!" Mrs. Rust said. "I don't know! That's down to him to decide, and if he's kept his own counsel with you, he's not going to tell me, is he?"

Lily headed to the door. "Come on, Malkin," she said. "We have to catch him."

"Don't you try and stop him going, if that's what he's resolved to do," Mrs. Rust called after her.

"I *will* try," Lily called back, rushing across the yard in her slippers, with Malkin at her heels. "But if I can't change his mind, then I want to at least be there to say goodbye!"

Robert stood on the airstation platform with his ma and Caddy. Had it really been only seven days he'd known them? They'd grown close even in that short amount of time. He and Lily had shown Caddy the manor and its gardens, Brackenbridge village, and the old churchyard where Da was buried. Then, last of all, he'd shown Ma the shop.

She'd cried when she saw it, and he had too. Somehow seeing that damaged place had brought her losses home to her. Robert understood. He knew it could take a thing that big, that physically real, to make you realize that what you were missing was gone forever.

"Townsend's is yours, if you want it, Robbie," his ma had said as she dried her eyes. But then, as they walked away, she'd stopped and taken his hand. "Or," she said quietly, "you could come with us?"

Robert sighed. He'd hoped in his heart that she and Caddy might stay, but her words told him that wasn't to be the case.

In the few days since, Selena hadn't changed her mind. She had bookings for her show lined up in London and the provinces, she said. Plus contracts and opportunities she claimed she couldn't turn down.

Last night she packed their things once more, with Caddy and Robert looking on sadly. And John had agreed that, in the morning, when the time came, Robert would go with Caddy and Ma to the airstation to see them both off.

Now the moment of their departure had arrived, and for a second Robert thought about taking off with them. The opportunity had been playing on his mind, but this would be his last chance to actually take it, to disregard everything of his past and become part of a performing family in a life completely different from his own.

Selena put a hand on his shoulder. "Have you made your decision?" she asked.

"I don't know," Robert replied, and he recognized that much was true; the choice had been like a rock, weighing on him. "This past week…I feel as if I've got closer to you both. But there's John and Lily to think of, and Malkin, Mrs. Rust and the rest. The Hartmans saved me when I had nowhere to go. They looked after me when no one loved me and I'd no one to love. They're like family."

It was the same thought he'd had in the tunnels, and it was true; family wasn't flesh and blood, or the branches of a withered tree. Family was who you loved and who loved you. And though he'd made a connection with Selena and Caddy, it wasn't the same feeling he had for Lily, or John, or Malkin and the mechanicals.

"We do love you, Robert," Selena said. "But I understand. It's a hard choice, and I've put you on the spot by leaving so soon."

"Love and trust," Robert said, "they're not always the same thing. And I don't know if I can trust you yet… I don't think I can go."

"You're right," Selena said. "I've been neglectful. It's far too little, too late. I see that now. You don't have to come with us, but, before I go, I want to at least give you something to remember me by." She unhooked the Moonlocket from around her neck, and handed it to him.

Robert took it. The locket's shape and weight felt familiar in his hand.

"Open it," she said.

He flicked the catch and the two halves opened to reveal the painted miniature of baby Robert and his ma and da in one half and, in the other, a tiny photograph of baby Caddy held by his ma, a few years later.

"Your da painted that portrait of us," Selena explained; she half-closed her eyes and spoke softly as she remembered. "The photograph of Caddy and me was taken when she was newborn. With a box camera I borrowed."

She leaned in close, examining both pictures. Robert smelled her perfume, fresh and summery. "At last I can go back to doing my show with Caddy, and make a new life for us, without the bad reputation of Jack and the Door family hanging over me."

Selena took Caddy's hand. Then she kissed Robert's cheek, and stepped away from him. "We have to go. But we'll be back soon, I promise."

Robert nodded. "I understand."

He went to break the locket apart, to give Caddy back her half, but she shook her head. "You keep both pieces, to remember us by. That way you'll always have us close to your heart. A happy, united family."

Robert saw that she was right; the two pictures in the locket did make a whole family. A family that would never be complete without Da, not really, but a family that he could think of as his own nonetheless.

He tucked the locket inside his shirt, where it hung around his neck, his skin slowly warming the metal, and looked up to find Selena watching him.

She blinked a few times and he wondered if she might be crying, but she merely wiped her eyes and, still holding Caddy's hand, turned and walked up the gangplank to the entrance of the airship.

"Wait!" he cried when they were nearly at the door, and they turned and gazed back at him one last time.

"I shall miss you," he shouted. "I shall miss you as the sun misses the moon!"

Selena smiled and said something in return.

"What?" he hollered, for he could barely hear her over the drone of the airship's engine.

She came to the edge of the boarding platform and stood leaning over the rail, like she was on a stage—the grandest stage in the world, and he was an audience of one.

"It's the other way around," she said, raising her arms to him. "I shall miss you as the moon misses the sun. The sun illuminates the moon, without it she'd disappear. It's that light that keeps her shining through her darkest nights!"

She stepped into the doorway of the airship, facing him all the way and bowing slowly as she went. Caddy followed behind her and, before she left, she turned to Robert and waved.

"I love you to the moon and back!" she called.

And then the mechanical porter shut the door on both of them and they were gone.

Robert waited on the platform while the gangplank was removed and the anchor rolled up. Then the zep rose slowly and softly into the sky.

Robert didn't take his eyes from it, and, when it finally disappeared into the clouds, for a long time he watched the space where it had been. How was it, he wondered, that something so big and so real could be there one minute and gone the next? It felt impossible, and yet it happened every day.

He held out the Moonlocket and the clouds parted, scattering shards of sunlight across its strange silver map and sending glittering rainbows across the surface of his fingers. When he looked up again to where the airship had been, he saw a ghostly waning moon had taken its place, paling slowly in the sky against the bright blue light of morning.

"Robert!" a voice sang, and he turned.

It was Lily, cycling toward him across the airfield. Malkin sat up in the basket on the front of her bicycle, his pointed nose sniffing the air in delight.

"I'm so glad you stayed," she said, as she skidded to a stop.

She jumped down off the saddle and threw the bike aside to give Robert the most enormous hug.

"Careful!" Malkin coughed angrily. He crawled from beneath the overturned frame and spinning wheels of the clattering machine and trotted over to Robert.

"I am glad you're still here too!" the mech-fox yapped and he licked at Robert's fingers for good measure.

Robert gave a deep sigh. "I'm not going anywhere," he said. "Not yet!"

"That's good," Lily replied. "Because there's so much more for us to do. Papa needs keeping an eye on, plus the mechanicals have to be taken care of—I couldn't do all that without you! You're my best friend, Robert. And we made a pact, remember: whatever comes our way, good or bad, we shall look after each other.

"Come on." She picked up the bike once more and swung a leg over its crossbar.

"Are you wearing slippers?" Robert asked her.

"What if I am?" she said. "I didn't have time to change properly, that's all. Come on, we'll ride back together.

You can sit on the saddle, if you like, and I'll stand and do the pedaling. Malkin, you can get back in the basket and navigate."

"I don't see why I have to ride in the basket always?" Malkin said. "I mean, it's not as if I'm a loaf of bread."

"It's because no one else is small enough to fit in," Lily said.

Malkin growled a complaint that sounded like a curse, but still he jumped into the basket willingly enough, and bobbed his head up and lolled his tongue out to signal he was ready to go.

Lily rode them down the lane, weaving the bicycle unsteadily along, and her heart soared with the knowledge that Robert had decided to stay, as well she'd guessed he might.

The Cogheart… With this new adventure, Lily felt as if she was closer to discovering the truth of it. Since she'd first learned she had it eight months ago, it had sometimes felt like an alien fragment, or a foreign object inside her, something that explained why she felt so different from other people.

She had often found herself wondering if someone with such a heart could really offer friendship or love. But now she saw that that simply wasn't true. She had plenty of friends around her, and she loved each and every one of them dearly, most especially Robert.

The Cogheart was hers. As much a part of her as an arm or leg, or her thoughts or feelings. Integral to who she was and who she would become. Sometimes it ached for those she'd lost, and sometimes it soared with joy for those she'd found. But either way she felt one with it at last.

And it wasn't just the heart she was connected to, Lily reflected, but everything. If you didn't divide it up, carve things into categories, it was all one and the same anyway—waves and oceans, dawns and sunsets, noise and silence. Life was a single connected river that ran through mechanicals, people, animals, planets. Everything that ever was or would be, all mixed together in a soup of being; of shouting and jumping, moving and bumping. Echoes of the great creation, the let-there-be-light—she was that and more. One continuing, amazing instant; a single spark, burning a long trail that would go on forever, until the last ember of time burned out.

They were approaching Brackenbridge Manor. Robert put an arm around Lily and leaned back on the bicycle, staring up at the sky.

Above him, somewhere in the wild blue yonder, his ma and Caddy were sailing away.

In their time together he'd felt a deep, diamond-bright connection to them. It had filled every sinew and bone of his body, radiating out to the four corners of his soul. But still, he had decided to stay in Brackenbridge. He was sure it was the best choice for now. Selena and Caddy would be back soon, perhaps with new stories to tell—for the first time in his life he didn't doubt that was true. There'd always be a twist of longing, of course. A small wish he'd gone with them, but that wasn't a risk he was ready to take. Not yet. Not today. Selena had let him down so deeply in the past, and he needed to stand on his own two feet, walk his own path.

The choice he'd made was to stay with Lily, and John, Malkin and the mechanicals. Though this adventure was over he was certain they would find another. They were his family, Brackenbridge his home—the place where he belonged. A place where he could walk into a room and feel those around him were his friends and had his best interests at heart. A place of good company, where there was plenty of joy and affection to go around. A place filled with smiling faces telling him: *Robert, you are a free spirit like your mother; an artist like your father; and warm-hearted like your sister. We're true family—without you we'd be broken in pieces, but with you we carry on.*

And one face in particular meant more to him than any other. A face that belonged to a beautiful girl named Lily, a friend who loved him.

Shoots of green growth sprouted from the hedgerows;

Robert stuck out a hand and batted them from their path. A summer breeze tugged at his shirtsleeves, jangling the locket chain around his neck.

Lily's curls spread out across the sky, like blood-red ribbons. He held onto her tightly as she turned and rode them up the lane, and it felt almost as if they were flying home.

A dictionary of curious words

A glossary of words that may be uncommon to the reader

Automaton: a self-operating mechanical device.

Bazalgette: not a "what" but a "who." Joseph Bazalgette was a civil engineer who devised London's sewer network, which helped stop the spread of cholera across the city. The London sewer network is seen as one of the modern industrial wonders of the world (though Lily and Robert might disagree after their ordeal).

Chronometer: a timepiece that has been specially tested to meet a certain standard of precision. ("Cogs and chronometers!")

Costermonger: someone who sells goods—such as fruit and vegetables—from a cart in the street. You might well expect to see (and hear!) one or two costermongers milling around Brackenbridge.

Escapologist: an escapologist is an entertainer of sorts, who escapes from a variety of different dangers, such as handcuffs and ropes— or in the case of the notorious Jack Door, the police!

Howdah: a seat used for riding on the back of an elephant, either real or mechanical.

Hybrid: someone who is part-mech, part-human.

Mechanimal: a mechanical animal, such as Malkin.

Oakum shed: oakum is a type of tarred material used mainly in shipbuilding. In Victorian prisons, the prisoners would be

made to pick apart old tarred ropes to make this material...
although Jack Door preferred to simply pick up the oakum for
his daring escape.

Peelers (or The Peelers): a "peeler" is a nickname for a policeman.
It came from the name of the man who first introduced police
officers (first in Ireland in 1817, and then in England in 1822)—
Sir Robert Peel.

Penny dreadful: exciting tales of famous criminals, detectives,
or supernatural mysteries, these magazines were
published weekly and cost one penny (which gave them their
name). They are not considered proper, but if you're sneaky,
you can hide one rolled up in your pocket for when your parents
aren't looking.

Perpetual motion machine: a machine that will run forever,
without the need for an external source of energy.

Working Lads' Mission: a charitable organization who would
take in boys and young men, educate them, and help them find
jobs, instead of leaving them to live on the streets. It was Tolly's
saving grace!

Zeppelin: a type of airship. It has an oval-shaped "balloon,"
beneath which is a rigid metal framework filled with bags of gas
to keep the ship afloat. The passenger and crew area—or
gondola—is usually situated under the main balloon, and can
be quite roomy. (Unless you're hitching a ride in the *Ladybird*,
in which case it's a little bit cozy.)

Thanks to my agent Jo Williamson, and my editors Rebecca Hill and Becky Walker, for guiding me through the difficult second book with aplomb. To Kath Millichope, Sarah Cronin, and Becca Stadtlander for the gorgeous cover, type, design, and illustrations. To Sarah Stewart, Stephanie King, and Anne Finnis for edits and advice on the last drafts. To publicity and marketing mavens Amy Dobson, Stevie Hopwood, and Alesha Bonser; plus the entire Usborne team—you've been a joy to work with once again. To Mari Kesselring and the team at Jolly Fish Press, Katelyn Detweiler at Jill Grinberg Literary, and Barbara and Sarah at Blue Slip Media—thank you for your stellar work on the US edition. To my mum, dad, family, and Michael—for driving me crazy and keeping me sane through the final push to finish—I love you all to the moon and back.

Originally I intended Jack to be a Dawkins, which is the real name of the Artful Dodger in Charles Dickens's amazing *Oliver Twist*. Then on a whim—and a jackdaw pun—I changed it to Door, which is also a character name in Neil Gaiman's brilliant *Neverwhere*. So thanks to those two fantastic writers for unknowingly providing me with half a name each; plus every other awesome author who's inspired me over the years.

Finally, I'd like to thank the stellar bloggers, librarians, teachers, and many young readers who've told me how much they adored *Cogheart*. I hope you feel the same way about this one!

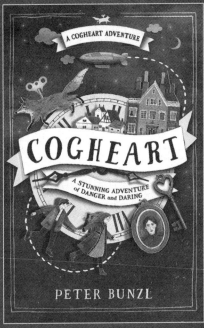